MW01087845

THE UNMERCIFUL SEA

The
Unmerciful
Sea

Islanders of the time will say to anyone that this did not occur. Therefor, this is a work of fiction. Names, characters, places, and incidents either are the product of the author's imagination or are used fictitiously. Any resemblance to actual persons, living or dead, events, or locales is entirely coincidental.

Copyright © John Martell/Gravity Well Books 2019

ISBN-13: 978-0-9980968-2-7

All rights reserved. No part of this book may be reproduced in any form on by an electronic or mechanical means, including information storage and retrieval systems, without permission in writing from the publisher, except by a reviewer who may quote brief passages in a review.

First paperback edition 2019

Cover design by Barb Noel

Published by Gravity Well Books

TABLE OF CONTENTS

PROLOGUE

5:56 P.M. MARCH 29, 1942

OFF THE CAPE HATTERAS COAST

Captain Johannes Sullivans kept a nervous watch at the helm of his ship. The *City of Savannah* was boiling through the churning waters of the Graveyard of the Atlantic in the early evening of March 29, 1942. The *Savannah* was a passenger-freighter, carrying in addition to the ore, rare wood, and paper products that stocked her holds bumper full, a compliment of 45 passengers, 90 crew members, and 8 members of the U.S. Navy Armed Guard. The majority of the passengers had either finished or were finishing dinner in the mess, served by impeccably dressed white coated waiters who treated the passengers with deference given to old money. The waiters saved their greatest respect for the off duty young men, truly pedestrian, some would even say hayseeds, who crewed the single weapon on the stern of the ship, a 3 inch .50 caliber deck gun that was their only hope of warding off evil that waited in the night for all the ships

1

that passed by the promontory of Cape Hatteras. The paying passengers ate their food with tempered indifference.

Captain Sullivans was not hungry.

A steady call of SSSS had been coming through the ship radio throughout their trip north to New York City. It was a relatively new call, replacing the everyday call of S O S for only certain types of emergencies. The four S call, a simple dit-dih-dih on the signal, meant that the ship was under attack by submarine. It wasn't the sound, but the prevalence of its use. Ships were being attacked regularly by the Nazi U-boats in a wholesale turkey shoot, a cold blooded slaughter in the cold waters of the Atlantic Ocean. And the most likely place for the attack was where the *Savannah* was right now.

Sullivans had hoped his ship would avoid a similar fate due to her speed, and ran her at full throttle through the night. He attempted to get the *Savannah*, all 450 feet of her, through the dangerous waters of Cape Hatteras without being spotted, and maybe make the run into Norfolk to meet into more secure waters with a convoy or protective Navy ship. Sullivans had set a straight course, not running tacks or zigzagging the way the U.S. Navy suggested.

He had made only one mistake. He had radioed his position earlier, under the mistaken idea that he was under attack. Unbeknownst to him, his position was heard not only by the U.S. Coast Guard and the Navy, but by the hunters he was so desperately trying to outrun. An hour later, he was in exactly the location the captain of U-857 had predicted the *Savannah* would be.

Katy Bunch sat at the small dining table in the passengers' mess hall. Adorned with soft white linen and decked with tiny crystal salt and pepper shakers, the setting made for a simple but elegant evening. The meal was pleasant enough, a flavorful roast with onions, fresh peas, and roasted potatoes. She cared little for what she ate, though, as she paid more attention to her dining companion.

John Gale sat across from her, laughing closed lipped as he tried not to spit out a roll. The two had hit it off well on the return trip. They were both single, traveling alone, with no intention on romance on board a ship. They were also solidly middle class in a room full of the snooty rich and the substantially poor. The rich held their names like they held their noses, up and away. The poorer of the travelers had too many z's and ic's in their names to be counted by the rich. The groups paired off quickly aboard the ship, leaving Katy and John to themselves, happily regaling each other with polite jokes and pleasant games.

It had made the trip so much easier for the two once the captain ordered daily lifeboat drills.

No matter how anyone pretended, they knew the ship was sailing in shark infested waters. Great metal sharks, hidden in the black of night, hunters looking for easy prey. The crew made it seem like a safety drill, like the ship might get stranded, but everyone knew.

Everyone knew, but it was still a surprise when the first torpedo hit.

Oddly for the passengers, it was less destructive sounding than they would have thought. There was a solid muffled *whump*! as the torpedo slammed into the starboard waterline toward the stern. Some merely thought the ship had hit something.

Captain Sullivans and the crew knew better. The enormous explosion to the starboard side was proof enough. When the metal hull of the ship started cavitating and shivering as broken bits from her insides shook the craft, he knew the *City of Savannah* was doomed. It took him less than ten seconds to order the evacuation and assign crew to the lifeboats.

The evacuation was orderly, as the passengers followed their long practiced procedure, made difficult from the debris strewn across the deck from the explosion. The crew worked the lines of the lifeboats as best as they could considering some were severely injured. Passengers walked to their assigned stations, balancing precariously as the ship began to list sideways. The crew knew what the passengers were slowly learning. The *Savannah* had been pierced open and was flooding with water. Whatever stress the passengers felt was less than the terror below decks as crew that survived the initial attack tried to fight off drowning in an icy spring sea. It was a fight none would win. The crew members caught below decks would all drown as the Atlantic flooded in and trapped them in the broken hull.

Katy and John rushed to their lifeboat station. The ship was leaning greatly now, both to the starboard side and to the stern. John looked aft when he heard the coughing crack of the deck gun. Three men were on the 50 caliber cannon, unloading shell after shell at the direction of the U-boat. He wasn't sure what good it would do. The men of the U.S. Navy Armed Guard pumped shells downrange at a target they could only barely see, firing with uncanny accuracy, but at a target almost impossible to hit.

John turned back to his job. He climbed in the lifeboat and began helping to lower the craft into the choppy and dark water. They were on the starboard side, and it seemed like the ocean was going to rise up to get them, the way the *Savannah* listed. It was difficult to keep the lifeboat level on the ropes, as they slipped through wet and salty pulleys. Katy fell backwards from her seat into the well of the lifeboat, banging the back of her head. She could feel the abrasion on her back, the warm well of blood on her head mixing with salt water. The wound added to the terror. She had no idea what had happened to her, but she knew that she was injured. This wasn't supposed to happen, she thought. Why would people do this to one another? They were just passengers. There were no soldiers, no tanks, no planes, no bombs on board. Her eyes manifested a look of sheer trauma on her face. John looked down at her. He saw the fear, the sudden discovery that nothing was going to be alright. That there

4

was a good chance that they would die that night, and the death would be long, slow, and horrible. He reached down with one free hand to help her back up, to steady her, to give her that one little bit of hope.

That was when the second torpedo hit.

Water splashed like a geyser into the little boat. The torpedo had struck amidships, breaking the back of the stricken *City of Savannah*. John and Katy's lifeboat was tossed up, then down, twisted by the ropes, sending the refugees of the lost steamer into a cold and merciless sea. It took time, but John found a large balsa wood life raft, a cheap alternative with no aesthetic value that would keep him and other victims from drowning. He pulled a shocked and gasping Katy Bunch toward the ring, and secured her to it.

Looking back, he saw the broken *City of Savannah* go down. On the stern, the last thing to disappear was the deck gun. The dark barrel winked out the flash of an explosive shell, time after time, over and over, manned by brave young men whom he would never know. Until they, too, succumbed to the deep.

Aboard U-857, *Kapitänleutnant* Reinhardt Krieg looked out the periscope at the dwindling *City of Savannah*. He had launched his second torpedo even though the passengers were abandoning ship, and the hull was severely breached. The flash of the deck gun connected with the harsh thumps of shells exploding close by in the water, yet he had pursued the ship anyway. He now watched as the ship burned, then sank. He didn't care about the people in the lifeboats. It didn't matter to him that his victims were elderly, women, children, foreign, refugees, pregnant, or civilian.

His Nazi cold-bloodedness would cost him dearly in the next few weeks, and for long after that.

1

10:00 P.M. SEPTEMBER 26, 1985

OCRACOKE, NC

Adam Howard looked out his window at the darkened sky that covered Ocracoke village, his home of all of his 12 years. Where lights usually dotted the calm harbor of Silver Lake, all was black. The houses along the village were only black on black, dark as pitch. Dark as death.

Outside, the wind screamed and squealed, getting louder and higher pitched with each gust. Hurricanes did that. They whirled their winds up, faster and faster, each gust building on the last. The wind would wail, and the house would shudder. Then another gust, not relenting, came after, a higher squeal, a thousand ghosts screaming to be let in. It sounded like pure bedlam outside, just aching to do damage to his poor home.

And every time, another rush of rain pelted the sides. Far from a sheet or curtain of rain, they were like waves washing against the house. It was more like being in a boat than a home. Adam felt the house finally shake with one tremendous push. The rain waves smashed against the house in surges that created a deep dull roar that absolutely did not go with the high pitched sound of the wind. Every time the wind and rain lashed the old house, it was nothing short of a promise to the poor 12 year old alone in his room. Any minute, the world was going to end. Washed away in a woman's fury as Hurricane Gloria bared down right on Adam's home.

Exhaustion mingled with his fear in Adam's gut. He had known, everyone had known, that this hurricane was coming. They knew days ago. And everyone that knew had left the island the day before. Ocracoke had gone from a population of 800 to less than 50 overnight, as the ferry to Swan Quarter filled with locals heading inland to stay with family or in a cheap motel near Greenville or Williamston. All that were left were a few diehards, people who stayed through every hurricane and weren't going to be run out by this one. Dave White sat alone in the Pony Island Hotel, empty of tourists as summer left the coast. Jody Spence came down from Hatteras to be with his mother, who refused to leave. Chief Boatswain's Mate Jennifer Stone was in the radio room of the Coast Guard station, drinking bitter coffee and listening to the constant ramble of ships conversing, with the unending report of the hurricane blaring through NOAA's VHF broadcasts in the background. Two Park Rangers were trapped on nearby Portsmouth Island, locked safely inside the old Methodist church. Two sheriff's deputies, a few volunteer firefighters, and an EMT from the mainland of Hyde County sat fitfully in the firehouse next to the small school that served every one of the 42 kids from kindergarten to twelfth grade. The rest of the remaining village residents, a mishmash of fishermen and descendants of pirates of long ago, all huddled in equanimous stress against a storm which they cannot turn back.

None of the other residents were on Adam's mind right at that moment. A 12 year old's world ended pretty much at his driveway, and right then all that really mattered to him was whether or not his house would survive the night. More specifically, he was worried about the old live oak tree that grew right outside his window. For hundreds of years, the twisted oak tree had grown freely, both shaped by the winds and unmoved by the storms of centuries past. He knew in his heart that the tree wouldn't come crashing through his window onto his bed while he slept, that the old tree would stand for years to come, but still, something in the back of his head just kept calling to him, some irrational fear that actually made perfect sense to a little kid. The regular worries that most people would have during a storm were often supplanted by the worst, most irrational terrors in a kid's mind. For Adam it was always going to be the strangest and most horrific incident that was the most likely. And that meant to him that the old oak tree would crash through his window, raining glass and thick branches down on his body, pinning him to his bed with the sharp shards of glass and long broken limbs, then crushing him in the night.

But Adam had a solution to his fear. He was exhausted from cleaning up anything that could fly away in the hurricane, all the preparations he did with his father down at the docks, and collecting drinking water. Sleep competed with terror in Adam, and sleep was going to win. Adam simply picked up his mattress and leaned it up against his window, wrapping his curtains around it in the vain attempt to hold the mattress up in case the tree fell in. It seemed to be a perfect and elegant answer to Adam's problem in his mind. Thus saved, he curled up with a blanket and pillow on the box springs and fell into a fitful sleep, dreaming of ghost pirates on the wind.

Hurricane Gloria skirted Ocracoke Island in the middle of the night, making landfall across Hatteras, with her eye passing over the iconic lighthouse at one o'clock in the morning. While the islands slept, the storm raged. Winds whipped at over 100 miles an hour, knocking over gas station canopies and flooding the sound. Gloria turned and crossed back into the Atlantic at Nags Head before heading north to do what damage she could around New York and up through New England. Her spiral finally spun itself out over Greenland, but the remnants of the storm would end up affecting Europe.

None of this was to be known by the few people remaining on Ocracoke over the next few days. They had something much worse to worry about.

2

Hurricane Gloria had been surprisingly forgiving for such a strong hurricane. She had lashed at the beach of Ocracoke, but only delivered a glancing blow. Blessed with a waxing moon and a waning tide, the storm surge had pulled itself up the beach, only breaking through the small holes in the low dunes that made up the barrier between ocean and island. Sand spilled like a fan, the heavy pebbles dropping out first, then the crystals and bits of shell, and finally the softest, finest loam, a delicate black powder like a gritty graphite ended the decorative washover. Farther up Highway 12, on the only road into the village, a dune had collapsed at a weak point. Waves came through in a surge as the hills could not hold all the water back. More sand from the sides of the dunes added to the mess. The road got underwashed as water eroded the base under the blacktop, and it cracked and

11

heaved, turning the road into an unsavory brittle, frosted with salt and sand. No one was getting out that way.

The village fared slightly better. The locals knew to count their blessings. Anything could be fixed, given time and money, but they still hoped for the best. Best was a relative term for the islanders.

The sound had flooded, as was expected, and had done damage in the harbor to the boats and gear still left there before the storm. Tree branches lay strewn about the yards, along with a littering of pine needles thick enough to cover the roads to the point of camouflage. Gloria may have snatched the odd item from one person's yard and deposited it into another's, which would be returned or kept depending upon its usefulness or value.

After the massively low pressure of a hurricane, a high pressure crossed over from the mainland to sit on the islands, bringing only a few light high clouds flitting around mostly blue skies, with a bright hot sun beating down on the people venturing out to begin the inevitable cleanup of trees, branches, and other detritus that always comes with a hurricane. A cool dry land breeze blew hard out of the west, which did nothing to improve the comfort of the residents, but did bring a swampy stench from the stirred up waters of the marshes, as well as blow swarms of biting black flies out in droves.

Adam awoke early that morning, unable to get back to sleep once the sun began to peek up above the horizon. His room was hot and still. The air did not move. It felt stuffy and sticky inside. He slipped on his pants quickly, wanting to get outside and see the damage done by the storm. Force of habit made him flick the switch to the upstairs hall light. Nothing happened. He then noticed the stillness of the house, the absence of the normal sounds of electricity, like the TV, the refrigerator, or the air conditioning. The storm had knocked the power out. This was normal, even expected, on the island.

Running downstairs, his shirt still over his head, he met his mother in the hallway leading into the kitchen.

"Good morning!" Michelle Howard greeted her son as he barged his way through the once silent house. She was no worse for wear from a night in the storm. Already dressed, she had fixed a cold breakfast of cereal for herself, and set a bowl out for her son. A battery operated radio cranked out a static filled station from the mainland listing all the damage from the night before. The hollow emptiness of the house made the radio sound especially old.

"G'mornin'," Adam answered. He tried to straighten his hair and focus on the bright morning light outside to see the damage. "Can I go outside? I want to see what fell."

His mother knew her son's desire to see the destruction outside, and she didn't have the strength to bother with insisting he eat breakfast first. "Alright, but put your shoes on. Not your flip flops! Your father is already at the harbor. Don't go down there and bother him."

Adam's father, Dan, was the harbormaster for Silver Lake. "He's got his hands full down there, some of the boats came loose last noight." Adam's mother slipped into her Elizabethan brogue, a strange patois of English with Irish accents and a mix of Ocracoke slang only heard along this narrow part of the Outer Banks. Adam had made a point of shaking the brogue as best he could.

Slipping out the front door, he was confronted by the wondrous sights and smells that only come after a hurricane. Tree branches covered Howard Street, a sandy road now mixed with a blanket of green pine needles. The air smelled of sap and salt. A pinch of tropics hung in the air, a leftover of Gloria's travels up from warmer waters. Adam looked around, noticing that the only way to tell where the roads were was the line of trees that skirted the curbs of the village lanes. He could see where his father had driven his pickup out of the driveway toward the bay where he worked. Two wheel tracks left a shiny mashed trail in the wet pine needles along their road.

The sun hit his face. It was a familiar, but at the same time altogether unique feeling. Adam realized at that moment that he was alone on the island. Normally, people would be out already, raking, cleaning, sawing, the typical activities after a storm. But because of the ferocious threat of Gloria, most of the population had evacuated. He realized that he may be the only kid left on Ocracoke. And that realization led him to a decision. The island was his for the taking. He could explore freely, searching the coast for all the flotsam that would wash up every time the waves got big. There were no high school kids out giving him the eye while they prowled the beach, no adults scavenging for anything of value, no old bitties collecting all the shells and beach glass.

No one to else make a claim to fame of being the first out after the storm.

Adam grabbed his bike from inside the shed and began riding.

It was a wondrous feeling, the brightness of the sun in a high blue sky. Even this early in the morning, the sun was already way up, losing all of its red and yellow fireball in the first few minutes of dawn to rise up into a clear day. Adam pedaled his bike up to speed, then let it coast, as kids do, slowly twisting the handlebars as he sped down the main road of Highway 12, letting the breeze change directions with every turn. The world was his oyster, if only for a day, and he was going to find a pearl.

The trip to the beach was easy. Sand had washed over the roads only to have the high winds blow it all off into the sides, making wonderful drifts, natural sculptures of sand waves, frozen in a moment of time until the will of man could come and plow them all down. That would be later; this was for now, thought Adam.

He pedaled hard into the beach access by the town's local airstrip. It was a simple piece of bumpy macadam, roughly north-south, that served a few planes every summer. Instead of stopping at the tiny pilot's shack, Adam continued to pedal, letting his bike plow into the thick unmolested sand that had spilled over the beach access. It took only a few feet for the bike to become hopelessly mired in the sand, and Adam kicked the bike down, jumping off at a run and letting his bike fall where it stopped. There was no need to hide it. No one else was out there that morning.

He plodded through the soft smooth sand. Looking through the cut in the dunes, he could see the beach and ocean. Even though it was just past high tide, the waves were pushed back. For over one hundred yards, the surf rolled over shallow sandbars, making waves of only about a foot tall. Sand had been pushed in from the Atlantic by the storm, as well as pulled off the beach by the surge. The sand had filled in the near shore to make a wide sandbar just off the shore break. The water was only ankle deep far out into the sea, and dry tiny islands of sand dotted the coastline.

Adam hit the dune at a run, crashing through the seagrass stalks in order to get to the high ground, all five feet of it, so he could get a wider view of the beach. Who knew what would be scattered all over the sand? People had found pieces of shipwrecks, unchained buoys, beer cans with strange writing on them, light bulbs thrown from ships when they were changed. Adam had found an air conditioner once. And one time a ship had lost several containers of cargo, including strange melons destined for Canada, large balsa wood blocks, and bags of Doritos. Rumors told of a container that held a Ford Mustang that had somehow escaped its ship, and was serenely floating its way to whatever owner could first find it.

Adam had all those things and more on his mind when he crested the low dune. What he saw was so much more amazing than anything he could imagine.

He saw it, easily, even though it was a quarter of a mile down the beach from him, a long dark tube with a short stubby chimney sticking up at a haphazard angle from the middle of it. It had beached on one of the sandbars just offshore. It was unbelievable, but it was also right there. It had a bow like the nose of a shark, and looked eerily similar to the predator. Only many orders of magnitude larger than any fish that swam in the ocean. Its nose was only a hundred yards or so from the breakers and dry land.

As impossible as it was, Adam knew, during the storm a submarine had beached itself upon Ocracoke's shore.

Adam ran out to the beach, never once looking down, no longer caring what treasures were at his feet. This was bigger than anything, an entire submarine. His vision bounced as he ran, tears filled his eyes from the wind and sun and the unbelievable feeling he had at making this discovery. Through the tears he could see that the craft was only slightly damaged in the stranding. The nose was dented, the railing along the bow crinkled. The stern was worse off, with bits that looked like a twisted wad of aluminum foil. If there were screws back there, Adam couldn't see them, as the waves swished along the stern, making a milkshake where they roiled around the giant boat.

As Adam got closer, he kept noticing something, but he couldn't quite put his finger on it. Something nagged at him, and it weighted down his feet, heavy in his shoes on the wet beach. His feet slowed, as if trying to stop the rest of him from getting too close. He found he couldn't move but so fast. Adam stopped before he came to the wet sand of the beach, with the boat out in the water. It looked precariously balanced on its keel, as if it could rock and tip over at the next wave. There was just something wrong with the dirty gray ship, the strange conning tower and bridge, and ... deck gun. "Submarines were supposed to be black, weren't they?" he thought to himself. "American ones were..." It was a known secret among the locals that the US Navy had a base up near Cape Hatteras, listening for Soviet submarines off the coast. What if these were the Soviets? And... why weren't they coming out? He had this delightfully terrible fear of Commie sailors pouring out onto the deck, loading the gun and taking aim at him. It sent shivers down his spine to think of him all alone on the beach, running for his life as explosions popped all around him. He forced his feet back to life, running back to the airport, back to his bike, to get back to the village.

He made it to his bike, sweating and exhausted. He was barely able to make it go, and he stumbled several times, putting his foot out to catch himself before he fell. There was just something so wrong with all this, he thought to himself. Submarines don't have deck guns anymore.

Where was the crew?

3

7:50 A.M.

SILVER LAKE

   Dan Howard had wasted all his curses in the first
minutes of arriving at Silver Lake. The harbor's name was
mostly a tourism promotion. Originally called Cockle Creek,
Silver Lake was definitely not a lake, and only vaguely silver.
At this moment, it had none of the attractive varieties that
were so usually applied to the location. Not only had two
boats cut loose from their lines in the night, one had piled up
at the mouth of the harbor when the sound had reversed
direction and sucked all the water out. When the hurricane
passed by, it had blown the water away from the sound side
of the island. As Gloria moved upward along the barrier
islands, the water that had been pushed away came back in a
rush, only to pour back out as the harbor slowly leveled itself.

It was like tipping a giant glass, and watching the drink inside splash back and forth.

The fishing boat was inexorably tangled in lines and nets, cranes and masts, as well as being half full of water. "Look on the bright side," Dan said to himself, "It's half full, at least."

It wasn't as if any other boats were coming in to moor in the harbor anytime soon. The Coast Guard boat that normally berthed in the harbor every summer season had steamed out before the storm, along with many other fishing vessels to be ported in hurricane holes inland. The ferries had all steamed away to be tied down to more secure docks. Dan knew that soon enough the North Carolina Division of Transportation would be sending out boats to check the shoaling of the sandbars along the sound. He wasn't sure, but he figured that the shoals would probably have shifted, and the channels needed to be checked and deepened before a ferry came back through that way.

He had no idea what Highway 12 was like heading to the docks for Hatteras, but that road was overwashed regularly, and he doubted the road would be passable until someone got out there with a bulldozer.

Dan scratched his head under his cap. His soft curls of black hair were hidden by a baseball cap. He hadn't showered yet, and his hair felt tangled and course. He had always set an example for his son to look his best. Dan's hand went down his jaw to scratch at his chin. He hadn't shaved either. "Oh, well," his brain just couldn't care but so much this early, after so little sleep. He stretched his stiff back. Tall and thin, he generally had a better concern for his looks. He was the face of the island around the harbor. Sailors, locals, business people all saw the jovial, smiling harbormaster wandering the docks, white teeth in a good natured smile, At 38 years old, he was old enough to command respect, and young enough that he wasn't seen as a crusty old salt.

While standing over the mess in his harbor, Dan was joined by Chief Bosun's Mate Jennifer Stone, who came walking over from the Coast Guard station, tired and worn from being up all night. She couldn't sleep in the storm. "Dan," she greeted the harbormaster with a tip of her cap.

"Chief," answered Dan in a low growl. The two stared at the mess of boats wordlessly. "Where do ya start with a pile like this? Damn." Dan let the curse out, a light and delicate oath considering his sailing heritage. Dan's ancestors, like half of the people on the island, were descendants of the original owner, William Howard, who was quartermaster of Blackbeard's ship when the dreaded pirate was beheaded nearby at Teach's Hole. Dan wondered if Uncle William ever had to deal with this mess.

The two scratched their heads, a ritual that all seafarers do when faced with a task.

Their silent consternation was interrupted by Adam pedaling furiously up to the harbor house, red in the face and more than a little shaken. "Daddy! Daddy!" he yelled.

"Adam! What's wrong?!" The gamut of a father and husband's fears ran through his body, his veins like ice water. When his son looked like this, he figured it must be the worst. "Is your mother okay? Is Shelly alright?"

"Yeah, yeah… it's…" Adam gasped and tried to catch his breath. "You won't believe it, Daddy. There's a shipwreck on the beach! It's a submarine!"

Dan, relieved but also a little disappointed and angry now, tried to steady his son. "Wait a minute, son, what do you mean, a submarine? Is it a boat out there or what?" He looked at Chief Stone with a little disbelief.

"No, Daddy, really. It's a submarine! A whole submarine! It's huge! It's right out by the airstrip! You gotta come see!" He tugged at his father's arm. Adam worried that the thing might float away in the moments he was gone. Someone had to see it with him.

"Alright, alright... C'mon, Chiefy, let's go see what it is. These things ain't going anywhere," he waved his hand dismissively at the wreck on the harbor mouth. "C'mon, pile in, boy, we'll take my truck."

Dan drove slowly and carefully over the roads. He knew his way well. He could pass through Ocracoke in the dark with his lights off if he wanted, but he still had to be cautious. Adam sat in the cab, in the middle of the bench seat, sweating in the heat as the air conditioning slowly began to cool down. "Why wouldn't he go faster?" Adam thought. They had to see it. Before anyone else did.

They parked at the end of the road by the airstrip. Dan got out and started to air down his tires, but Adam pulled on him. "You can see it from here. C'mon, you'll see it from the dune!"

"You know," Chief Stone told Adam, "It can't really be a submarine. They never get that close to shore, except to go into port. There's no ports around here. It's probably a container that washed up, or a barge or something."

Adam looked at her quizzically, squinting his eyes. "I know what a submarine looks like. This was a sub." Adam ran ahead. "It has the conning tower, the deck gun. It's a sub!"

Chief Stone stopped in her tracks. "A deck gun..." she thought. "Submarines don't have deck guns anymore." She forced herself to move, to catch up to the other two. The father and boy had just crested the dune, and Chief Stone saw them stop, their body language communicating what she would soon feel, too. Dan, frozen like a statue, his son sprung tight like a twisted band about to pop. She climbed the dune and saw it.

The big gray submarine sat there, immovable by the waves that washed against it.

4

11:00 A.M.

OCRACOKE BEACH

By mid morning, about ten people were standing out on the beach staring at the improbable boat sitting on a drying sandbar on an ebb tide. Forgotten was the cleanup needed in the town and the rest of the island. Crusty fishermen and the few town employees stood at the water's edge, all with looks of stupefaction and incredulity on their faces. Invariably a hand would go up under a salty soiled cap, scratch a head, and give it a shake. No one had an idea what to do about this.

Chief Stone felt herself repeating the same story over and over, every time someone would come storming down the beach in their truck, stop, get out, and all expressed some form of "What the Hell?!" Everyone turned to Chief Stone for an answer. The Chief was tall, broad shouldered, athletic, brought on from a disciplined life at sea and on land. Her tanned face peppered with freckles on her cheeks matched well with her straw blonde hair. She could fool some people into thinking she was a windsurfer when she was out of uniform, but right now the crisp and tight light blue shirt and long slacks gave her an All-American poster print of the US Coast Guard. She looked strong yet youthfully innocent, so it was a surprise to the locals to see her become a doting caretaker for the British cemetery on the island.

The village held a plot of land where four British sailors were buried after their ship was torpedoed by a Nazi U-boat in the early days of World War II, when the U.S. was woefully unprepared for German wolfpacks lying in wait for convoys steaming their cargo from the states over to Great Britain. Cape Hatteras was a favorite place for the U-boats, as the targeted ships passed close to land and were often silhouetted by the lights of the towns, making a torpedo run easier than practice. The Germans took almost 400 ships to the bottom of the sea, killing over 5000 men. The sailors died horribly, by explosions from torpedoes or deck cannons, burning fires of oil laden tankers, and the horror of drowning, either trapped in the ships as they sank, or pulled under Atlantic's waves to a cold unmarked grave.

Chief Stone had become an expert on the history of the events along the barrier islands, in tribute to the lives and deaths of the people whom she tended. So people looked to her for answers.

"What the hell?!" growled Andy King, the latest to show up. "Is that an American submarine?"

"No," answered Chief Stone. She repeated her mantra, now long practiced. She hoped that sometime soon someone else would explain this to the rest of the people on the island, or to the thousands that would come to see it in the future. "It looks like a German U-boat, from World War II. Must have been washed loose from being sunk during the storm. There were seven U-boats sunk around here, and this is probably one of them. Look at the stern. Probably took a depth charge there and it sank in shallow waters. All this sand here, it got

24

stirred up by onshore surge, lifted off the boat and it just sorta rolled with the waves.

"At least, I guess that's what happened."

Andy looked at the beached sub, scratched his head under his cap, and said, "A Natzi sub, huh? Well... damnhell."

"Oi wonder if we could lift it offa there and tow it around the back soide of the oiland," said another fisherman. Jeff Beasley, the EMT, huffed at the idea.

"No way you're going to lift it off that sandbar that easy. And even then, it ain't gonna float." He and the few other volunteer firefighters that stayed on the island stood around with the calm confidence of something that wasn't their problem.

"Oi say we get on board and see what's in there," old Bill Howard said. "Let's see whut them Nutzis got on this thing." Old Bill was always hawking on ways to make money off the tourists. People rumored that he knew where Blackbeard's treasure was buried. He ran a tourist shop and a gas station, and never missed an opportunity to make a buck. "Hey, that makes me think..." He spoiled around in the back of his truck and found a sheet of rope, coiled up in a figure eight. Throwing it over his shoulder, he began tromping out into the shallows toward the boat.

"Hey, what the hell does he think he's doing?" yelled Dan. Old Bill made his way through the tiny rivulets of waves. Low tide was not for another hour, but already the water had receded to where the ship was only 200 feet from the dry shore, and the sandbar upon which the submarine rested was high and dry. Bill made his way through the shallow breakers to the bow of the ship. The prow, pointed sharknose-like, bared down on him silently, a promised threat that if this thing could somehow come back to life, if its batteries would ever recharge, if its diesel would fire one more time, it would reach out and eat him and any boat in its way. But the thing was long dead, just a hulk of metal that had its best, and worst, days behind it. It was a big dead fish, Old Bill told himself, it just didn't stink yet.

He uncoiled his rope and threw one end over some exposed railing at the bow, caught the end, and tied a knot. The rope secure, he began walking back to the beach.

Sloshing ashore, one of the others on the beach teased the old man. "Now, all ya gotta do is pull real hard!"

"Pull nothin'," Old Bill spat. He dropped the line on the sand and went to his truck. In the bed he pulled an old Danforth anchor out. He tied the other end of the line onto the eye of the anchor, and threw the tiny anchor into the sand just above the high tide mark. The line fell slack in the water, washing around like a thin yellow snake.

"That anchor isn't going to keep that ship there," commented Jeff Beasley. Many others were thinking the same thing.

"It don't hafta," said Old Bill. "That thing's moine now!"

Chief Stone and Dan smiled at each other, just a half smile of understanding. The same way people tolerate the superstitions of their elders, so did they honor the old maritime laws of, essentially, finders keepers. If a ship was abandoned of crew, all someone had to do was secure it, essentially by tying a rope and anchor to it, and they could claim the ship as salvage.

"What's he mean, that's his now? I found it first!" cried Adam.

"What were you gonna do with it, boy?" responded Old Bill. He was crusty and ill tempered with kids. Adults, too, unless they had money in their hands. Adam had no response. He never thought that far. "Alroight," said Old Bill. "Let's go see what's on this thing." He went back to his truck and grabbed a greasy black old wrench, made for turning big bolts. He then snatched up a long silver flashlight. Clicking it on and off, he started walking toward "his" boat.

"Wait!" Chief Stone called. "W... you just can't do that! We need to wait for someone from ..." she thought. Who would she call for this? East Carolina University? They would have the proper team for archaeological research. The Navy? They probably would be the only ones to be able to move the thing. Who? Well, at least the Germans probably didn't have claim to the thing. No one was on board anymore. No one alive, anyway.

"Wait! C'mon!" she gestured to Dan. "The old fool will conk his head open on the deck!" There were probably still explosives on board, too.

Dan told his son to go back to the truck and get his flashlight, then he took off after the old man and the Coast Guard officer. The three splashed into the waves, short breakers that barely washed up to Dan's shorts. They reached the submarine sitting on the dry sandbar easily. It listed slightly to starboard. The three of them walked up to the lower side.

Old Bill headed toward the conning tower. Chief Stone called to him. "No, this way. There's a forward hatch that will be easier to access!"

Bill waved his hand over his shoulder, not even looking back. "Eeeeaahhh... I wanna see where the captain's chair is!"

Let the old man do what he wants. Chief Stone wasn't in the mood to argue with the crank. She and Dan began to climb the side of the sub, using footholds and ducts along the side to ascend to the weather deck.

The two found the exterior hatch on the forward hull. "This should lead us to the gangway for the officer's quarters," Stone said. She had a basic idea of what these U-boats looked like, but had no idea where the hatch would open to. It may be the torpedo room, supply storage, quarters, who knew? Her morbid curiosity ran wild with what she might find. The two turned the hatch wheel and pulled.

"Put yer back into it, Chiefy!" Dan grunted as they pulled. It gave way slightly, which surprised the two. It should have been stuck fast after all this time. Dan thought that they could use a pry bar, or a big wrench. If the tower hatch was this loose, Old Bill was probably inside already. The two pulled again, Dan pulling with his back while Jen bent her muscles into lifting the wheel. "Watch your feet!" she reminded Dan.

The hatch finally broke free of its seal, and the two lifted it on its hinge to the deck. "Make sure," Jen said, pointing to the hatch, "that doesn't close on us. The last thing we want is to have it closed and get us stuck down there." Light spilled in the shaft that led from the deck to the inner seal. Chief Stone jumped down the accessway to the inner hatch. The second hatch cracked open easily. The steel levers were ice cold to the touch, but turned smoothly, and the Chief was able to secure it open. Dan turned his plastic flashlight on, and let a feeble yellow beam shine down the hatchway.

Even with the weak light, Chief Stone cursed the darkness. A submarine was going to be tight enough. It was only going to be worse in the dark, and leaning sideways. She slipped her way into the gloom of the old abandoned boat.

Her sandy boat shoes found purchase on the rungs of the steps that lead down into the bow of the ship. Chief Stone found it hard to think of in ship's terms. "This thing wasn't made to go in the water," she thought. Anyone who spent time on a surface fleet found the idea of purposefully going inside a metal tube and sinking it to be beyond crazy. There was barely anywhere to go on a normal, what, day? Night? Shift? Time didn't matter on a submarine, she guessed. Two steps down and the walls were already closing in on her, she realized.

The hatch led from the front torpedo room and toward the wardrooms of the boat's officers, with a tiny hall of sorts, barely able to squeeze one person into. Dan shrugged himself in behind the chief as they slid their way into what passed as the U-boat's common area. Chief Stone, familiar with the history of the German U-boats if not their actual innards, wondered how the Nazis could pass through the tiny craft. The Germans had long promoted their now failed vision of the Master Race, the tall, muscular, blue eyed blond haired model of perfection, that in Stone's mental eye would not fit on board the confines of this boat. The narrow beauty of the Nazi hero would be dashed on the head and shins, bent on the tiny bunks, covered in oil, diesel, sweat, grime.

And blood.

So much blood.

The history poured into Chief Stone's heart now. The U-boat commanders brought death to the coast, and delighted in their bloodlust. So many died. Most of the bodies were never recovered, just left to the sea. Some made it to shore, just waterlogged corpses with little hope of ever finding their way home. Two small plots of land were dedicated to some British sailors who died during one of the attacks. Jen managed the plot on Ocracoke, a tiny spot of land belonging to Great Britain on a tiny island in North Carolina. It gave a tiny hope that maybe the spirits of the dead can rest in peace on slightly native soil.

Somehow the ghostly ship brought all the history, all the destruction and carnage of those early cold days of 1942 into the forefront of her mind. She shivered and froze in the narrow passageway, the realization that she was treading on blasphemous ground passed through her in a sulfurous wave.

"Chiefy… You alright?" Dan bumped into the chief when she stopped suddenly in the passage. Dan Howard had been following so closely he didn't have time to react when the Coast Guardsman came up short. The dim yellow beam shone off Stone's face, tiny diamonds of sweat beading on her forehead. The chief's face held a worried rictus.

29

"Yeah, I know," responded Dan to a statement not said. "Kinda wrong to be on this thing. Boats supposed to float, not sink.

"And definitely not sink other boats."

Belatedly, the chief spat on the deck, and Dan added to it.

They made their way aft, past the small stateroom doors of the officers. All closed, noticed the chief. Oddly, the boat seemed remarkably shipshape for a submarine blasted into the ocean floor for almost 45 years. There should be more damage, she thought. Then she had a more sobering contemplation. Where were the bodies?

Stone walked past the last doors on the passage, shining a light on the door, with a notation that read *Kapitänleutnant*. Tempted to open the door, she wondered what she would find behind it. Nazi treasures, swastikas, flags of the Third Reich, all the instruments of the unholy worship in a church that Chief Stone just couldn't understand. She also wondered if the captain was still there, going down with his ship. His body could be still resting in state, a martyred pilgrim on a malevolent crusade.

Chief Stone left that door closed. Of all the things she would see on this thing, that was probably the last. She hoped the bastard suffered.

They were at the final hatch to the middle of the submarine, which would lead to the helm and control room. The door was sealed tight, and locked with four pressure locks in addition to the hatch wheel. The chief rapped on the door with her knuckles. As if in response, the sub shifted slightly. Of all the things that could happen, this was the least of their worries. Old salts both of them, they knew the feeling of a wave and sand under a keel, and the rocking of a boat. A large wave probably slammed into the damaged aft section, then rolled down the keel, bringing a rush of sand across the boat. The feeling was unsettling in the strange setting of the sub, but not unknown to the two sailors. The ship seemed to breathe slightly. Items shifted somewhere on board. A few unsecured chains or tags swayed somewhere, creating the soft sounds that motion would always cause. Probably a book slid off a shelf, or a plate would tumble somewhere in the mess. The distant sounds made the feeling of the boat even more spooky. It reminded Dan of a clowder of cats, wild and feral, scurrying from cardboard boxes in the dark of night as a kid spies them with a flashlight. Soft sounds, half imagined, ran through his head.

Stone leaned over and banged the heel of her hand on the bottom of the hatch, which responded with a hollow dull sound. There was no water behind that hatch and it was safe to open. The two took hold of the latches and began to pull. Straining, Jen said, "Don't let them break completely. The other two will just get too tight to open." Dan and Jen switched to the remaining two latches and cracked their seals, too. Then they were able to easily pop the latches open. All that remained was to turn the wheel.

"Let's find that old man and get the hell outta here," commented the chief as she began to spin the hatch open. The wheel broke its lock on the hatchway with a silent gasp as the last of the locks that held the door gave way. Chief Stone pushed the hatch in, and it opened on silent well oiled hinges.

Inside, the control room gave off a dingy gray haze, resplendent in its monotony of dull ashen color. All black, gray, with only bits of white where dials shown in an incoherent German that the boat lay dead, no electronic or combustion pulse showed on the control panels. A center post thick as a tree but made of metal streaked with a thin grease grew up in the middle.

Jen and Dan entered the room, swinging the light from side to side in the small deck. They saw empty seats where sailors would man what Dan figured was the helm for the craft, though something without a ship's wheel was just wrong to him. Jen played the light down where she stepped as she crossed around the periscope.

Where she stopped, frozen, visibly shaken, and terrified as to what to do next.

There, on the deck of the control room, near the aft hatchway, was Old Bill. He lay motionless on his back, his face a rictus of horror and pain. His body lay still and flat, not giving away any telltale motions of life that most bodies would. His eyes were open, looking up, but not seeing. His mouth formed what looked like the mix of a scream and a gasp, but it said nothing. All of those things in one way or another formed a very accurate picture of the current and forever state of Old Bill Howard.

Yet none of them were nearly as important as the fact that the back of his head, neatly midway between the top and neck, was caved in utterly and completely. Blood had poured out onto the deck and stopped, as his heart no longer had the ability to keep pressure. There was no doubt that Old Bill was massively and completely dead.

That, however, was not what froze Chief Jennifer Stone to the deck, her feet unable to move, her brain unable to grasp or make any coherent decisions. As she shone her light down the lifeless corpse of Bill Howard, she lifted it to find the rear hatch open. There, she saw, in the gloom, pale sunken eyes in pasty white faces, lips drawn back, small and gray in the darkness. The weathered visage of a young sailor, starved of light for over forty years, looked back at her, a look of fear, remorse, and resignation.

A hand came over the young man's shoulder, moving him back. Chief Stone and Dan Howard stared motionless, unsure of what would happen if they moved in any direction. Out of the darkness, the hand went up to shield the eyes of its owner. He, too, had a face of pallor, white and ashen as if from a fire long ago put out. He wore a cap on his head and the two Ocracokers recognized him immediately as the captain. His hat bore all the markings of an officer. The white top cover was stained with sweat, and the clustered oak leaves were worn of their gold color. Those things did not frighten the two.

What frightened them was the small gold eagle pin atop the hat. It was the unmistakable symbol of the *Kriegsmarine*, the old German submarine force.

What truly terrified the two people was that the metal bird clutched bravely and proudly in its talons a very small swastika.

"*Der Greis fiel und schlug mit dem Kopf auf die Luke. Wir haben ihm nichts getan.*

"*Wir sind unschuldig.*"

5

1:30 P.M.

OCRACOKE SCHOOL

The crew of the U-boat U-857, now late of the Third Reich, stood or sat as they chose along the basketball court of the Ocracoke School. The gymnasium was generally reserved for basketball games and assemblies. It was occasionally used for shelter and relief efforts during a hurricane, and they had room for about 40 cots to stretch out across the court.

Chief Jen Stone felt it was an abomination to host a group of Nazis on the same place that innocent children played, no matter how sullen they looked. Dan Howard merely hoped to get the men into the gym without having to deal with the gawkers coming in to look.

They got the crew in and did a head count while locking the doors to the outside. Dan no more wanted a group of Nazis in black uniforms strolling around the island than he wanted the locals in to see these strange ghosts of another time.

Jeff Beasley had just finished gathering the vitals on most of the sailors and officers. He walked up to Chief Stone. "It's a wonder," he said, shaking his head and talking in a sotto voce whisper. "I can't explain it. It's like they haven't aged a day since they sank."

Chief Stone asked the man, "How are they even alive?"

"Have no idea. They all have a pulse. Weak, but a pulse, like 20-30 bpm. Blood pressure is pretty much what you'd expect with that heart rate. They breathe, but never deep, never shallow. It's spooky, I tell ya. It's like their bodies just don't care. You know how you can breathe in deeply, like have a big sigh? They don't do that. Not at all.

"The only time I ever saw this was a patient whose body temp dropped real low. He was like a zombie. And he didn't last long like that."

"What's their temperature?" asked Dan.

"I dunno; my thermometer doesn't go that low. They seem like room temperature, if I had to say so. What the hell is going on here?"

"I wish I knew," Chief Stone put her hands on her hips and pouted over the problem she had. She was completely at odds with the circumstances, and she had no course of action. She couldn't let them sit here forever, but there was no way to get them off the island. She didn't need the place surrounded by locals trying to get an eye on the Nazis, either.

"Are they hungry?" Stone was trying to figure out how to feed them. The school had no cafeteria. How had they eaten for all those years?

Jeff shook his head. "I offered one a Snickers bar. He ate half of it and then put it down. I don't think he can taste anything. Who turns down a Snickers?" Jeff was used to having problems too difficult to solve. An EMT could do a lot to stabilize a patient, give IVs and injections, but sometimes he just needed a doctor. Sometimes he just needed a hospital.

Sometimes you just needed a hearse.

Right now, the only solution Jeff needed was a beer. Or five.

The islanders listened as the crew mumbled quietly in the familiar sound of guttural German. The captain and other officers had barked out a few commands, mostly to pay attention and be quiet. The words weren't familiar, but the tone was to any sailor or military veteran. The sailors would keep quiet until their situation was less in flux.

They seemed to be waiting for something, Dan thought.

"Too bad we don't speak German," Dan said.

"Oh, I do," responded Jeff. "I took it in college. I did it to read foreign medical journals. I can't understand much, of course. I listened to what they were saying while I treated them. Mostly they ask each other what's going on or what are they going to do. They seem to be a little fascinated with the basketball goals."

"Well, let's not let them know that you speak German just yet. And maybe we can get them some basketballs."

Dan knew that some of the officers spoke English. The crew would have been hearing English and French, along with their native German, at some time in their lives. The radio operators would have been fluent in it, having listened to the radio broadcasts along the coast and the ship to ship calls made by the freighters passing along the coastline, in order to determine their location. Dan didn't relish the idea of getting information out of the Nazis, or even being around them, but they still were sailors of a sort. They may have been a piratical scourge in the 1940s, but now they just seemed pathetic relics with no country to serve. He wondered if they still held the same ideology, or being trapped in a submarine for over four decades had changed them. They didn't have any comparisons to make. There was no one to show them the folly of their course or how loathsome their movement was. It was going to be a shock to them. Dan wondered if they would care.

He walked across the court to where the officers had gathered. At some time, he would have to offer them a billet, some form of respectful hospitality garnered for officers. It was a tradition that dated back to when shipwrecked crews came ashore on the Outer Banks. The sailors usually enjoyed roughing it on the beaches for a while, but the officers had earned a bit more than a modicum of accommodation. He'd put them in a rental home if he had to. And he would put the crew either in the Coast Guard barracks or in a motel. Dave White wouldn't like having sailors in his motel under normal circumstances, and the chief seemed nearly livid at having the U-boat crew, refugees, whatever they were, on the island, much less bunking in her hall.

"Find the leak, pump the bilge," thought Dan. First things first.

"Captain," Dan addressed the man in the cap he had seen come up from the depths of the sub when they had first discovered Old Bill's dead body. He didn't know if he should salute the sailor. The man looked about 25, not taking into account the years trapped aboard. Dan struggled to find an idea of how someone so young, relatively clean cut, could be in charge of an instrument of death so big. Then again, Dan had learned to sail before he knew how to walk. And he never made the choice to kill other people.

Kapitänleutnant Reinhardt Krieg stood at attention and saluted Dan. He had one officer behind him, most likely his Executive Officer, second in command on the sub, Dan guessed. Another officer was stationed with the crew, along with a few non commissioned officers that he could pick out. The bosun was easily distinguishable by a cold icy glare he kept on the crew to keep them quiet and docile. The other petty officers mostly seemed to whisper to the ratings, telling them that things would be okay. Dan had watched them pat other sailors on the shoulders and talk good-naturedly, keeping the crew in decent spirits. Dan was a little surprised they weren't more happy about being rescued.

Dan waited for the salute to end, and put out his hand. It was the best he could do. He had already introduced himself, for lack of any better way of greeting on a darkened and stranded sub, over a body. He wasn't really an officer, but he wasn't going to tell this guy that. Let them think he was in charge. He'd start with that.

"Again, I'm... I am Dan Howard. I'm the harbormaster in charge of the island here." Krieg would understand that.

"*Guten Nachmittag, Herr Hafenmeister*," Krieg responded. Dan almost expected the young man to tap his heels and give a raised arm salute.

"Please, Captain, I know you speak English. Even a little. I..." Dan wanted to say his German was bad, but he didn't want them to even think they could be understood. "None of us speak German."

"*Ja*, yes, of course," the man's tone was a strange mix of singsong lilt and callous uncaring. It made Dan's skin crawl. The captain and his crew were all but dead, with little emotion showing in them. When Krieg spoke in a kindly tone, it came across as fake and challenging at the same time.

"Can you tell me more about what happened to you and the crew? How did you end up like this?"

Krieg turned away from his crew, as if to hide what had happened to all of them. The two men stood shoulder to shoulder as Krieg found his words to tell the story.

"I have no idea what happened to give us this condition." He started with the obvious. "I can tell you of how we came to be stranded.

"We were halfway through our," he thought for the words, "*seereise*? Voyage? Yes, our voyage. We had expended most of our torpedoes and almost half of diesel, and needed to return to Lorient for fuel and armament. We were on the surface running the diesels to charge our batteries. One of your airplanes spotted us before we could dive. We were able to get under water but we were attacked. The starboard side was severely damaged and we took on water.

"I attempted to run the U-boat toward shallow water, but we took on water in the rear battery and diesel compartments. The ship would power, but it began sinking stern first. I was able to hold it at an angle with the bow up, hoping we could rise to the surface and abandon it without being attacked again in the water."

Dan cringed inwardly at the thought. It was hypocritical of a submarine commander to be concerned with being attacked in the water when they continually did the same thing to other unarmed ships. He didn't comment, but held on to the thought in his head.

"The boat settled to the bottom in deep water. Too deep to escape but above our crush depth.

"I ordered the men to begin repairs and pump out the water from the ballast. We used manual pumps to clear the boat, and kept the flooding to a minimum. It was my intention to find a way to re-power the boat and rise to the surface. We would then either abandon it or make our way by raft to the shore to surrender, if we could not call for help from another submarine."

"But what about this?!" Dan gestured with his hands to the rest of the crew. "How did all of you survive under water for forty years?"

"We don't know." Krieg looked Dan in the eye. "This should not have happened. We thought we would run out of air and go to sleep. We were resolved to die in the dark, our families never knowing what happened to us.

"It was not what these men chose to do, but they knew it was possible."

To Dan, it was still beyond him how any man could call himself a sailor and want to go in a craft that went under the water. He also wondered how this many people could choose to blow up ships and kill people. Sailors went out to catch fish. If someone was in trouble, sailors dropped their nets and came to the rescue. People just didn't do what these men did. How could they choose to do these things, and how could they glory in it?

"We first thought it was a disease..." Krieg added.

If the captain was looking for a reaction, he got it. Dan never considered that. The sailors caught some strange disease that penned itself up on the submarine, somehow stopping the aging process, slowing all functions on the body while keeping the brain working. But that was impossible. Unless they had been exposed to some strange virus from a ship they sank, coming from an exotic port. Like when the Europeans brought smallpox to South American natives. Perhaps it was a strange viral revenge on the Nazi sailors.

"What ships did you come in contact with? Did you pick up any survivors?"

"*Nein*, .. No, we did not take up anyone from the ships."

Dan continued to take in a big picture of the man, coldly killing and sinking. He had no problem saying that he did not rescue survivors, Dan thought.

"We did not come in contact with the ships we attacked. Except the last one. We had launched two torpedoes at a freighter which sank quickly in deep water. We did rise to find out what the ship carried and her name. She was," he seemed to think, trying to remember the English word and trying to focus on his translation, "the *Tullza*."

Dan thought about the name. Tullza.

"The *Tulsa*?"

"*Ja, Tullza*."

The name meant nothing to Dan. A ship, a freighter named after a city in Oklahoma. Most likely an American. Probably not a Navy vessel. The captain would have noted that. The *Tulsa* was just one of many that would go to the bottom of the Graveyard of the Atlantic at the time. Most likely the crew were lost. No one would remember the ship or her men.

41

"We surfaced and asked the name of the ship. We asked of her tonnage and freight."

"What about the crew?"

"We supplied them with water and food. They were in the shipping lanes, and as we were returning to Lorient they would be easily picked up.

"We were not under the duty to do rescue at the time, *Herr Hafenmeister*." Captain Krieg gave Dan a stern glare. Do not attempt to judge me, he implied.

Dan stared back. "There's that Nazi sonofabitch in there," he thought.

It took Chief Stone walking up into the silent debate to break the cold impasse of the two men. "Captain, how many men are under your command?" She couldn't keep the accusatory tome out of her voice.

Krieg replied, "We are a crew of fifty. I have an *oberleutnant* and my…" he struggled with the English words, "…engineer. Along with under officers?" he lightly directed his hands at the Chief's insignia, three stripes and a rocker, along with the fouled anchor and shield.

"Petty officers, non-commissioned," she answered to the unasked but implied question. She didn't know if it was meant to imply the captain outranked her, but she took it as a reminder that officers usually fouled up, and the chiefs still did the job to fix everything.

"*Ja*, petty officers, and thirty seven sailors."

Chief Stone was concerned, but she put a look of puzzled indifference on her face. "I only count forty five men here, Captain. Where is the rest of the crew?

Krieg looked down, hiding his eyes in shame for the incident he had to report. "We lost some men in the attack. Three men died in the explosion, and one of my officers was killed during our attempt to recover the ship. He was electrocuted."

"That accounts for four men, Captain," Chief Stone didn't necessarily feel bad about the men dying in the submarine, but it was a horrible way to go. She may not like this captain or what he stood for long ago, but she understood the love a person has for their crew.

"One of my officers could not stand the thought of being trapped on the submarine. He… he attempted to take his own life. Due to our condition, he was only partially successful. It took him ten days to die, no matter how we tried to help him. Or help him die." There was a look of shame upon the captain's face. Chief Stone couldn't tell if it was shame for the man for killing himself, or shame on the captain for having so weak a member of his crew. An officer, no less.

A cold shiver ran through the cadre, as the talk of death for sailors was not lighthearted in any case.

"My condolences, belated," Dan shared with Krieg. He wondered how well his compassion would be received. "On a better note, after tonight, we will see if we can provide you and the officers with more fitting accommodations. I think we can find a house to put you up in. Your crew can stay here until we figure out a billet."

"Will we not be going home?" the captain asked.

"Well, I don't know about that, and I'm not the one to make those decisions. Right now, no one's going anywhere. The waterways and the roads are blocked from the storm. We're all stuck here for the time being."

6

3:00 P.M.

OCRACOKE BEACH

Frankie Tillett thought about taking his shoes off in the sand. A sheriff's deputy was supposed to stay in uniform, complete with shoes and socks on while walking the beach. No one would see, he thought.

The beach was empty. Except for the giant submarine, of course. Frankie had come out to the beach, dragged by the Coast Guard chief almost, and had seen the same thing that everyone else had. He had the same reaction, too.

"Damn!"

It had taken time, but within an hour, he had grown accustomed to the behemoth. After an hour, he grew tired of telling the locals not to go out to the sub. He didn't know how dangerous it was, just that the chief had said there might be explosives on board, and that it was hazardous to go out there. Frankie liked that word, hazardous. Dangerous sounded like a challenge to these islanders. Hazardous sounded like a chemical spill. Hazardous kept most of them at bay. So after standing, then sitting, there for an hour or so, letting the rest of the locals come out, look, then shooing them off to take care of more mundane duties, Frankie got bored. He drew in the sand. He plucked the sea oats. He wandered to the shore, not even heeding his own warning. He wouldn't get close to that thing out there, but he did think about going to the water's edge and soaking his feet for a moment. The boredom and monotony sat in quickly. He might have been happier if he had stationed his subordinate deputy here, and he had stayed at the gym with the German sailors. There really wasn't anything for him to do in either place. So he actually welcomed the visitor he got next.

Adam Howard showed up on the dune as Frankie walked back to his spot on hill.

"Don't be going down there," Frankie warned the boy.

"I wasn't. I just wanted to see my submarine," Adam pointed at the U-boat. He didn't know what was going to happen to the thing, but he still saw it as finders, keepers.

"Your sub?!" Frankie was incredulous. This thing wasn't anybody's. Maybe the Navy's, maybe the Germans', but most likely no one's. He started hoping that the damned thing would wash back out to sea, fill with salt water, and rust to nothing. And there was no way he was going to let some kid play on the boat.

"Yeah, I found it!" Adam claimed. Frankie was dubious, as if the submarine could be "found." "I came to the beach and there it was. I saw it before anyone." Adam was rightly proud of his discovery. He didn't see any difference in the submarine and a particularly attractive sea shell, or a piece of driftwood. He knew little of the horror the beast would have caused in the 1940s. He just imagined a giant playhouse for him and his friends, a popular hangout, a place to camp out in the waning summer nights. It was old, but virginal in his eyes. It may have been an instrument of death, but Adam had

46

known no war in his lifetime, and this was yet another opportunity for something new to do on an island with very limited borders.

Frankie saw the sparkle in the boy's eyes, and gave in to the youngster's fantasy. Sure, kid, it's yours. Just stay away from it. Frankie sat down again, happy for some company.

Frankie moved back to drawing in the sand, his head down on his most recent temporary artwork. That was why he didn't see the other object that washed up farther down the beach, to the south. Adam was in the throes of imagination when he noticed the other dark shape washed onto the tide line. "Hey," he said, mostly to himself, "what's that?"

Frankie looked up, following the kid's gaze. About a quarter mile down the beach, well past the U-boat, was a small bit of flotsam. Small was a relative word with the giant submarine in the foreground. It was dark looking, but with some flash of white, curved or rounded, about the size of a table top. It looked like a big broken egg shell.The soft waves that rushed the shore tried to move it, but the thing simply spun lazily on its base.

"I dunno, kid." Frankie had seen everything wash up, especially with a U-boat a stone's throw from him. Sailboats, dead whales and sharks, old wooden ribs of ships, he saw an air conditioner once. It could be anything. "Hey, why don't you run down there and see what it is." Compared to the submarine, nothing could be that dangerous.

Hazardous, Frankie told himself, hazardous.

The boy's eyes perked up as he realized he was tasked with a job from the sheriff's department, on an exploration to find something else, in addition to the submarine."Really?!" he exclaimed.

"Sure," Frankie said. He watched as Adam got ready to run down the shore. "Only go up by the airstrip. Not down the beach!"

47

Adam jumped over the low sea grass and pounded his way down the sand covered tarmac. "And come back the same way!" Frankie yelled at the kid.

While Adam ran down toward the egg shell, Frankie stared at the strange object, wondering what it was. He shook his head slightly. Here he was wondering about a piece of plastic, and the giant submarine went unnoticed. That damned thing wasn't going anywhere. It was aground hard. It would probably take three tugboats and a bunch of bulldozers to move it off the shore.

Adam finally reached the flotsam wedged in the wet sand. He was a mere dot to Frankie, about a quarter of a mile away. Frankie watched the kid plod through the soft sand, still wet and clotted from the storm. He was probably exhausted from the run, but kids didn't care at that age. Frankie watched as Adam made it to the egg shell, touching it on the top edge. He began to rock it and pull, but the thing wasn't going anywhere. "Just leave it there, kid. You can't pull that all the way up the beach," Frankie sighed. He waved and yelled to Adam, telling him to come back. Frankie doubted the kid could hear him, but Adam would get the idea. Frankie saw the boy wave back excitedly, then run back up into the dunes.

It took him a few minutes to get back to Frankie, coming over the sand dune in a breathless rush.

"It's a …" he panted, trying to catch his breath. "… a piece of a ship…"

7

3:00 P.M.

SILVER LAKE

"Shit! Shitshitshitshitshit, dammit to hell!"

As if Dan didn't have enough problems.

The few residents left in the town slowly gave in to the needs of getting back to normal, a giant submarine on their collective front porch notwithstanding. The roads had to be cleared, trees that had fallen needed to be cut and pulled back, and especially plans had to be made to receive aid from Hatteras and the mainland. They would need bulldozers and dump trucks to clear the sand, haul it to the beach, as well as to pick up the branches, reeds, and other detritus that always comes with a hurricane. The islanders knew what to expect, even if they didn't like it.

The power was out. It had been out since the first big winds had hit. It always went out during a storm. Some places used gas generators, but most of the islanders found it just as easy to do what their ancestors did and burn candles or oil lamps, and just go to bed when it got dark. Battery operated radios worked. They barely picked up anything, being so far from most stations, and the ones that were close enough probably didn't have power, either. The nearest local station for the Outer Banks was up in Wanchese. WOBR would normally fill the FM airways with local ads and a mix of Top 40 and adult contemporary hits, but they were probably without power, or under water at their lonely station on Roanoke Island, or just off the air, as they only broadcast until sunset. It was unlikely they would be picked up this far south anyway.

The Coast Guard building had a backup generator. It did little good except to power the air conditioner, which no one would feel since almost all the sailors had left with the boat to ride out the storm in more favorable weather. Their communications were down, to an extent. The antenna had become mangled in the storm after getting pelted with shingles. It would work, but it was picking up little, and even if they were broadcasting, they couldn't tell if anyone was listening.

Most of the locals had already left for drier and higher land, either taking their boats or their cars with them. But the ferries weren't running. It would be days before the DOT and the Coast Guard figured out where the channel had gone to, and there had to be test runs before they loaded up with cars and equipment and headed into Silver Lake.

The harbor, not really a lake, and rarely silver, was already a problem. Most of the boats had either been snugly tied or taken to safer holes inland. A few had become untied, or damaged in the storm. This, too, was not only expected but pretty much taken as a given that it would happen during a hurricane, and the islanders dealt with it the best they could.

The problem wasn't just that the boats had become fouled or sunk, but that one in particular had become completely untied and had floated out in the waning waterline of the harbor as the hurricane winds pulled the water away, leaving the sound and harbor shallow and dry. The *Betsy D* was half sunk, half wedged in the entrance to Silver Lake. That would be a problem. The owner and captain would be even more of a problem.

"Shit! Shitshitshitshitshit, dammit to hell!" The curses emanated from a bedraggled shirtless man who stood aboard the boat. Eddie Gruber, captain of the hapless and waterlogged vessel, was moving and throwing things around in a useless but dramatic fashion, trying to figure out what to do about his boat. Dan Howard stood on the dock nearby. But not too near.

No one in town liked Eddie.

"Shit! What I am supposed to do now?!" Eddie cursed again. Dan winced a little. The island was mostly uninhabited now, but still, most people there didn't cuss in public, not like Eddie. The old salts may use colorful language to great effect, but usually only on the water, and around their own kind.

Dan also knew that he would be responsible to having to talk to Eddie, to explain things about how the boat would get removed. He cringed at having to even interact with the man.

Eddie Gruber wasn't an islander. Some called him a Woodser, a dingbatter, some just called him a jerk or an asshole, which was more fitting. He was from Alabama, which at least meant he wasn't a *damn* dingbatter, someone from up north. Eddie had sailed to North Carolina with his boat after leaving the Alabama waters for some reason. Divorce, a kid he hated, didn't want to sell his boat for child support or alimony, everyone knew it was something along those lines. They also suspected it was because everyone hated him where he was from, too. The only reason no one asked him was because no one wanted to talk to the prick any more than they had to.

Dan Howard didn't want to talk to Eddie cither.

"Look, Eddie, you gotta wait til we can get somethin' to lift the boat. We're gonna have to get a crane on a barge in here, and refloat it, and put it on the dock on a hook." Dan waited for the response, the vile spew that he knew would come from any captain whose boat got half sunk in a storm, and only made worse coming out of Eddie's lips.

"Like hell!" Here it comes. "Dammit, get me one a those other boats and a bilge pump and I'll get her out of here. I'm not waiting for no crane ner someone like Old Bill to come throw a chain around *Betsy*'s neck and try to claim her!" By now, everyone had heard of Old Bill's failed attempt at salvage.

"No one's gonna claim her." Dan sighed. He had to put up with this nonsense, even though it should be obvious enough. "Old Bill didn't want your boat. It would be more work to raise it and he can't do anything with it now. Hell," now he's got me doing it, Dan thought, "you oughta let someone salvage it. They'd have to sell it, and no one is gonna pay money for it." Crap, Dan thought, I bit it now. Shouldn't have said something about his boat.

"What the hell you mean?!" Eddie got his dander up, his Gulf patois coming out in an annoying ring that sent shivers up Dan's back. He knew the Ocracokers had a unique brogue, but that deep south dipstick twang grated on him. "Why wouldn't someone want to buy my boat?!"

"It's not that, Eddie." He had to calm the guy down before he blew a gasket and had to be treated. God knows what else was wrong inside that man's body besides his brain. "I'm just sayin', everyone else has a boat that needs one. No one is gonna buy another boat, and no one from off the island is gonna buy one either. They'll just buy one somewheres else."

That seemed to soothe Eddie, just a little.

"Look, just git one a those other boats over here, get me a bilge pump that I can run off there, and I'll get her floated."

"Now, I can't do that, Eddie. And don't you go messin' around other people's boats, neither," Dan scolded Eddie. Pictures of Eddie ran through Dan's mind, of him taking someone else's boat, stealing their gear, probably stealing their beer. He didn't put it past Eddie. Dan looked at the captain of the waterlogged boat, bedraggled, sweaty, unshaven, and began to imagine just what Eddie might try. The island was empty, pretty much. Eddie could have the run of the place, going into unlocked houses to steal money, or probably liquor. "Great," Dan thought, "another thing to worry about." He'd have to get someone to watch Eddie now. It would prey on his mind if he didn't. Deputy Tillett was around, somewhere. The chief was at the Coast Guard station, working on the radio. He knew that getting anyone to come watch Eddie would be a fool's undertaking. Most people had their own problems, and didn't want to be saddled with another one, especially Eddie. Dan had his own problems and everyone else's, too. He didn't want to add to his issues.

"Listen, Eddie, I'll go up and get the hand pump from the stockroom, and you can use that. Just come up onto the dock, okay?" Dan turned and walked away briskly. He knew what was to come, and steeled his body and his ears to not respond.

"Hell, I don't want that thing! Get me a motorized one and hook it to a boat!" Eddie tried to be furious, but it came out petulant. Dan had dealt with children before. His patience at the end of this storm was about gone, but he held fast and kept walking, ignoring the calls. He was going to give Eddie a task that would either keep him busy or tire the man out, but at least he wouldn't be doing anything else to cause more trouble.

It was a long walk to the other side of the harbor. Longer heading back with a bilge pump and hose in his arms. Dan hadn't eaten yet, and he had probably lost five pounds in the day between hunger and sweat. He got back to Eddie's stranded boat, where nothing had changed but the angle of the sun. "Here, naow come up here and pump'er aout!" His brogue slipped more and more as he became more tired. He needed a shower. He didn't need a single word from Eddie about his damned boat.

Eddie began his tirade all over again. "I don't want tha.."

"I swear to God, Eddie! One more word, and Oi will hang you by yer ankles and feed you to the fish, you say anything. You got more help than anyone else got around here. Now shut up and take care of your own!"

Eddie saw the look of hate in Dan's eyes. Eddie knew he would push too far, and sometimes did, just prove he could. He usually ended up on the bad end of his actions, but he didn't care. No one got to push him around. This time, however...

Dan's eyes glared red. Give me a reason, he pleaded silently to himself. At that moment, he plotted to pick up a long handled gaff, used to snag game fish, and run the bastard through. He could cut the guy's head off and stick it on the bowsprit like Maynard did to Blackbeard, and he'd end up a hero on the island. No one would care.

Dan turned before he committed a very justifiable homicide.

Eddie waited. He knew he probably dodged a very bloody bullet, but he couldn't let the old coot win. His lips pursed with habit, forming the beginning sound of an F. His head struggled with his dark heart. He knew that would bring Dan back. Dan would be high above, while he stood on a crooked and rickety boat half filled with water. His mind let him wonder for the second he needed to save himself from a beating sure to come. Was it worth it? A busted lip? A broken nose? Thrown overboard? No way to get treatment, no doctor on the island. Some form of self preservation in his mind clawed at his mouth, not to do it, while his pride pushed back hard.

The two found a compromise.

"Ahhh, fff… forget you," he muttered.

Dan didn't turn back. He could go back, beat the living crap out of the man. He could stare Eddie down, or flip him off, all the behaviors Eddie was looking for, to back him into a corner where he had to fight Dan. It didn't matter who won, and Eddie certainly wouldn't, but if he got someone to start it, Eddie was always the victor in his own mind.

Dan kept walking toward his truck.

8

4:00 P.M.

OCRACOKE COAST GUARD STATION

Deputy Frankie Tillett had given up and come in to the Coast Guard station, along with most of the officials on the island. They mostly wanted a little air conditioning, and a place to gripe.

"I'm not staying out there. It's too hot. No one is going near that thing. Hell, it's not even interesting anymore."

"Alright," Chief Stone had to agree. Everyone that had seen the U-boat had already left for more important things. It just sat there. The tide didn't even pull on it, the boat was stuck so fast. No one really cared about the U-boat, except to see what was inside, and she made it clear no one should go aboard that ghost ship until it was checked out. Torpedoes, artillery shells, explosives maybe, left by saboteurs, anything could be on board. And it wasn't like someone wouldn't notice that an islander somehow mysteriously gained access to a Nazi flag all of a sudden. When someone finally went back aboard and found that the boat had been ransacked, well, there would be holy hell to pay on the island, and everyone would get the bill. Considering half the residual population was either some form of government employee, a child or elderly, it was fairly easy to make that view stick.

The outside door opened, letting the steamy still hot air flow in and mingle with the dry coolness of the hallways and rooms. The evening breeze had succumbed to a still air that brought out the mosquitoes on the island. The two climates of inside and out seemed to do battle.

"Chiefy…?" Dan Howard's voice called into the room from the opening in the doorway.

"I was looking for Frankie," he pointed and nodded to the deputy. "I hate to say it, but someone's gonna need to keep an eye on that Gruber boy. I think he's gonna do something stupid. All these houses empty, no power, no lights, he may just think of breaking into one of these homes. His boat is all half sunk, and he may think of tryin' to raise some quick cash."

"Or steal someone's liquor," added Frankie.

Frankie may not have wanted to babysit a submarine in the dark, but he knew what his job as a deputy was. He wasn't going to let someone cause trouble on the island on his watch. He was tired but willing. "I'm on it. Where's he now?"

"I left him pumping out his boat, but he may be gone by now," Dan said. "If he isn't at the marina, he probably is at his house. I doubt he would start this early. But you never know with him."

Dan ticked a mental checkbox in his head.

When are we gonna hear from civilization?"

Chief Stone sighed. "I don't know, really. They probably won't bother to return the Coast Guard boat here now. Not with the channel blocked. The antenna blew down on the radio, and I'm not going up there to put it back. Above my pay grade. Anyone else got any reach?"

Dan didn't think anyone on the island would want to answer, even if they could. Most CB radios would reach no more than 15 miles or so on a good day, and while someone probably had a linear booster on their radio on the island, they would be loathe to admit it to what essentially was a T-man in the form of a Coast Guard noncom.

"I tried to call, but I don't have the range. I couldn't even drive up to the pony pens," Frankie explained. The deputy had tried earlier to go up the road on the coast to get closer to Hatteras and the ferry terminal, but he had been blocked by sand on the road near where the Ocracoke ponies, decedents of English horses lost by an early English exploration, were penned up to keep them from roaming across the island and into the village. "There was a blowout over the dunes. DOT is gonna need a bulldozer to clear that."

"You think Dare or Hyde will send a helicopter or something?" Jeff Beasley said. He was speaking what the others in the room were thinking. The walls were closing in on the little village. Having a U-boat and a bunch of Nazi sailors in the school gym made things edgier for the islanders.

"I doubt it," Dan answered. "Not yet, not until they get any emergency plan in place. They may be flooded up in Buxton and Manteo now. Have to wait til they get all that sorted out. We'll give them a day. A day won't break us."

Dan's assuredness rang slightly hollow in the old wooden room of the Coast Guard station. He knew it, and everyone else knew it, now, too. They were trapped on the island with no good communication. The harbor was blocked and the channels were filled with sand. The road to the ferries was blocked halfway up the island, and the ferries were securely docked at the terminal in Hatteras. The power was out and couldn't be fixed until someone from the Tideland electric corporation could get a truck in and commence repairs, which wasn't going to happen until the ferries ran.

"Look, let's worry about this stuff tomorrow. I'm tired and hungry, and I know you got things to tend to at home. I'm gonna get something to eat and hit the bunk." Chief Stone needed to get everyone out of her office and get a little peace. She sighed. No one wanted the mantle of responsibility on this, but she knew how to handle it. She just didn't like working with civilians who were not part of her corps. Well, Dan Howard was okay, he was a sailor, and they spoke the same language, so to speak. The rest were a mixed bag. And people like Eddie Gruber were just trouble. He was an itchy burlap bag, Stone thought. "I tell you what," she gave in, "if you need something, I'll be in the ward room. I'll set up a cot here tonight."

Dan nodded, a quiet note of thanks. He had worried that the few people left would be a difficult group to manage. They probably wouldn't turn on each other, he thought, but they would be out for themselves. Hurricanes made people fearful, and the aftereffects made them tired and grumpy at best. When the community came together as a whole, they looked out for each other. When there was no one to lean on, the job at hand got a whole lot harder. Dan figured he would need to make an effort to rectify that, and make things seem a little better than they were. "Tell you what, Frankie, I'll come out and find you tonight. I can come out maybe at 2 o'clock? I need a shower and some bed, too. You'll be beat by then. I can probably make it until 5 or so, til the sun comes up. Eddie won't be causing any trouble by that time anyway. Even he's going to be tired."

"Sounds fair," Frankie said. He hadn't joined the sheriff's department to become some TV detective staying up all night on a stakeout, eating peanuts and looking through binoculars. Stakeouts for him and his fellow deputies usually consisted of sitting in their car for an hour or two near a party to make sure no one drove home drunk or started a fight. This may be a long night for him, but at least it will be a peaceful one, Frankie thought.

"Now, what about our guests?" Dan asked the group.

""Guests, hell," Chief Stone nearly spat the words out. She was getting more uncomfortable by the moment with the idea of having the Nazis on the island.

"We need a place to put them. They can't stay in the gym." Dan said. He didn't like the idea of them being able to wander the island. There were about the same number of sailors as there were islanders. In addition, the near death bogeyman condition that they possessed made them a potential night terror for the people of Ocracoke. The thought of them walking freely across the land where they once attacked was an abomination, no matter how much of a group of sailors they seemed.

"We aren't putting them here, I'll tell you that." Chief Stone was getting her dander up. She had put drug dealers in her brig before, but she wasn't going to put Nazis, no matter how old, forlorn or waterlogged, in the same bunks as her crew. "I'd be just as happy putting them back on board their sub.

"Then shoving them back into the Atlantic."

Dan knew they couldn't do that. No matter the history or politics, a shipwrecked sailor had a level of rights coming to them. He didn't like the Nazis, and he certainly didn't trust the captain. It was a level of trouble the islanders didn't need, but it was what it was. If they tried to shove those Nazis back into a tube, even if the sailors would go, when the news got out in a day or two, it would look bad for the Ocracokers.

"Well, let's keep them in the gym tonight. Maybe we can move them into a motel or one of the rental homes until we can get them off the island once the roads are opened. Until then, let's make sure we have a couple of people there. Jeff, you mind just bunking there tonight? It might be good to have someone listening in on them."

61

Jeff nodded his head. The life of an EMT on the island wasn't too exciting, normally, so he could handle a long night. It he had to, he'd hook up an IV to perk himself up. "Sure, I can stay. I'll see if I can find a phone there that works so I can get any calls." Usually, the medical personnel on the island worked as a direct call. If someone needed help, they called the EMT himself.

"We can get one of the volunteer firemen to come over, too."

Chief Stone wondered how many men they might need over there. She also wondered if they needed to be armed. "Do we need to get some rifles for the guys?"

"I don't know if we want to show up with guns around these guys. Let's not spook them. We don't know what they will do if they get threatened. And we don't even know what a bullet will do to them." Dan wanted to make sure the island stayed peaceful and trouble free. There was no reason to bring in more trouble. Keeping a bunch of sailors trapped in a gym wouldn't be a very good start, but it was better than a shootout with a bunch of angry Nazis that were already dead.

"I'm pretty sure our 870s would make short work of those fellahs," Frankie chimed in. The local sheriff's deputies were armed with a 12 gauge Remington shotgun in addition to their personal sidearm, the .357 revolver. "If it ever came down to it." Frankie normally didn't even like the idea of pulling his pistol, but this wasn't normal. He felt bad about saying the words as soon as they came out of his mouth. He never wanted him or his other deputies to seem like they were gung ho gunslingers to the islanders. He didn't even think anyone had ever pulled the shotgun from their patrol vehicle except to lock it up or clean it. He also wasn't going to hand out armaments from the department to civilians. "I bet there are some duck hunting guns around here. They might even seem less threatening if we say we are using them for game, or something," he trailed off. He didn't know if the deflection would work.

Everyone in the building knew they were on edge with the circumstances. Dan spoke up to reassure the deputy, "Don't worry about that. Let's not worry about that stuff unless we have to. We haven't had any problem with them yet. I'm more worried about Eddie than those guys." It wasn't entirely true. Eddie could cause problems. A group of nearly fifty potentially enemy sailors from a time long past was infinitely more risky. "Look, we're all tired and hungry. Let's go home, make sure our lives are right, get something to eat. We'll think better after we have some time."

Chief Stone agreed. She wanted everyone out of her station anyway. The day had been long enough for her, and she needed a little peace. She didn't want them getting too used to the idea of free air conditioning, either. "Yeah, look, I need to work on the radio. I have no idea how I'm going to fix that antenna..."

"You want some help, Chief?" Jeff Beasley chimed in.

"No, I don't want any help, and I don't want anyone, especially me, climbing around on the roof. I'll figure something out after I get something to eat. You fellahs go home. Get some rest. We'll do more in the morning. Maybe someone will come down tomorrow from Hatteras." Just get out, she didn't say.

"Okay, Chiefy," Dan answered. "We'll get out of your hair."

Frankie spoke up, while thinking about how it would look if he was found asleep in his patrol car on a stakeout. "Yeah, you know what, that might be a good idea. Tell everyone you see not to go out tonight as well. At least that way I can see Dan's truck when he comes to spell me."

"You putting a curfew up, Frankie?"

"Hell no! I doubt I have the power to do that anyway. I'm just saying let's keep off the roads tonight. They aren't cleaned off and no one should be driving around at night in the dark anyway."

The rule of law for the islanders was somewhat secondary to common sense. Living in a tight knit community led to a basic understanding of both respect and openness. They didn't need any declaration of a curfew. It just made sense to do so. With the power out, when it got dark, the best thing to do was to go to bed and wait for the sun to come up.

"Alright, decided." Chief Stone verbally whisked the people out of her office. Just a little peace, she thought to herself. The meeting broke up.

The group headed outside, where the sticky humid air and still high sun beat onto them. The air conditioned skin that they had enjoyed disappeared in moments, forming the all too familiar layer of sweat on their arms, necks, and foreheads. It was the nature of the beast on the coastal island. That didn't mean the islanders liked it.

Off in the distance across the lake they could hear the steady stream of cursing from Eddie, still at work trying to right his boat. Involuntarily, they looked over as one to see the man, at a loss for what to do on board his boat, moving things indiscriminately. Eddie's black hair shook as he looked back across the water at the group. The crowd scattered quickly, avoiding glancing at the man, out of fear they would somehow be roped into helping Eddie.

Except Dan Howard. He stood looking over his harbor, staring at Eddie. Eddie looked back, so desperately wanting to say something, knowing he'd regret it. Finally, Eddie bent down and lifted up a cooler, setting it precariously along the raised port gunwale. He muttered something that carried in the wind, but didn't have the strength to say it in Dan's direction.

9

10:00 P.M.

LIGHTHOUSE ROAD

Frankie drove his patrol vehicle down the pine needle covered Lighthouse Road and stopped at Albert Styron's Store. The store was boarded up for the storm and the current owners left for higher ground. Albert Styron would not be coming back to open it. He opened the store in 1920 and ran it until he was lost at sea in 1956. The parking lot to the store gave Frankie a clear view of the side roads off of Lighthouse, including down the lane where Eddie's cluttered beach box home sat. An oil lamp of some sort sat in the window, flickering hazily on the salt coated glass as Eddie wandered through the house. He wasn't going anywhere soon, Frankie thought. He realized that if Eddie did something, he would have to arrest him, and then take care of him. Frankie didn't want to do that. He hoped Eddie went to bed soon.

10

HOWARD LANE

Dan Howard fell into a fitful sleep. He was dead tired, but at least he was clean from a cold outdoor shower. He had come home to a clean yard, courtesy of his wife and son. Adam had probably wanted to impress him in order to get a better chance at getting something on that sub, he thought. But Dan had come home late, and beat, and no one pressed him on what he had been doing, which was fine with him. Shelly and Adam had asked a little about the old U-boat. Dan had said that he gave up having any control over it to Chief Stone. He figured that the Coast Guard had priority, like if it was a lost buoy, or a shipwreck, which it pretty much was. He didn't care. The Germans could come and get it in the middle of the night, as long as they kept it quiet long enough to sleep til 2.

Dan tossed and turned in his sleep. His mind kept reminding him to wake up in the middle of the night to spell the deputy, and he worried he would sleep through his alarm.

Adam had turned his bed back over to a regular mattress. He had stayed out until after dark, raking the leaves and branches out of his yard, and from the road nearby. Part of the kid in him wanted to do the bare minimum work, raking right up to his property line, but no farther, and letting someone else deal with the rest. Another part still wanted to please his parents, and show he could do as good a job, if not better, than they could. He was growing up and needed to be more responsible. So he cleaned the driveway and road, picked up some of the big branches down the lane and moved them to the side, cleaned his mother's car of pine needles, and raked the road. He even pulled out his camping lantern to light up the twilight to keep working into the night if need be. His mother finally called it quits when she realized he was working in the dark.

Now he fell asleep in his dark, quiet room. The usual hum of electricity that surged throughout the house was gone. There was no sound of the air conditioner rattling on, the whir of the refrigerator, or the babble of the TV. The still night of the clear high pressure that moseyed in after a hurricane didn't even leave a breeze to blow through the open window. Not that it mattered. For the first time in his short life, his feet ached from standing all day. He had heard of adults complaining about sore feet, but never experienced it himself, until now. This was the first time he remembered a bed being truly a place of rest instead of a de facto punishment. It was time to go to bed, and Adam didn't mind at all.

11

MIDNIGHT SEPTEMBER. 28

LIGHTHOUSE ROAD

Frankie felt his eyes droop past the point of keeping them open. He knew the feeling of exhaustion. He was seeing small animals peek from behind the bushes, only to disappear when he looked straight at them. His brain told him to just sleep, just a little, it would be alright. Then he would find himself slumped over five minutes later. His body was done with staying awake. He knew he had to make a decision. He reached for his radio.

"Jimmy, Jimmy, Over," Frankie put out a call to his subordinate. He had been loath to do so, hoping to keep Jimmy Gray out of the middle of the night so he could assist tomorrow. But Frankie couldn't stay awake another moment; he was done.

He called again. "Jimmy, Over." Deputy Gray should have been in his truck or in the gym, watching over the... prisoners?

"Go ahead, Over." Jimmy came on the line.

"What's your 10-20, Over?"

"I'm outside the school. Those guys are all asleep in there and we turned most of the lights off. Beasley is inside by the back doors and I'm out front. Pretty quiet for a while now. Over."

"Listen, Jimmy, I gotta go 10-7 'til morning. I'm out on my feet here. I need you to do something, okay? Wait 'til after 1 and then drive over to Eddie Gruber's house, make sure he's still in. And then just check out the beach front, make sure no one's out there by that sub. It's pretty quiet now, and I think he's gone to bed, but you never know with him. Just do a quick patrol. Over."

"10-4. Nothing is gonna be happening here anyway. Over."

"Also, Dan Howard may be out tonight. He said he would come help out. If you see his truck, just know that's why. You can probably just send him back to bed. Quiet as a tomb out here. Over."

"Roger that, Over and Out."

Blurry eyed and tired, Frankie put his car into gear and drove home, the road coming up to meet his slow pace as he drove by memory to his driveway, and closer to bed.

12

Dan awoke early. His body was not going to let him rest until his mind was at ease, and that wasn't going to happen tonight. He arose from his bed and dressed quietly into a clean blue work shirt and jeans. Soft and worn, they gave the false impression of both coolness and comfort. He would regret wearing them later, when it got hot, but right now he wanted something that would provide some measure of protection from the biting insects and scratchy things in the dark that would reach out and cut his shins. He tiptoed to the bedroom door, swinging it open quickly so as to minimize the squeaks of the hinges. His wife didn't stir on her side of the bed.

She probably would wake up for a moment when he started the truck, but there was little he could do about that.

He drove in silence, early for his meeting with the deputy, so he took his truck out to Silver Lake. It was quiet,

71

even for late at night. Silver Lake twinkled with the starlight and a full moon. No streetlight blurred the darkness, and no house spilled out the yellow tungsten lights from their lamps. His truck was the only vehicle to shine its lights across the road. It was an eerie feeling, as if a void of darkness was taking over the island. Dan turned off the engine as he parked and stepped out into the blackness.

The docks were familiar to him. The smell of creosote and diesel came to him like friendly ghosts. A light wind made the shrouds and stays of the boats tinkle in the breeze. The water in the harbor, usually well protected, was like glass tonight, without a swell or ripple. Farther across the harbor, the shadows of the few boats left formed a hazy and deformed pattern, like a sea monster rising from the depths late at night to hunt without fear of humans.

From somewhere in the ink of night, a ship's bell rang. Indistinct and without location in the blackness of the night, it clanged softly, once, twice, then with a diffuse thunk it was silenced.

The sound, though familiar to any seafarer, was disturbing to Dan. No one else was out at that time. No one he could see. A ship's bell ringing on its own was a very bad omen.

Dan felt something tread on his grave. He shivered even in the comfort of a warm night.

"Time to go," thought Dan to himself. "Before the monsters get out."

Unsure of where Deputy Tillett might be, Dan first drove down toward Lighthouse Road. "Eddie's house is as good a spot as any," he pondered in his head.

Dan turned down Lighthouse, slowly driving down the road, looking toward Eddie's darkened beach box. No lights, no candles or lanterns came from the windows. Nor was there a sheriff's vehicle waiting for Eddie's inevitable nighttime excursion. In the middle of the night, nothing came easy to Dan.

Deputy Tillett could be out following Eddie, or even have him at the sheriff's office. If Frankie was surreptitiously tailing the miscreant, Dan didn't want to give anything away. Still, he needed to make an attempt at finding the deputy.

Wheeling the truck around, he turned back and began heading toward the coast, toward the sheriff's office and the beach beyond.

The office was as dark as everything else on the island. It was a simple building, all square and government, with no soul or personalization outside of the Hyde County Sheriff's Department sign. It sat black and lifeless, like a tomb. The place probably had a generator, too, thought Dan, but Frankie hadn't been there all day, so he hadn't had the need to turn it on.

There was only one likely place left. The beach.

And that damned submarine.

Dan said a silent prayer that he didn't think even his own head could hear, let alone God. It was a quiet plea from his conscience for there to be nothing out there. If anyone heard it, they didn't listen.

Dan snapped the lights off the truck, driving by feel and the light of the moon. It was enough for any person who knew the island like he did. He drove to the beach access and saw what he expected. A patrol truck sat in the dark, pointed at the dune line and the hidden beach beyond. Dan stopped, turning the truck off, and waited for a moment in the silence.

There is something about a calm that all sailors know. It's a foreboding spirit. The calm before the storm was more than an expression to any fisherman. Many a waterman has fished at a spot, keeping a weather eye on the approaching dark clouds, hoping they will turn, the fear of the approaching storm tempered by the blinding run of fish filling the ship's hold. There was always the hope of one more cast, one more pull on the line, and then they felt it. The first cold wind of a front, the sign of the storm bearing down. This meant it was time to go, to get everything tied down and put away, start up the engines and get home. But it was always too late. The rain lashed, the wind stirred the water, and the boat rocked. The calm always disappeared.

Dan got out, flashlight in hand, but still off. "Frankie," he hissed through clenched teeth. No matter how quiet, he knew anyone there would have heard his door open and shut. The Ford had a distinct wrenching clank to its hinges and locks. Dan looked around in the darkness, looking for another vehicle. There was none around aside from the big Chevy Blazer. "Frankie," he called out, a sotto voce whisper that would carry to the dune, but hopefully no farther. Dan was jumpy enough, tired and strung out. He couldn't imagine how Frankie felt. And Dan remembered that Frankie was armed.

Dan walked slowly, almost stalking, as if it would help him in the dark. The night was exquisitely uncomfortable. The salt air was still warm and thick with humidity, and a diaphanous silt hung in the air, which seemed to take inanimate delight in clinging to Dan's sweaty neck. The sand at his feet still contained a bare modicum of the rain from the hurricane, which had made holes where the men had tromped through the sand to the beach the morning before. Now the sand crunched and slipped under Dan's work shoes. He stumbled in the darkness as the sand slid beneath his feet.

His discomfort was already at a knife edge when he stumbled and fell over something more substantial. An irrational fear worried at him that he had impaled himself on an old piece of shipwreck, with jagged rusty nails exposed. What he felt was much, much worse.

He placed his hand down to push himself up and felt something slightly soft, like a wet backpack. Without thinking he placed his hand up farther, and felt a strange mix of wet, warm, and scraggly. He thought at first he had placed his hand on a dead shore bird, its feathers torn and innards exposed. He flicked on the light in his other hand.

He saw his hand come back to his face, covered in a thick crimson, a bright red that he knew well, but had rarely seen in such copious amounts before the last morning. His light shown down and saw the source. In the path lay the body of a man, his clothes befitting a member of the sheriff's office. What was left of his head was covered in a mix of short blond hair streaked red with blood and bone. The back of the man's head was severely caved in. If his last thoughts could be seen by some horrid divining of entrails, the man's final emotion would have been one of terror and pain.

Dan stood up, shock and despair mixing with the rising bile in his stomach. "Ton...." Was all he could get out before he retched. He tried to hold in his stomach, but the stress proved too much as he disgorged what little contents he had left in him. Gasping for breath, he lay over the legs of the supine body. His hands held Dan up; he felt the sand cling between his fingers, but was unable to do anything about the gritty feel. His arms shivered as the first chill hit him. Sweat beaded and poured over his forehead. Finally emptied, he fell to his elbows, trying to keep himself out of his own retch, when he realized he was laying over the legs of a dead man.

Dan screamed, rolling himself off and away from the mess next to him. His flashlight was half buried in the sand, and its beam shone on the dead body's shoes and pants. Dan noticed the man's legs, slightly shorter and thinner than they should be. The image of the man's skull, crushed and opened, was sadly imprinted into Dan's mind, but something in it gnawed at him. The short blond cut was not Frankie's longer black hair. Dan got up, legs still shaking, and crawled over to the body. He kept the light off of the head so as not to see the hole, though the blood had poured down onto his back, and glistened in the yellow light. He took a shoulder in his hand and pushed. The body was heavy, with no give and no rigidity that usually came with the living trying to help. The body was fully dead weight. Dan pushed harder, and the head lolled, still staying face down in the sand. With a final push, the man's body turned over. Even covered in sand, the face was recognizable, and it wasn't Frankie. The eyes and mouth were open, filled with sand but staring and screaming in a silent rictus. Dan recognized Deputy Gray immediately.

Dan was able to walk back to the patrol car and his truck, his knees shaking and body dehydrated. He went to the sheriff's truck and pulled on the driver's handle. He had hoped to call on the radio to Frankie, to tell him, what? That Jimmy Gray was dead? That he had been killed?

The door was locked. Dan looked inside, but could see nothing. The car was turned off. Jimmy probably had the keys on him. He was damned sure he wasn't going to go through a dead man's pockets.

Dan went back into his truck and sat down. The night held him thick, the darkness closed in as the stars winked out of Dan's vision. He had no idea what to do. He couldn't bring himself to leave the body there, but he had no way to lift Jimmy by himself. Dan slammed his hand onto the rim of the steering wheel. He wanted to scream and curse into the night. Then he realized that Jimmy had been murdered, right there on the beach access. Jimmy had probably been walking around outside, following someone, when he was attacked in the dark. He was just left there in the sand.

And whoever did it might be out there in the darkness. Right now. Out there, looking at him. He closed the door to his truck and locked it, digging in his pocket for the keys. The truck was hot and cramped, unfamiliar and alien to him even though he had owned it for years. He smelled the oily mix and creosote of his life as they braided their scents with blood and vomit. As hot as it was, he didn't dare roll the window down. It provided some comfort of protection from the bogeymen that creeped and crawled outside, a horde of black clad murderers armed with dull instruments of death.

He put the truck in gear and backed his way out of there.

13

Eddie Gruber was stomping awkwardly back across the dune when he saw the black shape rushing toward him. He had no idea what it was, and he had little in the way of decision making skills in tight spots, so he did nothing more than stand there as the black thing rushed up and hit him across the face. He fell in a heap, cobwebs clouding his head, and stars filling the night in his vision. He dropped the duffel bag full of Nazi sailor uniforms and a U-boat pennant he had stolen from the stranded submarine. His hands patted the sand, still looking for his lost booty.

His brain couldn't focus on what had happened to him. He still was in a mode to steal, and escape. He couldn't fathom that he had been found, or attacked yet. It took the faint recognition of a voice, a sound in his ears, some mix of anger and barbarism, that led Eddie to realize he was in danger. The knee in his chest as the black shape pinned him down helped the awareness immensely. The voice cried out, a terrifying mosaic of high pitched shriek and guttural stabbing, "You sonof-" the rest of it, none too hard for Eddie to determine, was drowned out by a horrific cuff to his ear, causing this head to ring like a thousand wasps were swarming inside his hollow skull.

Eddie's hands, seemingly disengaged from any other part of his body, put up their own form of protection, trying to keep the swinging fists away from his head. His chest felt like it would pop, the pressure from the leg on his ribs was so great. Fists came flying in, left and right, trying to tear down Eddie's quickly weakening defenses. The wasps were having a field day in his brain, and his mouth, so normally ready for a smart comment, did what it could to keep itself shut, in hopes of protecting his teeth, and maybe his life.

"Get off!"

It wasn't Eddie saying this. Dan Howard called out, pulling the shape off of Eddie. Flashlights turned on, exposing the mess that Eddie was in. Dan had Frankie Tillett locked across the shoulders, holding him back from pummeling Eddie into the sand. Chief Stone shone a flashlight at Eddie, the glint of the light sparkling in the blood that dripped from his wounds on his face. Eddie was bleeding from his ear, probably torn partially, as well as from his nose, which was slightly crooked, though Stone wasn't sure if that had happened during the assault or it was just like that. And his lower lip was cracked and bleeding.

Considering what Eddie had done, he didn't look that bad.

"You killed Jimmy, you bastard!" screamed Frankie, pulling at Dan's restraints.

"What?!" Eddie blubbered. His head was still full of spiders and wasps. He couldn't think straight. "I didn't kill nobody!"

"Well, what have you been up to, Eddie?" Chief Stone shone the light on the duffel that had fallen beside Eddie in the sand. The mark of the Kriegsmarine and the broken spiraling cross of the Nazi swastika were printed upon it. He hadn't even bothered to bring his own bag. The red of a wartime ensign draped loosely out of the top of the duffel. Stone could see an officer's hat with a gold eagle inside. She couldn't make out the rank, not that it mattered.

"You went to that U-boat, didn't you, Eddie? We knew you would. When Deputy Gray followed you, you hit him on the head. Did you even know you killed him, Eddie?" Chief Stone was like ice. She didn't think anyone on the island was that cold blooded, to simply cave a man's skull in just to loot a ghost ship. Eddie was a problem. He started fights and got other people in trouble, but this was a new low for him.

"I didn't kill nobody! He's crazy! You're all crazy!" Eddie tried to get his head engaged into talking them out of this. Part of his mind thought they were going to kill him here, on the beach, in the middle of the night. His bluster, his desire to fight back and mock people until they were goaded into a confrontation was almost gone. It was replaced by a fear he didn't know since childhood. It was a helpless terror of being caught, and the punishment was going to be severe. Just like his father had done to him. Just like he had done to his...

"You're gonna cook, Eddie! I swear I'll see to it personally," Frankie pulled at Dan's armlock, but he knew his heart wasn't in it anymore. Jimmy was dead, and there was nothing Frankie could do about it, except see justice was done. "You'll get the fucking chair for this. And I'll be there. I'll watch you cook, you hear me! I'll watch you burn!"

Frankie was swamped with emotion. He had come out with Dan to find and recover Jimmy's body. The sight unnerved the deputy. It wasn't something that happened here. Assaults, domestic disputes, the general problems of an isolated island where people can rub each other wrong. But no one would commit murder here.

After having the body taken back to the village, to join Old Bill in the town ice house, it hadn't taken Frankie long to find Eddie's truck parked at the end of the airstrip, about 400 yards from the murder. They knew, Frankie, Dan, and the chief, that Eddie was out pilfering from the wreck. He had seen Deputy Gray following him when he drove to the beach, so Eddie turned his lights off, parked down the airstrip, had hidden, and snuck up behind Jimmy and smashed him on the back of the head. Eddie may not even had known he killed the man.

Chief Stone wondered why Eddie would have even done it. He should have known he would have been caught sooner or later. He couldn't have gotten off the island. Maybe Eddie thought it was like an old police show, hit him in the head, and half an hour later they get up rubbing their neck and everything's fine.

Still, the hit to the deputy's head was vicious. The back of the skull was caved in to the brain. Chief Stone was worried that they would have to come out at daybreak and clean up the rest of the poor man's remains. It was just too late, too dark, and everyone was tired and hurt from the incident. Though she doubted anyone would sleep tonight.

"Where's the weapon?" Chief Stone wondered.

14

8:00 A.M.

OCRACOKE COAST GUARD STATION

Chief Stone had slept fitfully for a few hours the night before, and had awoken from the strange visions in dreams as ethereal phantasms garbed in red and black had washed at the edge of her unconscious mind. Tired as she was, she preferred to be awake.

Hot coffee and breakfast helped some. She was glad to have power from a generator, and hot and cold food. She pictured the locals on camp stoves, or even burning driftwood in a fire to make some thick black java, suitable for cleaning the boats as much as drinking. Her coffee was strong and bitter, a deep brown with a bit of alkaline.

She stared out the window, looking east, as the full of the sun had already come up on the day. A new day, a new problem. She wondered how the island would handle it. She didn't know how the island would handle the next problem to show up when Dan walked in.

"Chiefy," Dan greeted the bosun's mate with somber reverence. The usual gruff lilt was gone, and the name tailed off, more of an *–eh* than an *–ee*.

And no wonder. The two had been witness to the current population of the island going down by approximately five percent in one day, with neither death by the hurricane.

"Any idea what we're gonna do with the day?" asked Dan.

The chief pondered for a moment, thinking of telling Dan the news she had gotten hours before when she woke up this morning. She decided to ease into it. "I got nothing. I thought of sending someone over to Hatteras in a bay boat to see if we could get some help, but I don't know what anyone could do. It would take all day, and they must have problems of their own there." Dan and Stone looked at each other silently. Not problems like ours, the two thought simultaneously. They doubted that Hatteras had a submarine with explosives just offshore, and a school full of Nazi sailors from forty years ago.

"Yeah, until we get all that shoaling sorted, they ain't getting anything bigger than a shovel in here."

"That's not our only problem." Chief Stone held up a portable weather radio and clicked it on. The broadcast was full of the typical static that came through the marine VHF frequency. When the usual blather continued unabated, an impatient Chief Stone just blurted out the news. "I've been tracking it. We're getting another storm."

Dan was dumbstruck. "Not another hurricane? There was nothing nearby to that storm."

"No, it's just the offshore remnants of a low, some tropical depression, but it looks bad. We'll get a lot of rain, lightning, and some onshore flow. It's just gonna sock us in for another day now. It probably is starting already with this high tide we're having," the chief said as she glanced at her tidal clock.

"Great. That's just all we need." Dan was already weighted with the worry of the whole island, two bodies in the ice house, a gym full of formerly enemy combatants who may or may not be diseased or cursed, he had no idea, and the fact that through all this he had shirked his responsibilities at home. He reminded himself to thank his son and wife. And hug them tight. All the work they did, and the storm would bring it all crashing back down upon them again tonight.

Dan wondered how it could get any worse.

Just then, Jeff Beasley came barging in the door. "Hey, you guys know who has access to any emergency food supplies? I think we're gonna have to feed those guys. They're getting hungry."

Careful what you wish for, Dan thought.

15

9:15 A.M.

OCRACOKE SCHOOL

Chief Stone watched in silence as the German sailors ate. The men had none of the childlike exuberance of the school kids that usually ate at their tables. There were no squeals or screams, none of the fake bletches of kids rejecting their food. Yet the sailors did not eat in silence either. The intercourse of German communication did not prattle like its English counterpart, coming instead in low, conspiratorial tones. Chief Stone couldn't tell if they were complaining about the food or plotting to attack Norfolk, as either seemed likely.

Officers stood watch at first, before settling in at their own table. All the ranks found their own level, a tidal flow of high ranking officers, non commissioned officers, and the bulk of the crew separately having their first meal in decades. Only Captain Krieg stood divorced of the group, letting his lower officers handle the mundane work. He glanced over at the group of men and woman standing by the door, watching his sailors eat. Five people, formidable, all fit and seemingly specialized. He knew the firefighter, the *Feuerwehrmann*, a bold yet happy young man, Aryan, and the, he pondered his terms... *Sanitaterunteroffizer*? He was some sort of medical corps service. The island people used a strange term he did not know. This man was always around, it seemed. Krieg wondered if the... doctor, would that be the right term? If the doctor was there in case the crew was diseased. What would those men do if they were? Another man, armed, in a uniform, *polizei*, stood arms akimbo, right hand in easy reach of a bright chromed pistol. A cowboy, Krieg thought, or, what had they heard on the American radio stations, a *Copper*. He was not sure why they called their *polizei* the name. The man looked ashen and stressed.

The last two were the ones with whom he was most concerned. The *kapitan*, a man in charge of the boats in the harbor, a harbormaster, he understood that. The man liked order, and Krieg and his crew threw him into disorder. Harbormasters ruled their water, and did not like their waters stirred. Sailors ingratiated themselves with the master. But this one... he liked rules, he liked order, he didn't like... problems. The harbormaster saw us as a problem, realized Krieg.

And the last. A sailor, yes, and a woman, but not a *kapitan*, though more in charge. Krieg knew this one. The disciplinarian. The one who ran the ship so that the *kapitan* could run the ship. He had seen the look from this one. This one had seen death before, and had seen the killers. Krieg knew of the American Coast Guard, and thought of them as more a coastal rescue group than a military. This woman, the Chief, she was called, put those thoughts in doubt. Tall, strong, athletic, she reminded Krieg slightly of a woman Olympian, only both more attractive, and less soft. She was a surface sailor, a deck hand, pulling the lines, hardened, not like his men. His men were oiled, dirty, thin for passing inside the cramped quarters. She was tougher, muscular.

She had the look of someone who was hard to kill, thought Krieg.

The captain watched as the cowboy said something to the harbormaster. The two left. Krieg decided the odds were better in his favor now and approached the remaining people. He watched as they stiffened, eyes tight on him. This was what he must look like when spying a ship through his periscope. It was eerily unsettling.

"*Oberbootsmann* Stone," the captain began his greeting before being cut off by the chief.

"I'm Chief Petty Officer," she said icily. The cold Teutonic ring of the German language out of a Nazi commander's mouth made even the close translation uncomfortable to the chief. She wasn't going to be compared in any way to these Nazis.

"*Ja*, Chief Petty Officer Stone, do you know how long we will stay here? The men are wanting to get out and see the island. We have not seen land in quite some time, you understand. The harbormaster said something about getting accommodations?"

"I don't know about that. You may have to stay here for the foreseeable future." The last thing Chief Stone wanted was to have these sailors wandering around Ocracoke. They weren't going to be able to get outside now anyway with the remnants of a hurricane bearing down on the island.

"Surely, you do not plan to keep us locked inside the school. We are not prisoners, are we? We are no longer at war." Krieg tested the Chief.

"No," Stone agreed. She sighed a shallow breath of resignation. She knew more than the U-boat captain, and didn't know how to explain it all to him. Forty three years. The history was still fresh for many. These sailors weren't there for most of it, the invasions of Africa, Italy, D-Day. The horrid slog of Europe. Hitler's monstrous scorched earth plan, sending children and blind men to die for him while he hid in some cave until he ate a bullet. The starvation, the separation of Germanies, the rise of the Communists and their own brand of hate. How much they didn't know. The chief was going to have to show him.

"You need to see something. Come with me," the Chief led the captain out of the school. Stone felt the hall go quieter as the two left.

16

9:30 A.M.

OCRACOKE BEACH

If visiting the place where Jimmy Gray was murdered was hard on Dan Howard, he thought how difficult it must have been on Deputy Tillett. Frankie had asked Dan to come with him, to investigate the spot, and, in an implied way, help clean up if any of Jimmy was left. Dan watched as Frankie looked around. The deputy looked crestfallen, as if he had failed his subordinate in some way. Frankie was sickened by the sight of the spot when Jimmy had fallen, but not ill. More like he was repulsed. It was a horrendous act, that only a monster could do. Frankie was more bent on vengeance, or at least consequences, for Eddie, than wanting to cry and throw up over the spot where his man was killed.

They had arrived separately, as the wind and rain began to pick up. The blue skies mixed with white and gray clouds. The ocean already began to pound the sand. There probably wouldn't be much damage from this storm, as the track of

89

Hurricane Henri, its remnants in the form of a disorganized low pressure, tacked offshore. Any houses up in Hatteras or farther north into Nags Head that were at risk of falling in after the last hurricane would surely tumble to the sea. Dan had often wondered what happened to the beach houses. Old homes owned by the same families for ages, or brand new, boxy, modern, ill fitted for the quaint beach life, neither ultimately stood a chance against the ravages of King Neptune. Would they fall down whole, washed away in one piece, only to become homes for fish who would swim through the living rooms looking at the chairs and sofas in confusion and wonder? Did they break apart like so many Lego pieces? Could, if someone was patient and skilled enough, walk the shore and gather each part, and painstakingly recraft the building, bit by bit? Or did they just fall to pieces, joining the freight train of water that was the Gulf Stream? Bits of North Carolina and families' lives being strewn to Nova Scotia, Iceland, and Great Britain beyond.

The warm rain splattered Dan's face, breaking his reverie. He looked down from the hill he stood on. Most of the markings of poor Jimmy's last moments alive were gone. The footprints of men blended into the sand. Pelting raindrops and blowing, stinging sand blotted out anything recognizable as far as clues or a pattern.

The only memoir of the traumatic event was a large stain of crimson where Jimmy's wound had bled out into the sand. And that, too, was slowly being beaten away to nothing by the oncoming storm.

"So, Jimmy tails Eddie, so Eddie turns off the side here," Frankie pointed south toward Eddie's old pickup, still left at the far end of the airstrip. "He hides," Frankie looked around, the clumps of sea oats making any spot a decent place to conceal a murderer. "Well, anywhere, it's dark. When Jimmy comes out to find Eddie on the sub, Eddie jumps from behind and kills him. That's about it, right."

"That's about it," Dan agreed.

Dan stared down at the truck. The wind was whipping up enough now that the salt spray was mixing with the rain, making it more difficult to see. The sky was trying desperately to cover the blue, and bring in the gloom. It was going to be another rough night. And it was still only morning.

"Except," Dan thought, "why did he park that far down? Why not just park here, since he was just going to hide anyway?"

"Eddie's a dumb asshole, that's why." Frankie had thought he hit the nail on the head with that one. "He parked his truck down there so he could haul off more stuff from that south access, that cut in the dunes where we found him."

"Yeah…" Dan thought that must be it. Eddie is an asshole, he had to admit. Hell, Dan had wanted to kill him less than a day ago. He wondered if Eddie had been smart enough to close the hatch on the U-boat. Then Dan wondered if he had even been smart enough when Dan and Stone first went on the boat. He thought back to discovering the crew, still preserved, on board the derelict craft. Dark and sullen, the crew still looked dutiful. He remembered the sailors dogging the hatches tight, and the way the officers stood watch over them. Duty and discipline still came first, even after decades.

Dan started to walk back up the dune, to stare out at the U-boat, half in hopes the damned thing had washed away, when Frankie asked him, "What do you think we should do about that?"

Dan turned to see what Frankie was talking about. The blood stain, slowly dissolving into the sand, right in the middle of the path that tourists would take to the pristine beach of Ocracoke island. Within a few years no tourist would even know that story. They will trudge over the spot, dragging rafts and kids and coolers, never realizing a good man died there. It was kind of like looking out over the ocean. It was just a vacation paradise, not the grave for many a sailor over hundreds of years.

Dan had to think. "You know what? Jimmy was an island boy. Not like you, Frankie. This was his beach. We'll let the storm take care of him. When it's done, we'll come out and fill in this cut, and build a walkway over the dunes somewhere else. He'll be part of the island. It's probably the best we can do for him."

With little ceremony, Frankie kicked soft wet sand over the last remains of Jimmy Gray.

Dan sighed. He didn't want to have this as part of his life. He never had any desire to deal with the extremes of life. He liked solving the problems of his island, and leaving the rest to others. But here it was, death had come to the island, and it felt to Dan like it wasn't going to leave. They were all trapped together. He climbed the dune line to look out at the ocean, the reason and call for so many to be on the coast. The trite expressions came and went. The ocean wasn't a fickle mistress, nor was she unpredictable. No sailor needed to treat the sea like a lady. You just needed to be prepared for anything. The ocean was career, recreation, and home, all in one. It's the things that wash up that cause the problems, Dan thought, as he eyed the U-boat, still stuck, unyielding to the waves. The damned thing will be there forever, he cursed.

The waves forced a spume up, the thin airy foam caused by the agitation of the waves mixing with the organic matter of summer algae. It blew across the beach in misty plumes, little beach tumbleweeds that got caught in the sargassum and reeds that blew in and took up residence on the beach. Dan scanned across the shore. He was familiar with the view, and looked for things that were out of place.

It didn't take him long to spot something. Some things.

"Frankie!" Dan cried. "Come on! I think we got some bodies out here!" Dan ran, heavy footed in the rain soaked sand as his boat shoes sank uncomfortably, twisting his ankles and making him run more slowly than he liked. He saw what at first had looked like three piles of sargassum washed up on the high tide line, lolling in the heavy surf. As they moved with the waves, they took on the distinct shape of waterlogged bodies, probably from a shipwreck offshore. It was likely, almost to the point of certainty, that the men were long dead. Dan didn't relish the idea of seeing the bodies, bloated with salt water and bruised until black, but he knew what to expect. The Outer Banks had once been the epicenter of bodies washing ashore; it was part of the islands' lore. It wasn't surprising to have it happen again.

Dan slowed upon approaching the shoreline. He had to be careful not to get caught by one of the waves and add to the rising body count. Still, it was his job, every islander's job, to go out and save anyone in danger. Or at least give them a chance to make it to dry land. "Dry land," Dan spit the rain and sand out of his mouth with the thought.

He knew the bodies would be damaged. He steeled his thoughts and stomach to what he would see. Pale skin, pasty, like old glue, clammy, the smell of salt and dead fish, decay. Sand in the nose, eyes, and ears, with no life to remove it. He reached down to roll the first body over, hardening himself, but not yet able to touch the bare arm. Instead, he grabbed a lapel of a jacket and pulled. The body felt funny, tense, as if the muscles were straining against him. Dan wasn't ready yet to look down. He simply pulled the body past the high tide line. Frankie was doing the same with another of the three.

Dan flopped the body down unceremoniously and went back for the last one. He was finally in it, the responses coming naturally to the sailor, like holding a fish as you killed it. He grabbed the last man by the wrist.

Dan flinched, "Ghaahh!" he clutched at his own hand, dropping the dead man's arm into the muddy shore.

"What's the matter?"Frankie looked at him. Dan held his wrist up close to his chest, his leg up and body turned sideways in a reflexive protective stance.

Dan shivered. "Damn. I swear it felt like he grabbed me." The body just lay there, unaffected by tide. Not a breath of life came from the corpse. Dan stared at the body. He couldn't figure what was making the corpse look so odd to him. Perhaps it was the idea that it felt like it grabbed him. That would shake even the strongest man.

Perhaps it was the clothes on the body. They certainly weren't fisherman's clothes. The corpse did not sport either the typical tourist attire of shorts and shirt, nor the workmanlike bib of a commercial fisherman. He had on long pants and a jacket. And leather shoes. It was like he fell off a cruise ship.

Dan reached back down gingerly, grabbed the man by the back of his jacket collar, and pulled the body roughly across the sand. He didn't care how the man got there. As long as Dan didn't get grabbed again. He threw the body down with the others.

Frankie looked down at the bodies, up at Dan, and back down again. "I don't know if we have enough body bags," he stated, half kidding and half serious. The weirdness of it all had finally gotten to the deputy. He began laughing, a dry laugh, heartless and without humor. "If this keeps up, we're gonna run out of room in the ice house."

17

9:30 A.M.

BRITISH CEMETERY

The weather was helping to make the point, thought Chief Stone. A gloomy day with rain coming in bursts and the clouds chasing off what was left of the blue sky was perfect for visiting a cemetery. She had brought Krieg here to show him the fruits of his labor. Krieg needed to know what the world thought of him, of the Nazis, and what they were in store for. So many of Krieg's brethren did their penance, dying for the Fatherland, or just dying under its oppressive yoke. If Krieg thought that years alone on his ship was some sort of baptismal forgiveness, he was sorely mistaken.

Krieg and Stone stood over the small cemetery, marked off physically by a low white picket fence. A marker identified the plot as the final resting place of sailors from the *HMT Bedfordshire*, a fishing trawler that had been converted by Great Britain to be a submarine hunter during the beginning of the war in Europe. It had crossed the ocean to help the woefully unprepared Americans fight the submarine attacks on the U.S. coast before it was sunk. Four sailors were interred, with only two identified. The land was permanently leased to Great Britain so that the sailors would rest in their home soil, even if they were thousands of miles away from their native land.

Krieg looked up at the empty flag pole. The British Union Jack had been taken down before Hurricane Gloria, and no one had bothered to come out and put it back up. To Chief Stone, that didn't matter so much. The flag was mostly a curiosity to tourists. It used to get stolen once a week in the summer, it seemed. The history of the men buried in the ground was much more important.

"The U.S. wasn't prepared for your attacks. You know that," Chief Stone stated the obvious to a somewhat smug Captain Krieg. The Nazi tried, and failed, to stifle a grin. The hunting for Allied merchant vessels had been so good, and so easy, that the Nazis referred to it as Happy Time. Stone gave the captain no satisfaction of recognizing the look of satisfaction. Krieg had been sunk, anyway. He had no reason to be proud. Stone continued. "So the British sent some armed trawlers here to help fight off the U-boats, including the *Bedfordshire*. No one even knows when they got sunk. The ship just disappeared. The bodies washed up days later.

"The only way they were able to identify the captain here, Lieutenant Thomas Cunningham, was that the man in charge of grave detail had met him. He was down in Morehead City," the wind whipped up and the rain began coming down in earnest, the clouds taking over the sky, pushing the blue out and turning everything gray. It only added to the menace and tragedy of Stone's words. "He met with Cunningham to get some ensigns or flags for caskets. They ended up drinking together. Cunningham was celebrating his becoming a father for the first time."

"You do not need to lecture me on the casualties of war, *Fräulein* Stone. We have all seen its loss." Krieg was adamant about that.

"But you only saw it from the other side. From a periscope. They were just a microcosm of a bigger picture. Yes, this was a warship, a threat. And some other ships were armed. But most of what the Germans sank were merchant and passenger ships. They may have carried wood, ore, some exotic supplies from the tropics, but they also carried people. You broke ships and let the fuel spill out, people burned in the water," Stone was almost yelling now, partly over the wind, but mostly because of the anger she had for what had happened so long ago. "They all had families, they had lives.

"You only saw tonnage."

Krieg lost his smirk at that. "It was our duty. We had to stop the supply of war materiel going to England! These were our orders, I will not be judged for doing my job well!"

"But you didn't. The first ship sunk here carried paper. One carried bananas. All carried people who never wore a uniform against you."

Krieg fought back. "The English were willing to slaughter the civilians to get to us. I'm sure that throughout the war, many people died like this."

"You have no idea," Stone shook her head. The losses were staggering. How could she explain what was started by people like Krieg, and his superiors, Donitz, Rommel, or even his beloved *Fuehrer?* How the generals and the soldiers became monsters? Stone knew the horror of war, more than most. Even the average citizen had only a mundane idea of what really happened in Europe. But Stone knew that everyone still had hatred for the men that started the war decades ago. The word *Nazi* was like poison on the tongue to Americans, especially here, where the war came home.

"These people," she continued, gesturing to take in the island, "saw firsthand what you did. America felt the hurt, we gave up so much, so many people came back to wives that didn't recognize them, came back injured, many didn't come back, and families had to be happy with a cross in France." She no longer cared if Krieg didn't understand the reference. The submarine would have been sunk long before D-Day. "They saw the bodies wash ashore, the empty lifeboats, hell, look at these graves. To this day no one knows who two of the men were. They will never have a name, their children will only know they were lost.

"And everyone will see that in you."

Krieg should have been deflated, crestfallen. But he never had the chance to learn to be forgiven. He had steamed inside a coffin, doing penance but never knowing that he had sinned. He didn't see the reparations, the hairshirt of sin worn by the Germans for so long. Even today, with the division of the Germanies, how the East Germans lost their culture to the Soviets, or how the Nazis had suffered by the Soviet occupation, Krieg knew none of it. Germany had rejected all that was the nationalism of Nazism, banned the idea from their culture, and he never saw it. He only boiled in his pride.

"Are you saying we will not be treated fairly? Is this a threat?" the captain used his words as a pointed sword. He only saw the danger to himself.

"No," Stone reflected on her words. She was angry, and tried to show Krieg what people saw in them. Take off the uniform, and take off all the Nazi hate and pride. The super men idea fell about midway through the war in Italy, Stone thought. "I'm just saying that you need to wash yourself of the crimes that your nation did. If people see you as a sailor who suffered and was cleaned, you can be forgiven. But if you walk around like some ubersailor, the world will push back. Push you back into the ocean. Your kind isn't welcome now. Your time has gone.

"You have to change."

The wind whipped around the two, chilling them both, for different reasons. The rain began to lash in currents, making the scene a miserable one. Two sailors, both used to a hard life at sea, were unaffected by the rain. The social climate was what was not hospitable to either.

Stone looked at Krieg. She saw an angry dog, freed from his back yard, but afraid to bite at anything, because he didn't know what was a threat. Learn to be fed, Stone thought. Forget your past, be free from those chains.

Krieg looked back. He saw a threat. A strong and capable person, powerful physically, unlike the thin captain. Krieg thought of how he sank ships, by sneaking up on them at night, from the rear. That was the way to stop this woman. If they all saw him and his sailors as only a cluster of ghosts from a bygone time, and they would never see anything more, they would be in danger. Yes, this woman was strong, but flesh and bone.

He was made of steel.

The two walked back to the shelter of the school in silence.

18

10:15 A.M.

HIGHWAY 12

Frankie drove back alone in his Blazer. The rain came down heavy and gray, as the windshield wipers beat a rhythmic tattoo on the glass, splattering the thick drops to the side. The steady *thunk thunk* was familiar comfort to him as he drove from the beach. Even as the wipers failed to completely clear his windshield, the intimacy of the truck interior to the driver, with the cold air conditioner drying out his uniform, still thick with the rain and salt, gave him a vague and murky solace. Frankie's neck still itched from the salt spray. He was sure it was that, and definitely not from the idea of an island littered with strange dead bodies washing ashore after live ones.

Dan had offered to take the bodies they found back to be put on ice in the cold house near the harbor. He had made the unconvincing tale of having the keys, and not wanting to put them in the back of the police Blazer, riding in the rain in the back of Dan's old pickup instead. Frankie knew it really was only to spare the deputy the need of seeing the frozen remains of poor Jimmy Gray wrapped up in a bag.

Which reminded him that he needed to stop at the jail to check on his prisoner.

Frankie's eyes watered, and he blamed the A/C unit blowing in his face, but there was no one else in the truck to see him, no one to accept this plausible deflection.

Slighted as his vision was, Frankie still held his police officer's edge. The hurricane had already blown most everything away that hadn't been tied down, so noticing something moving around at the nearby campground store made him perk up. Driving up the dirt and gravel drive, he stopped before the gas pumps. The entire store had the feeling of death and stillness even within the winds of the new storm. The pumps were lifeless without the lights on over them, and the windows were dark without the neon glow of beer advertisements. The wood shakes that covered the store were soaked with water, rendering the usually milk chocolate color a dull coffee. Frankie spotted the figures running away from the back, so he pulled around the far side and shone his spotlight into the ever glooming rain.

Four men in dark clothes froze in the light, unsure of what to do. Frankie could see the men look from the light to the markings on the car. Frankie knew everyone on the island, and had a good sense of who was where after the evacuation. Seeing four people together out in the storm was surprising for the deputy. He stepped out of the Blazer into the storm, hand on his hip where he had already unsnapped his pistol. The bright spotlight shone on the men, all dressed in the same…

"Uniforms?" thought Frankie.

Black turtlenecks and wool slacks were poor choices for a September storm, unless you wanted to hide in the dark.

The gaunt faces, shielded from the glare by thin, pale hands, over sheared heads, peered in a mix of confusion, trepidation, and expectance. Frankie noticed two things quickly. Three of the men continually glanced between him and one of their own, standing in the front and middle of the group, as if waiting for an order.

And that none had the look that all people did when caught in his spotlight while out doing something they shouldn't. None had the look of fear.

Frankie reached for his pistol and leveled it at the group. He recognized them, their uniforms, and their general decrepit appearance. They were part of the Nazi sub sailors. What they were doing out in this storm was anyone's guess.

Well, he wasn't going to have them prowling around his island in a storm, breaking into stores, whether they were looking for Twinkies or shelter he didn't care. About all the German he knew was from watching reruns of Hogan's Heroes, but that was probably enough. He motioned with his pistol. In his best Sergeant Schultz impression he could muster he growled out, "RRRRRAUS! Move!" He had no idea what it meant, but it got Robert Crane moving. "Lets go, over here!"

The men seemed to deflate, also confused at the poor mixture of English and German. Two even moved toward the truck, partly hoping to be out of the rain. The man in the middle, Frankie quickly assumed he was an officer of sorts, spoke. His accent mixed in Teutonic professor and Yankee sailor, a strange patois of salt water and classroom discipline that said all of "I know better than you."

"I believe the words you are looking for, *Herr Ordnungspolizei*, is *'Komm hierher'*."

Not wavering his voice, vision, nor weapon, Frankie responded, "You speak English. Good. Tell them to get over."

Frankie motioned to the rear of the Blazer.

"You get in the back."

Having a group of wet Nazis in his truck during a storm was not going to take the edge off of Frankie. They wouldn't all fit anyway. He kept one hand on his short barrel 870 shotgun's pump handle as he climbed in the front seat. He had no idea how he could pull it and accurately discharge the weapon within the confines of the truck, but he hoped the threat was enough. He wondered if the sailors even knew the power of the weapon. They may recognize the barrel of a shotgun, but did they even have pump weapons during World War II? He spoke loudly to the English speaking sailor in the back seat.

"I have to take you all at my office. I will," he spoke slowly to make sure the German understood him, " get one of your officers and another... auto... to come take you back to the school. But I can't have you all in here. Some of you will have to walk over in the rain. It's that building right there." Frankie pointed up the road. Even with the storm raging, the building was close enough to see.

"What were you doing out there, anyway?"

The English speaker, Frankie assumed an officer, spoke from the back. "We were trapped out in the storm. We were looking for a place out of the wind."

"Uh huh," Frankie grunted nonchalantly. He knew when someone was lying, and when they used the truth to be deceptive. The sheriff's office was only a few buildings down from the campground. He just needed to get them into the building without them feeling threatened.

Or emboldened.

Frankie drove his Blazer down to the sheriff's department after the officer explained what his men were expected to do. They seemed to think he was arrested, but the words he spoke, gibberish to Frankie, soothed them. It only made the deputy more uncomfortable, and he toyed with his shotgun the whole way.

He parked in front of the offices. "I have a prisoner in here I have to check on. Come in and I can give you a place

104

to sit, dry off, and I have some food, too." The promise of shelter and board seemed promising to most of the men. The officer tried to act nonplussed. Opening the door, Frankie carried the shotgun loosely out of its holder. He attempted to find a way to make the weapon both a threat and not at the same time. "I'll take one of you with me back to the school, so you can tell the others where you are, okay? Then come back with a bus or something. It will take, like, ten minutes." Frankie oversold the time, but he wanted them comfortable. Once he could secure them, things would go better for everybody. The last thing he wanted was to have splattered Nazi brains all over his office, or his truck. Try explaining that to the sheriff.

Frankie entered the office first, leading enough that the sailors would not be near him as he went inside. The rest came in, first to a small anteroom in front of a small office. To the back were two cells and a holding room. One cell was occupied by a rather upset Eddie Gruber.

"Hey, Hell, man, you can't keep me here al-" his shouting cut short as Eddie saw first the deputy and the shotgun in his hand. Murderer or not, Eddie's brain knew better than to antagonize a man with a shotgun.

"Shut up, Eddie."

Eddie fought for some sort of comeback. All he could settle for was, "How about some fuckin' breakfast?"

The other members of the group piled in the station, and Eddie stood agape at the Nazi sailors. They stared back at the scruffy, long haired prisoner.

"Ask nicely, Eddie. We got guests." Frankie's voice was ice cold. He didn't care if Eddie ever got a meal again, but he had to make sure Eddie had no legitimate complaints, even if they were under extreme circumstances.

"Okay, how about some fuckin' breakfast, PLEASE?!"

The sheriff's office was prepared for short term stays until prisoners could be transferred, and usually just got a hot meal locally. With the power out, Frankie had to go with a backup choice. He opened a pack from a case of Meals Ready To Eat, sealed packages of high calorie foods normally used by the military when mess halls were not available.

"What the hell's that? Hey, how about some eggs, man?" Eddie whined, trying again to find his edge with the deputy.

"You'll get what you get." Frankie took the time to look through quickly, though, to skip the spaghetti and found something that seemed like an omelet. "You guys hungry?" Frankie addressed the Germans. He couldn't remember if they ate or not.

The sailors looked at the officer, who did not want to acquiesce, but also didn't want his men to starve. They hadn't eaten for so long. They also hadn't been free for so long. Need won over want.

"*Ja*, yes."

Scooping up five more packs at random, he carried them over to the front where the men stood, unsure of where to go. Frankie opened the first pack, the one for Eddie, and showed the sailors the goodies inside. Shaking out the smaller packages from the large brown plastic bag, Frankie organized the items.

"Entrée, main dish," he wondered if the sailors knew the words, French or English. "Side dish, bread, spread, dessert, candy," he held up a pack of Chuckles, sticky and colorful, "drink mix, I'll get you water, salt and pepper, fork, uh…" he held up the toilet paper, "tissue, napkins."

Frankie tore open Eddie's omelet and showed the insides to the Germans. Then he took the omelette pack, along with a side, and a bread and margarine spread packet, over to Eddie.

"C'mon, gimme the rest! At least heat it up!" Frankie wasn't about to give Eddie anything he could use, matches, plastic knife, hot sauce.

"If you don't want it…" trailed off the deputy.

"Okay, alright, g'damn, man," Eddie waited as Frankie shoved the food to him on a paper plate.

The Germans had already mimicked Frankie's example and were opening the packages to sample what they got. "You can heat them up in these," he held up a translucent bag with a chemically reactive pad that heated when water was poured in the pocket.

The sailors ate in relative silence, at first. Guttural approval of their meals led to compliments and complaints, typical of all military, as the men sampled each others food. The officer ate in judgmental silence, watching and listening, while eyeing the deputy suspiciously. Frankie motioned to him.

"Look, I know you are in charge," the colloquial 'look' may have made the officer glance around at first, but he understood the meaning. Frankie continued. "I need to get you back to the school where you were. You can't stay out here, with a prisoner, while I'm not here. But I can't take you all back."

"What do you propose, *Herr Ordnungspolizei?*" the officer was suspicious, but unsure as to what to do while his men grazed gleefully at the first meal in four decades.

"I need them to stay in the cell or in that holding room. I can't have them walking around the office with a prisoner. I can give you a key, and you come with me to get a bus or van or something. We can be back in just a few minutes. It's either that or you walk in the rain. You need to tell them it's alright.

"Or you can send one of your men with me and you stay. I don't care. I just need to get you out of here and back with your crew."

Which is exactly what the officer wanted to hear. And do.

"I will stay with the men," the officer said. Remaining in the station would give him more time to look around, and possibly gain the trust of the *polizei*. "Peter will go with you. He speaks some English.

"Peter!" the officer called, his voice a high pitched stubble, used inside a submarine to be heard among the noises and rattles. "*Geh mit dem polizei. Erzähle dem Kapitän Krieg, dass wir in Sicherheit sind und werde ihn bald begleiten. Wir sind nicht gefangen. Wir kehren nur zurück, um unsere Aufträge auszuführen.*"

Frankie watched the sailor as he stiffened, seemingly wanting to salute. Frankie wondered if the men kept up with their *Sieg Heil*s on board the cramped confines of the U-boat, or were they constantly smashing their fingers into the hull. The sailor merely glanced at the deputy and gave a muffled, "*whol.*"

"I told him to report back to *Kapitan* Krieg that we were safe and would be returning. That we were not being held against our will and would arrive soon. Is that acceptable, *Herr*...?"

Frankie realized he was asking for a name. "Tillett. Deputy Tillett. Yes, thank you..." Frankie had little idea how to prompt for this officer's name. The man came through with a smile that cut through the storm.

"*Oberbootsmann Kurt Schacht.* It is a pleasure. We shall remain here in wait for you."

Chief Bosun Schacht seemed all too happy to just wait, Frankie thought.

19

10:30 A.M.

HYDE COUNTY SHERIFF'S OFFICE

"Hey.

"Hey, you guys from the sub?" Eddie didn't grasp the obliviousness of the question to three men dressed in Kriegsmarine uniforms. It was merely his way of starting a conversation. The men in the other cell pretended not to hear him. He seemed more wild creature than human. Eddie was long haired, black and curly, with bronzed leathery skin, and more beard than stubble after days without shaving. He looked like a cave man to the submariners.

"C'mon. You're the guys, right?" Eddie had little in the way of a plan. He just knew to engage anyone he met, for good or ill. Maybe a little of both. "What are you going to do with the boat? You gonna give it to these guys?"

That got the attention of Schacht. "No..." The Chief Bosun thought that this might be a way to gain the insight of the locals. He could get more out of this man than he would give. "No, the U-boat is seaworthy. We will need fuel to power it. We will wait for diesel to be supplied, and we will sail it to a safer port."

"Diesel, huh?" Eddie smiled. Schacht recognized the smile as a bastardized version of the way those inclined for power within his military service would look.

"I know where you can get plenty of diesel fuel."

20

11:00 A.M.

OCRACOKE BEACH

The storm ripped into the Ocracoke coast, bringing twisted sheets of rain. The ocean waves mixed into the air, causing the atmosphere to have a salty swampy mélange of fish and brine and rot. Algal foam rolled around in the ocean, only to be caught by dead reeds and then pummeled into a damp brown web. Nothing good would be out in this weather.

A storm surge pushed waves farther and farther toward the weakened and carved dunes of the beach. They carried every bit of the trash they could pick up right to the sand, throwing up the detritus like a disease. The ocean did not want this in its insides, and it pushed the garbage out. The Nazi U-boat took a pounding. The ocean was especially displeased with the submarine, pushing and turning the monstrosity. The boat turned, lifted slightly from the now submerged sandbar, and pointed south. It settled, rocking with every hate filled wave, in a narrow deep channel with its prow resting on a submerged bar far off the beach.

After regurgitating the first bodies earlier, the Atlantic gave up ten more. The corpses, darkened from bruises and paled from the salt water, were flung higher and higher upon the shore. All lay on their chests, faces buried deep into the wet pliable mud. Lifeless arms stretched out, not clutching, no life in them, keeping the bodies from rolling more, until the next wave overcame the wet anchors of limb and clothing. The bodies rolled farther up, tangled into the mass of sargassum and reeds. The pencil thin bamboo-like switches jammed themselves thoughtlessly into any orifice they could, mouth, gums, eyelid, ear, throat, or hands. They neither cared nor thought of how they damaged the corpses. The bodies cared even less.

It took time for the bodies to find rest on the beach. Once firmly stuck at the high tide line, the surge could no longer move them. There they remained for almost an hour.

The first body lifted itself from the broken spiked reeds and began to crawl. A sharp twig embedded itself firmly into the heel of its left hand as the arm reached forward. The corpse made no notice of pain, and continued crawling toward the dune.

The other nine bodies soon joined it in the effort.

The first corpse reached the carved dune, a niche dug out by the waves of the last hurricane. Rain sheets swatted at its face, lifeless eyes not feeling the sting of salt or sand as they embedded into unblinking pupils. It looked at its hand, and with a surprising fine dexterity, removed the offending reed from the green but unbleeding wound. Within moments, the other nine corpses joined the first at the dune line, all sharing the same indifference to the weather.

The corpses were different in face and figure, but the same in bloat and bruise. What all had in common were that they wore the same uniform, a sailor's stevedores worn by merchant sailors for decades. The only difference was that, besides the soaked cloth, these uniforms were over forty years old.

The corpses sat at the edge of the dune. Feeling neither pain nor fatigue, they were not resting.

They were waiting.

21

Deputy Tillett was able to drop off the German sailor Peter and go back for Schacht and the rest of the sailors to deliver them to an unsmiling Captain Krieg. The skipper seemed none too pleased to have his missing sailors reunited with the rest of the crew. He was less pleased by the questions that invariably came with the discovery of the men out in the storm.

Chief Stone had shown up soon after her German counterpart had arrived. Captain Krieg made a decidedly overt showing of noticing the chief's firearm on her hip. Stone concurrently didn't downplay the weapon. After their last discussion, the two had lost any sense of pretense in their relationship. Let threats be threats.

"You said that you lost five men in the battle. That their bodies were buried at sea." Stone made the accusation stick like a knife.

Krieg received the knife as if it had butter. "Would you reveal your men's location, on a possibly hostile land? We did not know what to expect. The island may have been entirely deserted, for all we could see by the *periskop*. They volunteered to explore the land and report back. They were trapped by the storm and could not find us, nor were they sure of their safety. My sailors commend your constable for his calm discretion, and providing comfort, I may add." Krieg wanted to imply that everyone else was at ease with his sailors. Stone should soothe herself as well.

Stone was having none of that, and she knew the skipper was lying.

"Where's the last officer? This makes forty nine, out of fifty."

Krieg stiffened uncomfortably. "What I told you was true. *Oberbootsmann Schacht* was injured during the attack, along with others. And one of our officers unfortunately did kill himself." The grimace on Krieg's face made Stone think most of this was true, though she still wondered about the officer committing suicide.

"Do you know any more about the storm? When will we be able to leave?" Krieg made it clear the other issue was closed.

"Hopefully in a day. Maybe two. It depends on the weather after this, the tides, how the channel has moved." The islands of the Outer Banks could change almost daily, with no real way to predict them. There were no rigid coastlines, waterways, or deep harbors on this part of the Atlantic, unlike the French shores the captain was used to. "You're still in a better place than the rest of us on the island."

Krieg doubted that. He was not wearing a sidearm.

The two officers dismissed each other without the permission of the other, both happy to be rid of their counterpart. Every time Stone spoke to the Nazi U-boat captain, she felt more and more as if she needed a bath. Or even a walk in the thick rain outside. And Krieg needed time to talk with his sailors that had been out along the island, to find out what they knew.

Krieg walked among his sailors, milling about in the gymnasium, pointedly not looking over his shoulder to see if Stone had left. "*Weiter Reden,*" he spoke sotto voce to his crew, having them keep up the Teutonic chatter. He counted silently to one hundred in his head after hearing the door close to the outside as Chief Stone passed into the storm. He then eyed the only islander left in the room, the tired and bedraggled corpsman who no longer seemed to care what the sailors did. Sufficed of his relative privacy, Krieg made a beeline to Schacht and the men with him.

"*Herr Kapitän,*" Schacht almost saluted before Krieg gestured to relax the formalities. There was no desire to draw attention to themselves from now on. "*Was hast du gefunden?*" the captain asked quietly.

"*Die insel ist größtenteils leer. Im Norden gibt es viele häuser, in denen wir uns verstecken können.*" Schacht could barely contain his excitement over his next news, though he had been sent to secure shelter and perhaps a way off, he knew the ultimate goal. "*Und, Kapitän, wir wissen, wo Dieselkraftstoff ist! Genug, um das Boot für eine volle Seefahrt zu füllen!*"

"*Wo wird der Diesel aufbewahrt?*"

"*In der Nähe des Fähranlegers. Es ist auf einem kleinen Schiff untergebracht, das die Fähren vom Festland mit Treibstoff versorgt. Es gibt auch andere große Boote hier. Stark genug, um unser Boot in See zu stechen.*"

"*Gut. Wir werden die Insel sichern müssen, bevor wir den Treibstoff holen und das U-Boot wieder aufstellen können. Der Bootsmann sagt, dass es mindestens einen Tag dauern wird, bevor es Kontakt mit anderen aus anderen Teilen des Landes gibt. Wir werden ihn am ehesten fangen müssen. Er, der Hafenmeister und die Polizei sind unsere größte Bedrohung."*

"Sie können eine größere Bedrohung sein, als wir uns vorstellen."

"Wir brauchen vielleicht den Hafenmeister, aber die anderen beiden sind unwichtig. Wir müssen sie vielleicht töten, wenn sie Schwierigkeiten mit unseren Plänen verursachen."

Krieg's second in command spoke up. *"Denkst du das ist weise? Die Leute auf dieser Insel könnten reagieren, wenn wir ihre Beamten ermorden?"*

"Er ist die größte Bedrohung für uns auf der Insel. Und wir werden ihn nicht im Weg stehen lassen. Wir werden nicht von den Amerikanern gefangen gehalten. Wenn er uns im Weg steht werden wir ihn durchgehen."

The submariners broke up their conspiracy quietly and went to discuss their plans with the rest of their crew. The approaching of evening and the storm would be perfect coverage for their escape.

22

4:00 P.M.

HIGHWAY 12

Frankie Tillett had a duty in his job, a very specific part of his job, that he really didn't like. He had to go back to the jail and feed Eddie dinner. It was something he very pointedly did not relish, and he wasn't sure if he could go there without either starving the prisoner, or just killing him outright. It had taken time to get over the shock, but now Frankie felt the complete emptiness of the job, how the only other law on the island, and the person who served under him, was dead. It just wasn't something that happened here. Not this way.

He had asked Dan Howard to come along. Having a bit of moral support from an O'cocker like him helped, and having a witness may have tamed the rasher ideas in Frankie's head. Dan seemed like the only person on the island who could tolerate the guy.

They drove in relative silence from the village down Highway 12 toward the jail. The rain was an unrelenting monsoon, and the wipers beat out a quick marching tattoo on the windshield. The high speed setting only unnerved the men, as it does to all people stuck in heavy rain. The fast *click clack* of the wipers and their ever present blocking of the driver's view was always discomforting. Whenever the wipers were on that high, it was a promise that things were bad, and the car had nothing left to give if it got worse.

"What the hell?!" Dan exclaimed, as Frankie saw them, too. Three black figures, walking up the highway, dead in the middle of the road. They had blended in with the scrub brush until the truck had gotten close enough that they could be seen as separate. Three men, all trudging along in the storm, oblivious to the wind and the approaching truck.

"More goddam Nazis? I'm sick of this shit!" Frankie put the car in park and reached for his riot gun. "They can walk in the fucking rain back to the school for all I care." He pulled on his hood and drew his raincoat up around him. Dan zipped up his own slicker. He stared through the windshield at the visages before getting out. He didn't want to be out in this weather, that was for sure. And he started to wonder why these men were out, too. They didn't look like the sailors from the U-boat, and all of those men should have been accounted for. "Hey, Deputy…" he called as Frankie stepped out into the wind.

Frankie didn't hear the call as the wind cascaded over him. The strong east torrent pushed into his hood, splashing rain into his eyes. He leveled the short barreled shotgun at the approaching men. "Stop! Hands up!" He didn't give a damn if they understood English or German or Greek, they were going to understand the barrel of his shotgun. Everyone knew the business end of looking into the mouth of hell and what it would unleash, Frankie thought.

The men continued to approach. Dan got out of the other side of the big Chevy. "Frankie..." he called again, louder, with a bit of urgency in his voice.

"Stop!" Frankie racked a shell into the shotgun. The sound was unmistakable to people who had heard it before.

"Frankie!" Dan shouted. "I don't think those are Germans!" The men were about fifteen feet from the truck by now, and Dan had walked around the back of the truck so as not to be in the line of fire.

Frankie, tired and bitter and angry, still had no desire to fire. They hadn't done anything wrong, but they weren't heeding his call, either. It could be a stalemate except that the men continued to advance, not slowing their pace, but not speeding up, either.

Dan could tell there was definitely something wrong with these men, but the rain, driven by the wind into stinging droplets pelting him, making him cold and blinded, created a fog that obscured his thinking. He looked for their faces, to see menace or pleading, but could see nothing. They had eyes, large dark almond shapes, but they were not looking. Mouths, pale lips parted so slightly, but not speaking. Their whole bodies moved with a slow, inexorable intent. And he and Frankie were in their way.

"Halt! Stop where you are!" at ten feet away, even the storm could not keep the air of menace from between the two groups. Three men, pale, scarred, walked with intent toward Dan and Frankie, with the same intent to stop them. Frankie leveled his shotgun at the road a few feet in front of them and fired.

The blast from the shotgun alone was deafening, leaving a ringing in Dan's ears. Frankie, more accustomed to the sound, was just as affected, but was able to keep his focus on the men approaching. The shotgun blast did nothing to slow them. If anything, it quickened their step and made them focus their attention on Frankie and Dan. The pellets had blasted a hole in the road, with some rebounding into the ghastly stalkers. Steel and asphalt tore into one man's leg, making him stumble but not fall. Dan looked on in awe as the figure took no notice of his wound.

"Frankie, get in the truck!" The figures were moving faster now, closing in on Frankie and Dan. Frankie was encumbered by his weapon, long raincoat, and a slippery door. Dan ran back around to try to get in the passenger side. The truck was still running, air conditioned in comfort, an inanimate object unaware of the danger and terror. Neither man had that good option.

Frankie tried to get in and close the door before the first man, thing, could get to him. It closed the gap with surprising speed, grabbing at the door's window frame and pulling back. Frankie could see its face now. It was a man, but without any form of recognition on its face. Just anger. The stench of sea life, salt, and death, were overpowering, but Frankie had no time to gag. He stared into the man's face, trying to find some reason for the attack. Nothing stared back, nothing more than a ghoul, missing all soul except a desire for violence. It pulled and ripped at the door to get to Frankie.

Dan did no better, not even being able to get to the door before another ghoul was on him. It approached and grabbed for Dan, leaving him to stumble away in fear. Black, damaged teeth bared in an open mouth growl, the sound of salt water being choked down and thrown back up. Hands grabbed at Dan's rain slicker, finding a strange wet purchase, pulling him close. Dan grasped the creature's arm, repulsed as he twisted at the wrist. The forearm was wet from more than rain. It was cold and slick, the way a boat gets covered with an algal film. Dan found no grip as he tried to pull the ghoul's hand away.

The creature pulled Dan closer, with a mix of strength and brittleness that unnerved Dan. Unable to escape, and not sure what the ghoul was going to do, Dan feared it would bite him, Dan squared up his body, one foot in front of the other, and tucked in his arm, fist curled flat and heavy. The punch came first from the shoulder, a twisting motion that added impetus to the short tight throw of his arm. His bicep tightened, adding to the punch. Finally, his body, hips swiveling, put its entire weight into the swiftly moving knuckles, large and protruding through tight skin, like barnacles on a boat. The punch connected perfectly, landing hard and solid on the cheek, between the two jaws. A punch like that would dislocate the bone, remove teeth, cloud the eyes, and rattle the brain. A head struck like that would turn, then turn more, too far, twisting the spine until the nerves gave out. The brain would become momentarily disconnected, causing the recipient to immediately lose consciousness. It was a powerful, knockout blow.

The ghoul's head turned with the blow, and Dan felt its body and bones snap. The grip released as the ghoul was forcefully moved away by the punch, still clenched fingers slipping off the wet jacket. Its head was turned at a too awkward angle to be anything but right. The chin had moved just past the shoulder, as if the creature was somehow able to look completely over its shoulder. He should have been out on the wet road, thought Dan. He shouldn't be alive, not with his neck turned that far.

Dan hadn't tried to kill the man. He merely responded in fear. The blow was spurred by adrenaline. It was one punch, to knock the thing down, maybe out, just to get away. But the hit spun the ghoul's head around. It snapped bone and tooth and skull and spine. Dan had felt it. The life should have gone out of the thing.

It merely straightened up and turned its body so that the head could stare at Dan.

Frankie had no better luck with his assailant, though he had a modicum of protection with the door of the Blazer between the two of them. Pushing back at the white and black pockmarked arms that grabbed for him, he took the butt of his shotgun and shoved it toward the grotesque head leaning in, closer and closer. It smelled horrid. Decay, rot, the sickly wooden smell of a ship left to die, all these things permeated the air, mixing with the tumult of the storm. Frankie didn't hold back, not worrying about how hard he hit the ghoul. The rubber butt of the shotgun connected with the forehead of the man, pushing his head back, making it stagger. Not waiting, Frankie struck again, harder. The blow caught the ghoul higher in the forehead, pounding into the hard part of the skull and skipping up, over the man's wet and bedraggled hairline. It tore away the hair and scalp, exposing the flesh and bone underneath. The creature fell away, letting go of the door long enough for Frankie to shut it. Immediately, the thing came at him, banging on the window. In shock, Frankie saw the tremendous wound on the ghoul's head. It was split across the forehead, peeled back. But no blood poured from the wound. The man should be blinded by his own blood pouring down his face. There was nothing there except a mix of pink, white, and black flesh, and a large portion of white bone exposed from his skull.

He looked at the other two monsters. One was wounded, its leg giving out, but still trying to approach. Frankie then glanced at Dan's side. He saw the thing rising back up, just after the tremendous blow it had received.

Dan stood rooted to the spot. His body and brain could no longer take hold of what was happening. These were no men. They looked human, but also dead. They felt no pain, but exuded hate. Their bodies could be broken, but not stopped. The thing reached up to straighten its own head back onto its neck. Dan felt the rain dripping into his open mouth as his body froze in terror. He knew in a moment, the thing would reach for him, again.

Then, the face was gone. A blast tore through the rain, as the droplets moved aside for a greater force. A white light had blinded Dan in his left eye, but he still looked toward the Blazer, unable to even respond in time to the massive crashing sound. Out of the passenger window poked the end of Frankie's shotgun. Drops of water only began to bead on it after being fired. Dan looked back at the ghoul. The front half of its head was gone. The close end of the blast had torn through the center of its cheek, ripping off the nose, one eye, and the remnants of the broken jaw. Bits of the face lay scattered along the road, the storm already cleaning the mess.

"Get in, now!"

Dan shut and locked his door. Then he looked at the other two ghouls outside. He felt no safer. Frankie's attacker began to beat harder on the window. The glass was beginning to bow inward with the strikes from its hammer fists. Not a time to hold back, Frankie did what he had to do. He rolled down the window, stuck the barrel in the ghoul's face, and pulled the trigger.

The clap of the weapon was loud enough to deafen the two men. Their ears were past ringing into a hollow whine. In a second, the vague whiff of burnt toast came to them as the propellant's odor, smokeless even in the confines of the car, drifted to their noses.

Frankie's attacker was no longer there. The deputy wasted no time in wondering what had happened to him. He secured the shotgun, placed the still running Blazer into drive, and floored it into the remaining ghoul.

He then put the truck in reverse and backed up until two crunching thumps satisfied him. Frankie kept going, not worrying about what was behind him, until they were a safe distance away from the bodies.

The headlights helped little to make out the corpses, but neither man was going to get out yet to see what they were. From forty feet away they could see through the speeding *clackclackclack* of the windshield wipers the three bodies prone on the asphalt. One missing its head, another still vaguely intact, and a third crushed and splayed. The two men in the truck would wait to see if the bodies would keep moving.

They would wait a long time.

23

4:45 P.M.

OCRACOKE SCHOOL

Krieg knew he and his crew would have to act on the timetable of someone else. When the Coast Guard *bootsman* showed up, they would react and take her prisoner. The *polizei*, as well. Securing the officials on the island, the ones who seemed to be moving the most, would offer them a better ability to move about, especially in the storm. They needed to act now, before the darkness fell, in order to gain some view of the land and water. They also needed to gain the use of their collaborator.

When Chief Stone pulled up to the school, the sailors readied themselves. They needed to be prepared to restrain the woman before she could draw her weapon. It would do little good for her, as they were too numerous, but the captain did not want his crew killed unnecessarily. He needed as many as possible for the long voyage.

Stone's vehicle stopped at the gym's door, but she did not get out. In a few moments, the large truck that the *polizei* drove came in from the opposite direction. The two cars stopped, facing each other. Krieg was put off when the deputy got out with his weapon in his hand, the large bore rifle. The harbormaster exited, too, armed with a similar weapon.

"*Warten*! *Halt*!" Krieg yelled without thinking. He didn't want his crew responding when there were three armed people there. It would be a bloodbath. He watched as his sailors made a point to relax, to go in different directions. He then noticed the fire fighter, tense and surprised, as he looked first at the sailors, and then pointedly at the captain.

He is more of a problem than we first thought, Krieg said to himself.

"*Zeigen Sie einige Wiederholungen. Unsere Gastgeber sind hier,*" Krieg demanded of his crew, partly in attempt to cover for his last command, and also to see how the fire fighter would respond. The sailors all stopped, turned toward the door in a form of attention, and remained silent. Krieg watched as the firefighter observed what the men did, with a small amount of acquiescence. Krieg began to think the man had been left there to spy on the men, more than to guard them.

Krieg wondered as the armed people came into the gym, if they were there to move them to a prison, with the show of arms. The three Americans walked in with grim faces, but not a threat, Krieg felt. More like… concern? Dread?

Fear?

The three came in, wary, two still glancing over their shoulders at the door to the outside.

"Captain," Dan spoke first, "we need you to come with us. We need some help with something, and you may be in, well, a better place than us to figure this out."

Two trucks drove the narrow lane of School Road, splashing deep puddles of rainwater that had nowhere left to go in the storm soaked land. Frankie navigated mostly by feel and memory, trusting the road would be where it always was, and hoping not to run into anything hidden in the sheets of rain that poured down. Dan sat next to him, shotgun propped in his lap. Captain Krieg rode in the back. He found himself mesmerized by how cold the vehicle was, so used to being in a hot and stuffy submarine. And the strange material of the seats, a thick and firm hide, like leather, but a a harder pelt, almost like rubber. The water that dripped from him beaded on it.

Chief Stone drove separately. She had not said anything, but her demeanour showed that she was not going to ride in the same truck as the U-boat captain. Her white Bronco, adorned with the Coast Guard symbols and bright red flash, followed apace. She was unsure of what she was going to see. The harbormaster and deputy seemed put aback to adequately describe what had happened.

Stone couldn't see what was ahead of the deputy's Blazer, only the bright tail lights as they lit up red when it came to a stop still hundreds of feet from the sheriff's department. She put her Bronco in park and watched as the deputy climbed out, shotgun dangling over one arm. Stone zipped up her slicker, put a salt rimed cap on her head, and climbed out.

As Stone approached, she saw Frankie reach into his coat pocket. "Here, Dan," he said, handing over a green cylinder to the harbormaster. Stone watched, curiously, as the two men put the shotgun shells into the actions of their weapons. She felt oddly helpless at that moment. Her own service pistol was fully loaded Beretta M9, new to her and all members of the Coast Guard. What was not new was keeping the chamber empty unless there was business to be done. It looked like Dan Howard and Deputy Tillett were open for business.

"What's with the boarding guns?" Stone asked, a dry humor referring to the shotguns as old blunderbusses, meant for clearing pirates off of decks of ships. Actually, she thought ruefully, that's what her job still was.

"We got attacked by three men here, just a little while ago," Frankie pointed down the road. Stone focused on three blurry lumps along Highway 12. She noticed that they were bodies, unmoving and twisted.

"What?! How did that… who are, … were they?!" she stammered.

"That's what we want to know," Dan Howard chimed in. "Chief, you need to know something, before we go there. They didn't seem, well, all human."

Krieg thumped on the window of the Blazer. He had no way of letting himself out of the back seat. Frankie walked behind Stone to open the door.

"Yeah, these guys, they were like... look, I'm not open to spooky shit or anything, but, these fellers were like zombies or something."

Dan continued. "They weren't fazed by pain. They didn't speak. They just looked so abnormal."

"We brought you here just for support. And we figured, well, the captain here has some experience with, sorry Captain, life and death." Frankie finished with a troubled nod to the German.

"And I ain't getting too close without one up the spout," Frankie patted his shotgun.

All four people walked warily toward the spot where the bodies lay. Frankie stopped no closer than fifteen feet before saying, "Don't get too close. They are stronger than the look."

Krieg scoffed as he closed in. "Don't be foolish," he said, "These men are clearly dead."

And dead they were. Two were only vaguely still remnants of a human form. Frankie's first assailant was missing most of his head, and what was left had a clean, bloodless look. The upper spine protruded from the neck. The rain and storm had carried off bits of his head. The body in the middle of the road fared even less well, mashed to a gory pulp by the Blazer's tires, it resembled more the guts of a cooked fish, crushed and spread along the asphalt. The yellow center line created a division between upper and lower halves of what once was its body. The third body, Dan's attacker, fared best from the onslaught, though left the worst visage on the three men. His face was gone, exposing brain and bone. Eyeless, the remains of the flesh were more a mealy white, glistening with rain and fluid. The head was severely turned on its neck, a most unnatural position, after being pummeled both right and left.

In response to Krieg's comment, Frankie said, "Yeah, you'd think that." He kept his shotgun level, finger over the trigger guard.

"Are these more of your sailors, Captain?" Dan only half questioned, and half accused the captain.

"*Nein*, ah, no," Krieg responded.

Before he could explain, Stone barged in. "Are you sure?! You didn't tell us about the missing men we just found."

"I tell you, you have accounted for all my living men." Stone saw Krieg tighten. Three men were out with weapons, and he stood alone in the rain, unarmed.

"Who are they?" Dan spoke up. "You run into anything like this? Did your men ever get to this point, unfeeling, mad?"

Stone walked closer, now curious. These weren't sailors from the U-boat, she could now tell. Maybe shipwrecked in the storm. Maybe they were hungry, or delirious. They could be foreign, not speaking English, on a ship from another country. She pondered these things as she got closer to the bodies, wiping rain from her eyes, and staring at their clothes.

"No," Krieg went on, but his voice was lost in the wind to Stone, "I have never seen..."

"These aren't his sailors," Stone hastily interrupted. "But you have seen these men before. I recognize the uniforms."

They were all wearing the same clothes, heavy cloth dungarees with warm coats for cold nights on the Atlantic. But sailors hadn't worn these clothes for years. Decades.

"They're all merchant seamen. They sailed on the ships you were sinking. Forty years ago."

All four people stood silent at the revelation, three in disbelief.

"That's impossible."

Dan Howard spoke for all. He looked around, first at Chief Stone, hard faced, assured in her knowledge, though grimly terrified at the thought. Then at Frankie Tillett, who had no idea what to believe. He was inclined to trust the chief, the more knowledgeable person. Frankie merely shrugged at Dan, and then jerked his thumb at the German. Nothing is impossible right now, his silent exclamation said.

Chief Stone patted the pockets down, looking for any source of identity or personal effects. Any rings would have slipped off of bony fingers by now, and the little paper that was found in the corpses' pockets was long soaked to the consistency of pulp. The sailors almost never carried wallets on board, for fear of losing them to the sea. There was nothing to distinguish the men, even from each other, outside of the severity of their wounds.

The bodies were wrapped in tarps and tied unceremoniously to keep the disfigured remains in place. Frankie made an offhand comment about how he was tired of putting bodies away, but that it was becoming second nature. He didn't like the idea of having to go back to the ice house where his friend's body was rapidly freezing. He was even less sure of driving back with three corpses that may rise up from the rear of his truck.

"Man, I ain't looking forward to this drive," Frankie rubbed the back of his neck. "I can feel these guys on me already. The hair's standing up on the back of my head."

"You don't have to worry about these guys," Stone grunted, lifting the last body. "They aren't getting back up from the job you did on them."

"Yeah? Well, … you deliver'em."

Stone didn't blame the deputy. Her skin crawled at the thought of seeing these men, still alive, and coming after her. "I'll follow you up."

Dan spoke up, "Look, I dunno who these guys were, shipwrecks, zombies, whatever. I'm just saying that it's more likely some ship broke up in this storm, and these guys were from a life raft. We need to go check the coast for survivors."

The words hit Stone in her core. It was her prevailing job as a Coast Guardsman, even if the job had changed recently to chasing down drug dealers, to go out and save people on the ocean. Only she figured that she was about four decades too late to do this job.

"Alright, we'll run the Bronco up to the airstrip and look. Frankie, you go back to the harbor and wait there. We'll be back soon to help you. If we don't get back in a few minutes, check back at the gym for us. Then come back here to the beach if we're not there."

Frankie looked up into the rain. He glared and pleaded a silent prayer, wishing the storm to stop. Then he reached up to wipe out the sand that just blew into his eyes. The sky stayed gray.

24

The storm wasn't about to let up. Rain came down in swaths, drenching the windshield of Stone's Ford. It was as if waves were thrown against the truck. The chief didn't seem to care, or even notice, the splattering rain. It was still better than many nights she had spent at sea.

The windows of the truck would go from glaucoma translucent to clear with each swipe of the wipers, but the view did not change. Leaden clouds choked the sky, a mix of ash and burnt smoke color. The stubborn scrub brush that grew fitfully across the island, sharing the nutrient poor sandy soil with spindly, serrated edged sea grasses and waving sea oats, added a cast of pallor to their normally green surfaces. Even the sand, normally a warm yellow, was a sickly brown, pocked constantly by the rain into an extraterrestrial landscape.

The parking lot for the airstrip was still covered with beach overwash, with even the tire marks from the locals' visit the day before erased from its memory. Across the edge of the land, running north and south, was the dune line, an effort of Man to hold back the tide, made long ago by bulldozers and men when the island became a national park. The sandy access had been breached by the occasional wave and surge that did not give up its energy entirely. There was a hole in the dune where the softer sand, carried by the waves, had belched up through the walking path that locals and tourists would use to visit the beach.

Stone stopped her truck well away from the end of the road, not wanting to get near the sand. She had little desire to get out. The rain had lessened after her truck had stopped. Now it just seemed like the usual coastal storm, heavy, downcast, wet and brutal as always. Thunder rolled from far off, the sky too leadened to spot the lightning. Ominous it seemed in Stone's mind. She had no fear of the rain and storm. She just wondered what else she would see.

"You sure you even want to go looking for more of those guys? Even if they are out there?" she jerked her thumb toward the front of the truck. "You're gonna regret it."

"I know what you think, Chiefy, but really, do you expect me to believe you when you say that those were old merchant seamen sailing here from forty years ago?" Dan's incredulous tone dripped down to a realization of who sat in the back seat. Stone only stared at him, a twisted moue on her face, with a sideways glance at the Nazi in the truck.

The three stared out into the storm. The dune stared back, hiding the beach and pounding surf beyond it. Wet seagrass, pocked with the occasional wild yucca plant, tall and spiked, waited in the wind for them, daring them to come out into a hostile environment that the plants thrived upon. To put point to sentence, the wind threw a lash of water at the truck. A bully pushing the weak kid.

"We just gotta know. C'mon," Dan opened the door as Stone pointedly took the keys from the ignition and got out.

She slammed her door shut. Even in the wind, it seemed like the storm stopped to look at them, to see where the noise came from. Stone immediately got a chill, like she was watched. She looked over her shoulder, but she was sure the threat was ahead of her. She noticed that the captain still had not gotten out. She glanced at Dan.

"I know. Someone stepped on my grave."

Dan wiped the rain from his face. He tried to clear his vision before setting off to the top of the dune. Shipwreck or no shipwreck, he wasn't about to walk out onto the beach. He would climb the dune and scan the shore for flotsam. Or bodies.

"Wait."

Stone put out a hand, steel on Dan's arm. "What's that?"

She pointed to one of the yucca plants standing in the dune. They watched as it turned. It looked at them. Two more dark shapes rose up from the dune, no longer hidden in the salt grass. What they had thought were the base of yucca plants were men, standing along the dunes, with more appearing by the moment.

Krieg got out of the back of the truck to see them.

It seemed like his presence was a trigger, as more of the shaded, ghostly figures appeared on the dune. Some rose from low spots, others trudged up from the beach, staggering in the storm, caught by the tight weave of grass, stumbling in the low dips of the hills. But they found their way to the top. They all stopped and stared at the three people.

Dan and Chief Stone stood rigid. Their feet were immobile, but their heads swiveled as they scanned left to right, north to south. It looked like one hundred men, starved, wet, bedraggled from the water and storm, stood on the crest of the dune. Stone could feel them all, a sense of hate and anger, all looking her way, as if glaring at something on her shoulder. She realized that Captain Krieg stood behind her.

Stone and Dan followed an invisible line, drawn from the glare of one hundred pairs of eyes, right to Krieg, still wearing his dirty captain's hat, emblazoned with a screaming eagle and Nazi swastika.

Stone was the first to respond to the threat. Still unable to react physically, her brain started first. She counted the number of bullets in her pistol, thinking about how inaccurate the thing would be except at close quarters, and even then if it would do anything to stop these ghouls. She noticed that Dan still held the spare 870 shotgun that he had gotten from the deputy. It might do better, but again only at close quarters. Nine bullets and maybe five shells between them, with no idea if they would be of any effect.

Dan responded quite differently. He looked back at the ghouls on the dune. He now could make out their faces, mostly pale, sickly, white. But now they were staring with open eyes. Through the rain, Dan could see the eyes, all glaring, red, bright. Full of hate. He half heard, half imagined the sound he felt in his gut. His body tensed, but too little too late, as a warm stream of urine poured down his pants leg. He didn't even care.

Stone either didn't notice or just didn't judge. "Let's get the hell outta here," she mumbled, too worried to speak loudly enough to set off an impending avalanche.

The three scrambled to the doors of the Bronco, Stone with her hand in a wet pocket, fumbling for the keys. As soon as they were in, they saw the wraiths take their first steps forward.

25

5:15 P.M.

THE ICE HOUSE

Frankie's back felt like jelly as he stopped to unload the three bodies. His arms shook, like from too much coffee, but only if it was mixed with sheer terror. "Get this done," he said to no one in particular. Being alone out there only made him more nervous.

He drug the three bodies out of the back of his sheriff's Blazer. He let the bodies fall unceremoniously to the gravel ground. "To Hell with these guys," he thought. He didn't care if they got bounced around some. He left the wrapped corpses where they lay while he went to open the doors.

Frankie crossed to the back of the building, which faced Silver Lake, only to discover the door open, clicking at its gate in the wind. First wary, worried that someone would come and defile the dead already inside, then wondering if he had inadvertently left the door open, he approached with apprehension. He mostly worried to find the ice melted and tainted from the rain, or the bodies spoiled. He had seen too much gore in the past day. He pulled and latched the outer door open and peered inside.

The interior did not seem disturbed. He went to glance at his deputy's body, hopefully still at peace, not disturbed, but he was taken aback by the three empty body bags on the opposite side. The bags were still there, all opened and empty. Stunned at the missing corpses, he went to look closer, as if the bodies could somehow hide in the small folds of the black bags. The smell of salt, decay, an acrid odor of chemicals and burning, all hit Frankie. He decided not to look closer. Who would come out in this storm and steal dead bodies? he wondered. Why would they want these, and what were they going to do with them? There was nothing of value on the corpses when they found them. And there was no place for anyone to keep them, since this was the only cold place on the island right now.

Frankie felt it get colder than it should inside the ice house. He shivered. It's as if they got up and walked away.

Frankie got out of the ice house, welcoming the warmth of the storm for once. He closed the door, jammed the pin in the latch, and wedged a piece of wood under the handle. In or out, he no longer cared. He ran around the opposite side of the building so that he could avoid the corpses at the back of his truck, still trussed in tarps, for now, he thought. Frankie jammed the Blazer into drive and punched it out of the gravel and dirt road. He didn't care if he kicked sand and rock on the dead attackers he left in the lot. "To Hell with those guys," he said again.

26

5:25 P.M.

OCRACOKE SCHOOL

"Are you insane?!" Stone had to bring her shout to a thin whisper, too late in the hollow confines of the gymnasium. "I am *not* arming a bunch of Nazis," she hissed.

"What else can we do?" Dan Howard was worried, too. He felt the island was threatened by the horde that stood on the dunes of the Atlantic Ocean. "Any moment those things could come walking into the village. We don't have an army. Hell, we're down a deputy now as it is."

Chief Stone grabbed Dan by the coat and pulled him close. "Listen, there's no way I'm giving weapons to a bunch of … Nazis," she whispered the word, a taste of battery acid and scarred knife edge on her tongue from it.

"Plus, we don't have the weapons. Between you, me," she jerked her thumb at Frankie, who looked cold and sick from his recent discovery at the ice house, "and Frankie here, we got all of, what, three weapons? A pistol, two riot guns?"

"We got a few more at the station," Frankie chimed in. "A couple of AR-15s, two more 870s," he nodded at the shotgun in Dan's hand, "plus ammo. Two more Berettas locked up."

"You wanna go get'em?" Dan asked sarcastically.

Frankie thought about it. One run in with those ghouls was one too many for him. For all he knew they were marching up Highway 12 right now. "Damn… Eddie…" he thought about his prisoner. There was little love lost for the man that killed Jimmy Gray, but… "If they get in there, and find him…" he let the thought hang. Partly he wanted to say, "Fuck that guy," but time and the circumstances of the day had scarred over his wound on his heart. "He better hope they don't find him."

"I don't think they are interested in him." Stone said. "I don't think they are even interested in you guys. I think that whatever kept Krieg and his sailors alive all this time has done one last favor to all the people he sank.

"I think they're after the Nazis."

As if on cue, the three looked up to find Krieg approaching them.

"If these men are a threat to us, you are going to help us defend ourselves from them, aren't you?" Krieg made it more a statement, the tone of the hypnotist, not a plea.

"You can do what you need to protect yourself, but we are not going to arm you, if that is what you think." Stone was adamant. She found it extremely difficult not to reach for her pistol.

"You cannot leave us here unprotected. What do you expect us to do, fight them with our bare hands?"

"No, of course not…" Dan tried to take a diplomatic tone.

"This is on you, what you did," Chief Stone spat out the words at Krieg. "We saw all the death, all the loss. They are here because of you. Don't expect us to do your dirty work!"

142

Frankie reached for Stone, to shut her up, as he looked out the glass doors. "Hey... Chief..."

All of them turned to look, some of the sailors running to the door, then backing off. Far down the street heading toward the school house was a slow moving wave of black. The ghouls had gathered and tracked down their prey. "It seems you will be part of the defense whether you wanted or not." Krieg commented coldly.

"Like hell. I'm not fighting against Americans, or Allies. Dead or alive. Not my job. We fought against people like you and won. I like their odds better than yours."

Dan and Frankie felt the edge and heat between them. Dan didn't like the idea of leaving people undefended, and Frankie just wanted to be out of there. Neither noticed the Nazis crowding around.

"If you will not be a participant, then you will be their victim," Krieg threatened.

Stone reached for her pistol.

Her arm gave out before she was able to undo the holster snap. It felt as if she had been jabbed with needle sharp glass. She reached for her shoulder, her body not working the way it should. Her arm felt like it was creaking, like it needed lubricant. But there was plenty of liquid, as Stone's hand came back covered in blood. She turned her head to find a small knife jabbed into her shoulder, tearing at the flesh. Only a small pocketknife, yet it caused enough pain and damage to stop her from reaching for her weapon.

Frankie and Dan had no time to respond, as arms grabbed at them and pulled their weapons from them.

Stone tried to hold back a scream as her arms were twisted behind her. She concentrated on the wound and the pain. Nothing tore, and her arm moved. Her mouth betrayed her with a muffled groan.

"Wait!" Dan called out. "You don't have to do this! You..." he had no idea what they were going to do. Fight off one hundred resurrected ghouls with a few small arms? What would they do to him?

Krieg barked out a command in German. "*Binde sie zusammen. Bringe sie zur Bühne und aus dem Weg.*"

The three Americans were shoved off, arms twisted behind them, and taken toward the stage to be tied to chairs.

"You won't get away with this!" yelled Stone. "You won't survive! Do you know how many people you killed? Thousands! And they will be at your door. All coming for you!"

A brutal slap came across Stone's face. It took a moment for the sting to set in, and her brain began to cobweb, stars twinkled in her eyes.

"Be quiet," came the words through fog. Stone tried to focus. A burly man, an officer, Stone tried to see who it was that hit her. To remember. The face came through the haze. It was the officer Frankie had picked up in the rain. Schacht. "The captain wanted us to kill you. I would suggest you find a reason to be alive, and not be dead." A skull's grin came across the Nazi officer's face. Stone spat blood, and wondered what he had to smile about.

"*Schacht, komme her.*" Krieg called. "*Lass die Männer sich ausbreiten. Blockieren Sie, was Türen mit Tischen können. Entferne die Beine von ihnen. Sie können nützliche Knüppel sein. Wir müssen den Eingang zum Gebäude begrenzen.*"

"*Whol.*"

"*Sobald wir ihren Zugang eingeschränkt haben, werden wir sie zu Öffnungen unserer Wahl leiten. Wir werden zuerst die Pistole benutzen und die größeren Waffen behalten, um unseren Rückzug zu decken. Weißt du, wohin wir von hier gehen können?*"

"*Ja. Es gibt Häuser, die unbesetzt sind. Wir werden uns im Schutz der Dunkelheit in ihnen verstecken können.*"

"*Gut. Setze unsere Männer ein.*"

Stone watched through tears she was unable to wipe with her hands tied behind her as the Nazis scurried about, upturning tables and breaking off the legs. The school table legs were not the fancy center screw kind that people would have at their homes, but large adjustable legs with a metal plate at the end to secure in the pressed wood tops. The German sailors practiced swinging them like clubs.

Stone was in too much pain to struggle with her bonds, but Dan and Frankie were already wiggling their wrists to loosen the knots. No matter how tight and secure the sailing knots were, the Nazis still had to use what was on hand, in this case, cheap nylon jump ropes from the gym supply. "It seems like they were ready for this all along," Dan said as he grunted.

"Yeah, we gotta get untied and outta here," Frankie seemed desperate, as a second encounter with the wraiths was a most undesirable option for him.

"I don't think we should move too quickly right now, with those Nazis keyed up like they are. They already think we're a threat. And I doubt we are in that much danger from those zombies, to tell you the truth.

"And I kind of think that Eddie wasn't the one to kill Jimmy, either, Frankie." Stone looked at the crestfallen deputy. "Eddie's an asshole, but I don't think he's dumb enough, or smart enough, for murdering a sheriff's deputy. I think it was those guys you picked up. That Schacht fellah looks like he'd be happy to bash someone's skull in." Stone eyed the *oberbootsman* who was armed with a large metal pipe of some sort, waiting at the set of double doors that lead out to the parking lot, and the wave of monsters somewhere outside.

"What do you mean?" Frankie stopped to gather his thoughts. It had been more than he was able to handle in so little time, and he had no time to grieve nor understand, before being thrown into the maelstrom happening now.

"I really think we need to get outta here!" Dan's voice pleaded. "If I could only reach my knife..." His folding pocket knife was still in his pocket. All watermen carried something to cut a line; it was part and parcel the costume of any sailor on the water. He thought of the small knife that must have been used on Stone's shoulder.

Stone had thought about the events leading up to now. "Did those ghouls attack you? Or was it only after you shot at them? See, they only showed up after the Nazis. This storm and the Hitler Youth over there brought them all up, back to life. The Nazis were trapped, cursed to live their sins out entombed. But they showed up now and..."

The first crash stopped her train of thought. Teutonic babble came through the hallways, barked orders and fearful cries. The Nazi Schacht and several sailors ran past the three captives and out the back of the gym. Stone could only see the little bit of light streaming through the gym's front doorway go dark, as the ghouls clogged the entrance outside. She had no clue what was happening in the other parts of the school.

27

5:30 P.M.

OCRACOKE SCHOOL

Schacht had taken a group of men away from the gym, as ordered by Krieg, and gone to the other side of the center traffic circle. The school had only a few entrances, including a doorway to the gym, and a walkway that led to the school offices and some classrooms farther inside the darkened building. As the ghouls flooded into the schoolyard, Schacht plotted to draw away as many of the zombies as possible. He would then use the narrow halls to bottle them up and strike.

Schacht stood up front, on a small raised walkway, and he waved his bar around to draw the ghouls to him. The men behind him, several frozen both in fear and in years, mere boys of perpetual eighteen or nineteen, stood in a stupefied shock as grizzled wraiths walked toward them. The wind pushed against the backs of the ghouls. Some had long and tangled twisted hairs, which blew up into the air. If the

Germans ever had known of the local legend of Blackbeard, and his affinity for his long locks to be twisted with cannon fuses, lit to create a smoldering hellish visage, they would still not have responded more terror to the trudging mass.

The incessant growling only made it worse.

The zombies looked at Schacht and the sailors beyond him. Red eyes glowed, as if lit by brimstone, burning crimson and hate.

Schacht bellowed so that his men could hear, "*Komm schon! Komm zu mir! Komm her! Kommen Sie!*"

He waved at the ghouls, a gesture meant to taunt, which may have worked against a living man. Schacht was tall, taught like twisted rope that would tie a submarine to the dock, with broad shoulders of a man brought up at sea. He held his pipe low, menacing, a promise that he wouldn't hold back with even his first swing. He didn't realize all his posturing would not matter against an attacker that was already dead.

When a large group of ghouls peeled off to pursue him, Schacht waited gleefully. He stood at the top of the steps as they approached. When the first of the ghouls got close enough, Schacht stepped out onto the stairs, raised his pipe and swung with all his might.

The leading ghoul met the pipe with the side of his head. A solid high pitched *thok* sprung out from the ghoul's head. The impact split the side of its skull, sending bone and butchered vital flesh out in a spray. Its head, almost halved from the side, lolled at the neck, broken and swiveling. One eye, still red, hung out of its socket. The body stopped but for a split second and stood still. Schacht was transfixed at the carnage and that the body didn't fall immediately. Finally the knees crumpled and the body collapsed. The other ghouls didn't notice one of them falling, except that now they had a target.

Three ghouls surrounded Schacht before he could bring his pipe to bear. He raised it high and brought it down straight, driving the short end down across the face of the center ghoul of the three. The open end of the pipe struck like a hammer at the forehead of a close cropped head, blotched with black spots and bruises. The waterlogged skin gave away easily, tearing down its face, breaking the forehead bone before ripping off the cartilage of the nose. The force of the blow drove the base of the pipe into the ghoul's jaw. Teeth, rotten and black, rattled with the contact, and shivered the pipe right through to Schacht's hands, before tearing the muscles of the jaw and ripping it almost completely off.

Schacht's sailors, scared and repulsed by the gore, saw the attack on their officer and leaped to save him. Two men swung table legs straight down at the zombies. One contacted his attacker fully on the top of the skull. The force of the blow cleaved its head, splitting it from the top. It released its grip on Schacht and fell immediately. The other Nazi aimed for the third ghoul's head and missed low, cracking into its neck as it leaned in toward Schacht.

The German officer stepped back, his bravado spent. With his free hand he felt fresh wounds, scratches that did little damage, and what looked like a bite to his shoulder, through his shirt. The wound ached less than it should, and barely wept blood. Schacht took the slight moment of freedom and called for his men to back up into the exterior hall. "*Zurück!*" he bellowed, waving his pipe to direct his men. They stepped cautiously into the darkened shelter.

Rain and wind made the view of the trudging ghouls an ominous parade, a mudslide of darkened bodies, wet, smelling of age old grease, salt, and rot. The tiny circle that held the school's empty flagpole was a natural dividing barrier for the onslaught. Most of the wraiths turned toward the gym, as some inexorable call drove them to the bulk of the sailors. But another group came toward the available threat, Schacht and his men. The three Nazi submariners were the only ones visible, but there were more hidden inside, waiting to dish out a bloody death.

"*Streik an ihren Köpfen!*" Schacht and his cohort of men stood in the darkened hall near the office, with only a table in the doorway to block the passage. Schacht only wanted to slow the ghouls down. The table would group them together, slow the horde, and allow his men to fight. It would be more difficult in the tight confines, but Schacht needed to keep as many ghouls on his side of the school as possible.

The horde came in, blackening the hallway as they blotted out the light from outside. One of the sailors turned on a battery operated lantern and threw it skittering under the table. It made the ghouls grow in size, long shadows casting upwards, arms reaching out through the walls. A few of the sailors whimpered in horror and crouched backwards in hope of escaping. One was forcefully held by his lapel by the grip of another. "*Wenn ich hier sterbe, bleibst du bei mir.*" one muttered to the other.

Four of the ghouls staggered to the table and began pushing. One tried to climb over the top. In the moment, Schacht screamed a cry and attacked. He swung his pipe down from close overhead. Schacht caught the ghoul in the back of the head, driving the body down into the table top as the skull crushed under the force of the blow. The lamp did little to enlighten his damage, but Schacht knew he struck well. He felt pieces of the head fly, bone, brain, or blood, he didn't care, as long as that thing didn't get back up.

His men struck just behind him, again with table legs. Two sailors ran toward the table, now inundated by the salt rimed undead coming for them. They attempted to push the table back but it could not stand the weight. The table flipped over, throwing the bodies back into the sea of ghouls and making a wall for the rest. The Nazis approached en masse, hoping to hold off the ghouls by poking into the horde with their blunt weapons. Metal made contact with the wet drooping faces, still mutilated by the light on the floor. Most of the ghouls had their faces caved in and their noses smashed, a black ooze dripping out, leaving a fetid stink in the confines of the hallway.

One of the sailors retched at the stench, burning acid bile coming up into his mouth. He turned away, choking and coughing, unable to spit or rid himself of the taste. His absence left a gap in the line, and one of the zombies lurched over to grab a sailor who flailed at its hands. More undead hands grabbed at the clothes of the man, pulling him into their clutches as they ripped bits of cloth from his uniform. He was pulled into the horde, screaming that became higher pitched until it reached an ululation. The rest of the sailors charged toward their lost comrade, grabbing his legs but finding their grip slipping easily as the far more determined ghouls pulled the Nazi to their side until he disappeared.

His screams didn't. The sailors had to listen as he was torn by the ghouls, the first punishment for a lifetime of loss. It didn't stop of with the first scream, or the second. It seemed like they were letting him suffer. The sailors became manic in their attack. They now knew the end result of not succeeding in this battle. "*Lieber Gott!*" one cried as the suffering shrieks continued. Two rows of Nazi sailors battled hand to hand with the monsters on the other end of a thin half wall. One of the submariners dug in and swung his club shoulder height, his backswing stabbing a crewmate under the eye, cracking the cheekbone. He didn't bother to look back at the damage he had done. He swung through, smashing open another head, soft and pulpy, with brains splattering in a guttural squish over everything near him.

Schacht thought that they had the creatures contained. The table still held them back, and the increasing pile of bodies, their gored and opened heads open and leaking, created an inhuman wall between the sailors and the ghouls. He stepped back, allowing another man to take his place as he watched and wiped the visceral fluids of the battle off of his face. It was then that he saw the mass of the horde surge.

The table moved, and with the pile of bodies, the ghouls were able to climb higher. One began to step over the edge of the table as a sailor swung at its head. An upraised arm was little defense, but it made the blow shift slightly, coming in contact with the thing's chin and jaw. Schacht watched as the head turned, the jaw opened, and snapped. Teeth rained out into the darkness, and the jawbone hung limp. But the creature was unfazed. It continued its climb, stumbling over the table as another of the Nazis brought a short crushing blow down on the back of its head. Then another, for good measure.

The body fell forward, and the table with it, allowing the ghouls to surge. The sailors seemed to want to stand fast against a still overwhelming tide, when Schacht yelled, "*Zurück! Komm zurück!*

"*Karl! Jetzt! Ziele hoch, für ihre Köpfe!*" It was a signal to the sailors, all of them, even as the order went to an anxious, taller young man that had waited in the darkness. Karl Brant strode through the rapidly retreating men, his compatriots that had done the dirty work, while he waited. Karl's father had been a young man in the first war, the *Weltkrieg*. He discussed with his son the trench battles, and how horrid the conditions were. Most feared among the Prussian soldiers was the horrid crashing cough sound of a weapon the infantry heard during the close combat, when the Americans came over and entered the trenches. What they feared so much was called by the Americans the trench broom. It was a fearsome weapon that spat out steel at close quarters in such volume as to render dead or dying soldiers by the dozens within seconds. So horrid was the weapon that the Germans strode to ban it from the battlefield, and threatened to have any enemy combatant found with the weapon or ammo to be shot on sight.

Karl understood its workings from his father's tales, and knew the destructive power. So he was given the shotgun taken from the *Polizei*. He approached and leveled it at the mass of ghouls, firing a blast into the middle. Fire struck out, and the hall shook with the death coming from the barrel. It met the soft heads of the wraiths, turning them into puffs of crimson smoke. The blast cleared a section three feet deep in the middle of the horde. The bodies were so struck that they tumbled backward into the others.

Karl did not wait to see his handiwork. He wasn't an artist at this time, but a simple butcher, ready to chop meat. He moved the barrel right, pumping the weapon's handle back, finger still on the trigger. The spent shell popped out. Pointed at the two ghouls on his right, he pushed the handle forward, allowing the weapon to fire automatically. The spout of steel crashed into the two creatures at the front, taking off most of their heads, spraying into a third behind them and splattering through the thin wall, streaking it with a glittering and sticky red comet from the brains of the ghouls. He swiveled and pumped again, to the left, letting the forend do its work, and setting off another blast into the crowd, with similar results.

The blasts still rang in his ears. He knew to back off to see where the threat now stood with his wounded crewmates. After a devastating assault, with what looked like twenty dead or dying ghouls laying on the floor in a pile, the small lantern battered into a corner but casting out its eerie gleam, Karl, and the men behind him, could see that they had whittled the horde down tremendously. There was no way that the horde they had just fought could win against them now, not after the final shocking blast that Karl had delivered. The floor shone with viscera, copious fluids pulled from the bodies and pooled on the cheap linoleum tiles. The strange cold crimson blood that seeped through the zombies lay thick on the floor and clung to the walls. The stack of bodies piled up in the tiny hallway, a disgusting heap of broken flesh.

Yet the remaining ghouls came on.

Schacht grabbed Karl, dumbfounded, by the shoulder and pulled him back. They should have been devastated, they should have run in fear, after the destruction and bloodletting that occurred. They should be terrified of us, Schacht thought. But they weren't, which sent a cold chill up his back, making the Nazi submariner rigid.

"Komm zurück. Wir werden sie im Inneren hinter uns schließen."

He pulled Karl away, the shotgun raised to fire, to cover them and possibly finish the remaining ghouls off. He had two shots left from the heartless broom he had fired, just like the Americans had done to his family decades before.

"Nein, warte, wir brauchen vielleicht später die Waffe." Schacht commanded him. They were threatened, but still had an escape plan. He did not want to waste his shots if he didn't need to. He hoped to save them for more impressive targets. A shotgun without any ammunition was merely a club, and a poor one at that.

"Wir müssen auf den Kapitän vor der Schule warten. Wir werden uns im Westen der Insel neu gruppieren und unseren ursprünglichen Plan fortsetzen." Schacht yelled to his men. They stood together near him, within the confines of the hall, looking at the remaining zombies now cresting a wave of gored dead bodies. Schacht pushed his men backward to lead them out the back way. A red EXIT sign wearily lit the doors to the outside. The last of the evening sun was completely choked out by the churning waves of clouds and rain. The sailors left the hall at a run, entering a tiny courtyard. It was a play area and field for the children, Schacht recognized. The last sailor out barred the doors as he was instructed.

The sailors in unison turned toward the gym as they heard a muffled yet familiar cough.

*
**

Krieg couldn't watch to see if Schacht had succeeded in drawing off any of the approaching undead marauders. He had no idea how these… men would respond to multiple threats. He knew to make his targets look one way while he attacked from another, and then to disappear into the depths, silently, and in the dark. He wasn't sure how to handle the more ominous threat of slowly being pursued by a relentless mob. He may be able to outrun the horde of zombies, but they were on an island. Where would they go? That had been the question in his mind from the moment they had been discovered and captured. He now had a way out, and the storm was the perfect cover, only to have his plans thrown to a churning sea by this undead group of… what were they… *Unmenschen*… ogres, beasts, monsters, not men.

He would not let his crew fall to them, the beasts he once sent to the bottom of the sea. He would send them back again, and find a way off the island.

The bulk of the horde seemed to crowd the hall that led to the gym. Krieg thought about having some of his men whittle the group down before reaching the interior doors, but he knew they would be sacrificed without any results. There were just too many of these *Unmenschen* to defeat quickly. There would be loss in the battle, but Krieg knew he could and would suffer less. He still needed his crew to man his boat.

He had instructed his men to clog the wide hall from the entrance to the gym with anything they could quickly get, desks and chairs, low tangling ropes, the basketballs from the courts. All would foul the walking corpses and allow his men to strike. He would create a bottleneck, and pick off the *Unmenschen* as they fought their way forward. When the hall became dark with the shapes of humans, it was time to put his plan to the test.

Krieg walked toward the maw of growling undead, their odor a horrid mix of salt and sea and death. He had smelled it before. He knew the smell from when he had surfaced to view the fruits of his labor, the burning oil and stink of the salted haze of a very one sided battle. Krieg hoped to keep it that way.

He raised the pistol he had removed from the Coast Guardsman. It was slightly unfamiliar, similar to early U.S. pistols, but thicker than his officer's Mauser. It functioned the same way, he commented to himself. He chambered a round into the action, and stepped close. He was not sure how the weapon would work. He thought his Mauser would not have the necessary power to stop one of these *Unmenschen* but this larger weapon, more modern, may deal a more deadly hand. He aimed at the most obvious target of a struggling *Unmensch,* its open black mouth, graying and rotted teeth hanging out an angle below red eyes glaring hate. Krieg squeezed the trigger and delivered hate back. The pistol whipcracked a crashing sound, a loud and short cough in the hallway. The split second tinkle of the spent shell casing hitting the wood floor was lost in the effect of the bullet as it flew the few feet toward its target. The bullet had flown true, going into the ghoul's mouth, only hitting a tooth, before striking the soft back of the throat. It took the tender flesh back to the spine before any major distortion occurred on the bullet. It mushroomed as it cracked through the spine, until exiting the back of the skull. The tumbling bullet popped almost softly into the eye of a ghoul behind the target. It rattled into the barely functioning brain, scrambling the waterlogged head of the zombie.

Krieg only noticed that his aim was true with the unfamiliar weapon. He began to fire repeatedly, counting to himself, while his feet danced backwards, keeping his aim calm instead of rushed, always staying the same distance away from the horde. At four he stood back to collect himself, to wait for his heartbeat to settle. Krieg saw the horde not slowing measurably, almost oblivious as they stepped on, over, and through the visceral remains of their dead.

Krieg moved to his right as the horde began to spread from the narrow hallway. He wanted to keep as many to the left, close to the wall of the gym, not in the open where they could move. He took a breath and aimed the pistol again.

"*Fünf...*" he counted as one more fell, a large, bulky sallow hulk of greasy dark hair in overalls.

"*Sechs...*" a bullet cracked through the cheekbone of a moving target. It was down but not out as its head twisted in shock.

"*Sieben...*" this shot rang true as it connected between the eyes of a thin *Schlappschwanz*, adding a third eye hole between its original beady two, and making a cloud of red mist puff out over the things behind him.

"*Acht...*" Krieg said it out loud, as if a code for his men, as one more ghoul fell to the weapon. Eight shots and the bodies mounted.

"*Einziehen!*" he commanded, and eight groups of four or five men approached the oncoming tide of death the zombies posed.

Unsure, the men simply lashed out at any single ghoul or group they could. The submariners slashed with their clubs or whatever weapon they had been able to arm themselves. It took them only moments to become organized, after the first flailing attacks. Two sailors in a group would come in at angles, swinging high at the zombie's head. They would then step back, allowing another to come straight in, slamming the end of a table leg or a folded chair into the bludgeoned wrecked face of the creature to push it back. The final members of the group would then attack with a *coup de grâce*, smashing the head in, putting the end to what consisted for life for the nightmarish beasts.

The first wave withered and crashed to the floor so quickly that the Nazis had a strange moment of rest, to stop and contemplate the threat, which only increased both their fear and response. The attack did not abate, and more of the ghouls spilled into the gym, trodding heavily on a butcher's floor littered with diseased, blackened brains. One creature, its head half caved in but its brain still willing it on, slipped and crawled on its knees in a desperate attempt to reach its prey. A German officer, muscles tensed, stepped forward with his whole body behind a swing, a hideous bloody slapshot across the side of the head, severing it from the body, sending what was left skittering in a slosh across the floor.

Feeling their success, the Nazis closed in on the tightened horde. Three groups approached the tiny hallway opening and began battering at the zombie seamen. One slipped in the oily blood. He fell to his back as the ghouls reached for him, pulling at his legs with clawlike hands. He screamed, a squawk of terror as he was pulled toward the maw of the horde. Instantly, his submariner comrades hacked through the wall while others pulled him away by his shoulders. It only took a moment for his legs to be scraped and shredded by the creatures. His blood ran thinly, but more red, an ominous difference that made the Nazi wince as he watched himself bleed for the first time in decades. It had been so long since he felt anything but the stuffy confines of their U-boat coffin. Now all he felt was the terrible chill of shock. The others pulled him by his collar and threw him unceremoniously behind the line onto the basketball court, where he panted, collapsed at the foul line.

"*Nein! Nein! Beweg dich nicht zurück! Halte sie zurück!*" Krieg screamed at his men as the flow of wet, dirty demons pressed forward. He couldn't afford to lose any of his sailors. He needed as many as possible to escape the island. These ghouls, eyes glowing red in the darkening gloom, seemed to have no such worry. They were not shocked by their losses, and kept pressing their attack. Krieg wondered if he killed them all, would the last one be as aggressive as the first. He may have to find out.

Two more groups of Nazi submariners charged in as the line widened. They had room to swing away at the heads and bodies of the ghouls now, and the Nazis used the space and speed to advantage. They chopped like madmen at the approaching ghouls. The bloodletting was so vicious that Krieg's men had to stop and step back to allow more to enter the gym, to have a new set of targets. Krieg watched, wondering if the line of creatures would ever stop. He looked at the pistol still in his hand. He had no time to check if he had any bullets left. His Mauser would be empty now. If he had more, Krieg thought, he may need what was left to make his escape. He still was thinking of escape. He counted the bodies. The number was so high he could only guess.

A scream became a choked cry. One of the sailors was caught, being pulled into the horde. Krieg watched as his body was pulled apart. The boy's death, just a young rating, was too much for the captain. His sailors, still repulsed, turned to the crowd, no longer looking to save the rating, but looking for vengeance, as they clubbed down the assailing ghouls. Knotted hair, clotted with blood, flew off the ends of the Nazi weapons. One officer plunged a fixed blade knife through the forehead of a growling, snarling zombie, all the way to the hilt. He pulled down, the knife embedded and holding fast, until the officer kicked at the undead ghoul. His knife freed from the skull in an arc of black syrupy blood. The line splattered a rope of crimson across the face and shirt of the officer. It looked like a disheveled bandolier.

Krieg watched from just beyond the line of his crew as they battled the demons. He watched as more of his sailors came back wounded. Most wanted back in, to avenge their injury, or at least to minimize the shame. Krieg waved them back. He needed them alive. He already lost one, and didn't know if any of Schacht's men survived. It was time.

"Jürgen," Krieg could wait no longer. He had given the two shotguns to his two largest men who knew how the weapons would function. They had hunted and fired the loud weapon before. They knew what it would do, especially at close range. *"Liefern die Hölle."*

Jürgen stepped forward with the police shotgun and pointed into the crowd, head high. With a shell already in the action, he leaned into the weapon as he squeezed the trigger. The blast was loud and hollow in the gymnasium, making the other submariners stop their attack, some dropping their weapons and covering their ears. One distracted sailor turned toward the sound, taking his eyes off the attackers long enough for three ghouls to lunge at him and grab his arm, pulling him into their grasp. Ten of his compatriots jumped to his rescue, pulling him away from the tight grasp. He screamed as his arm was wrenched and torn at. He came back bloody from the shoulder down.

The center of the horde had fallen in from the shot. Two of the ghouls went down in a spray of red blood and infected black gore. The blast may have stunned the Nazi sailors, but did not affect the ghouls in the least. A few in the middle fell over the decapitated bodies, a gore infested domino effect of zombies tumbling into their own carnage. Jürgen, less familiar with the weapon's ability, pumped a new shell into the action with his finger over the guard. He aimed into the right side of the crowd and delivered more hell into the mob. The second shot was aimed into the side of the heads of several of the demons. The shot took the back of one's skull off, while splattering across the face of another behind. Jürgen turned and fired to his left, taking down another zombie.

"Jürgen, ziele auf die Knie," Krieg commanded at a shout. He didn't know if Jürgen would be able to hear after firing the shotgun, but the large man kneeled with the weapon tucked tightly into his shoulder, the short barrel pointed into the bulk of the crowd at leg height. Krieg saw

160

that there were still so many of them. He needed to slow the horde down enough to escape. The shot spread through the crowd of zombies, cutting at their legs like a chain saw. The lead zombie had his kneecaps fold backward, a crashing of rotted flesh and ivory bone. Others mimicked the fall, all with similar wounds. They collapsed under their own weight, still moving, but unable to walk.

"*Speichere die letzte Einstellung. Vielleicht brauchen wir es, um zu entkommen.*" Krieg needed to think about escape, and freedom. He needed his men to hear it. But he also needed to get out. His men had whittled down the near eighty ghouls down to about thirty, maybe less. Still not good odds.

"*Verteilen. Bring sie dir. Nimm je zwei mehr heraus. Bleib zusammen, immer überzählig!*"

The sailors spread out across the court, making multiple targets of themselves and separating the remaining zombies. The groups were then able to bring their weapons to bear with gruesome effect.

"That's it!" Chief Stone knew when it was time to move. She had watched the gore fly as one of the Nazis, a blonde ogre that should have been too tall for submarine duty, had unloaded one of their shotguns on the group of zombies attacking him. "Time to go." She didn't want to do anything to attract attention to herself while the Germans could look over their shoulders. The zombies were going to keep the Nazis occupied now, and she doubted that Krieg and his goons would notice them gone, if anyone, Nazi or American, survived this onslaught.

161

The chief stood up, a cheap folding chair attached to her. Her shoulder had moved from a sharp ache to a continuous dull throb. It didn't matter now, anyway. The Nazis had tied their hands behind them to the chairs with the ropes, with the idea of keeping them docile, not so secure. Stone simply stood up and then rammed the chair backwards into the stage, bending the chair flat. It took little to shake the bent remains loose.

Her shoulder ached like hell. But she was free. Frankie attempted to do the same thing but only fell over with a clang. The noise did nothing to distract the Nazis in their fight. Chief Stone untied the nylon ropes from Dan Howard's wrists to free him, as Frankie wallowed on the floor.

"I coulda done better," he jested halfheartedly, trying to make himself not look bad. The other two didn't care. They were already in a bad spot. There wasn't time for judgement or embarrassment. Dan grabbed the deputy by the arm and picked him up. The three of them simply hopped upon the stage, Stone wincing again, and rolled under the cheap tall curtain. Just being out of sight of their captors and the attacking ghouls was some small measure of protection.

Until Dan stumbled over the body of Jeff Beasley, dead as a doornail. His eyes bulged out, along with a blackened tongue. The massive bruise across his throat showed how his windpipe had been crushed.

"Damnation!" Dan Howard cursed at the sight.

Dan had coddled and protected the men from the submarine. He had seen them as the victims, long trapped and cursed in darkness. They were sailors, people of the sea, just like him and his kind, Dan had thought. And then he had welcomed them to his island.

And they repaid his kindness by murdering poor Jeff Beasley.

And Jimmy Gray.

And old Bill Howard.

He was not terrified of the actions and blood spilling behind him on the gym floor. He was weak. He felt his knees buckle as his legs went limp. Always being a strong man, silent and stoic when misfortune came to him, like all islanders were supposed to be, he finally gave in. Silent sobs choked his throat as he looked at the lifeless body of Jeff, a man who had spent his adult life trying to make people better, from saving the life of a fisherman to holding the hand of a little lady worried about a cold. He never harmed a soul, and yet there he was, the life throttled out of him, his tongue black, swollen, and protruded from his mouth, a line of yellow bile already drying across his cheek. It was an ignoble death, devoid of any value or redemption. The Nazi sailors probably snuck up behind him and choked him to death with a rope.

Dan had defended them. He had let them onto the island, his island, thinking he was doing the right thing to protect and comfort the seamen from a different time and place. Falling to his knees, Dan held his head in his hands in numb realization. Behind him, cold and distant, he heard the violence of the sailors struggling against the zombie dead horde that overran the school. Even though one group was clean cut, the model of the marine sailor, and the other was a huge mob of demon eyed ogres, hair greasy with ancient black oil, clothing waterlogged, torn, and burned, bruised and blistered sickly flesh, rotted fingernails and teeth, Dan now knew which ones were the real monsters.

He staggered up and went to turn toward the curtain. His desire was to wade into the battle and tear apart the Nazis with his bare hands just as the zombies were doing right now. Chief Stone grabbed him by the shoulder. "No!" she hissed, a whisper that cut like a sharp chain, "We can't fight them here! We need to get out of here, get safe, protect the rest of the island. We need to get help!" Stone already had her hate up, but she knew better than to walk naked into that snake pit behind her, especially with her shoulder wound.

"C'mon, Dan!" Frankie all but pleaded. He had seen too much death. He was supposed to protect people, stop all this from happening, and he was powerless to do so. "We need to get out of here! We can't afford another body!" All this was happening without reason.

The two pulled Dan Howard toward the back of the school, through the back of the stage and into a darkened hall. Their best hope was to escape toward the back, head to the fire station and find someone there to boost their numbers, or seal themselves up just to get put back together.

28

6:00 P.M.

OCRACOKE SCHOOL PLAYGROUND

Schacht heard the sounds of a shotgun, the twin to the weapon that had done so much damage in the confined hallway where he had battled with the zombies. They had planned similar tactics, which meant that Schacht should expect the bulk of his crew to come out of the side door of the gym any moment.

He began to worry after three minutes passed.

The door he had barricaded rattled furiously, but held. There were only a few of those demons left on his side. He had no idea how well the rest of the crew had fared against the bulk of the zombies. His orders were to wait there for the crew to leave the gym and help necessitate escape. He held a wet and softened map he had found outside a store, a simple tourist cartoon drawing that showed a few places of interest and some restaurants along the village. More importantly to

Schacht it also clearly showed in large print with bright yellow lines the roads behind the school. That was where they would head when the rest of the crew joined them.

The wind still whipped across the island, sending the rain sideways and blinding the men. Across the field where the students would normally play was a basketball court and line of tall evergreen trees, all leaning at the tips, and bouncing back upright. They danced like giant cheerleaders in chorus to a game only they could see. Whoever was playing, the storm was winning.

Schacht thought he saw motion through the trees, but the darkness and fog of battle played tricks on him.

All of the sailors swiveled their heads to the *clickcluck* sound of doors opening. Familiar figures in familiar clothing came out.

"*Kapitän! Hier!*" Schacht called out to the men and their leader in the comfortable language they shared. The twilight sky darkened to the dark gray of pencil lead.

Schacht was unable to count the number of men that came out the door, but there seemed to be most, if not all, of the crew. He hoped they had lost no one. He cringed inwardly about the death of one of his charges. Every man down was a person he could not replace.

"*Kapitän?*" Schacht searched for and found Krieg. He almost patted the man down to see if he was injured. *"Kapitän, geht es dir gut? Hast du irgendwelche Männer verloren? Haben wir sie alle?"*

"Nein, wir haben eins, vielleicht zwei verloren. Wir müssen die Männer in Sicherheit bringen, um sich neu zu formieren." Captain Krieg regained his composure quickly and began to think like a U-boat commander again. *"Wir haben die Anzahl dieser Tiere stark reduziert, aber es gibt noch mehr. Sie scheinen nicht aufzugeben. Sie werden uns wahrscheinlich verfolgen."*

The Germans had planned to do battle in a confined space on their terms, like they would in the ocean, sneaking in for an attack in the darkness, then sneaking away. If they were pursued, they would run and hide, hoping to turn in the tides and attack the hunters in the dark. Only this time Krieg did not have his submarine, nor his weapons, and the enemy was past ruthless to be incomprehensible, or even irrational. That would not matter, Krieg thought. He would still win.

"*Sag den Männern, welchen Weg sie gehen sollen,*" Krieg commanded. Schacht hissed an order, pointing eastward, down Back Road as it was labeled on the map. Names didn't matter to him. He merely needed to put space between the crew and the zombies that were left. It would give him time to organize a counter attack. The sailors took off at a run, past the darkened school full of the undead, past a blacked out and empty fire station, before turning up the next road. In the failing light and through the rain the sign was not legible, but Schacht knew the road was Sunset.

29

Three people huddled in the darkness, afraid to use a light from the lanterns or from the generator, as they worried their presence would be discovered. They watched as a fast moving wall of men ran down the road, black on black tarmac against an ashen sky through the dark rain. The group moved surprisingly fast and silently. It was a horrific sight to see.

"You think that was the zombies?" Frankie whispered nervously, after the group had long gone. His leg twitched involuntarily, bouncing as the nerves sent uncontrollable shocks down his thigh. He wasn't scared so much as drained emotionally and physically, yet the situation would not let him sleep. God knows what he might dream, Frankie thought, and shuddered at the pictures in his head. He shook them out with a twist to his neck.

"No," whispered back Stone. "Too fast." The chief waited for the group to be long gone before she prowled around a medical kit do do something about her shoulder."Damn," she cursed and winced. Her shoulder throbbed, but her arm seemed to work. So did her tear ducts. Her eyes welled from the pain. She looked to find something she could take for the pain. "I'm gonna need some help with this. I can't see what I'm dealing with.

"Dan?"

Stone needed to give Dan Howard a job, and this was as good as any. Maybe better. Dan needed to do something, to fix something after he felt like he had screwed everything up. "Take a look, see what we're dealing with here. I got some sutures, and some butterflies," she held up a paper package of thin bandages, large winged adhesives with little in between, meant to pull cuts together. They would do on a pinch, but she feared she needed to be sewn back together. That would hurt, but probably no worse than it already did.

By the dimmed light of a flashlight with a cloth over the bulb, Dan inspected the wound. A stabbing cut, it went deep enough to do damage, but outside of a lot of seeping blood around Stone's shirt, it probably wasn't as bad as it looked. She'd need some antibiotics, stitches, and time to heal. Dan wondered if they would have a chance to get any of those.

"Jen…" Dan began, the quietude of the darkened firehouse lending an air of intimacy, "Listen,… I'm sorry… I should have seen this…" Dan tried to keep his voice calm, but felt the catch of phlegm in his throat, his voice raising higher as he kept himself from cracking.

"No. No, you shouldn't," Stone was angry and bitter at the circumstances, but she couldn't blame Dan for having a heart. It was in the nature of the islanders to stick a helping hand out, even if they were naturally distrusting of people off the island. When a sailor was in distress, it's a sailor that rescues them. Same in the Guard, Stone thought.

"No one could see this happening. No one's gonna believe it when it's all over. But it's not your fault that anyone got hurt, or got killed.

"It's theirs. It always has been. There's no way to paint a picture where the choices they made led to anything better. Those bastards are selfish, monstrous, and horrid. And I'm not talking about those waterlogged hoodoos, either."

Dan took a moment. He didn't completely buy in to Stone's words, but he felt better that at least one person wasn't going to blame him for bringing those Nazis onto the island. "You probably are gonna need stitches."

"Go ahead," Stone said gruffly.

The thickness of the air, full of stifling dust and humidity in the dark, did its best to muffle the cringes of pain.

30

7:00 P.M.

OCRACOKE COMMUNITY CEMETERY

Krieg had followed his men as the U-boat crew ran north up Sunset Road until they turned left onto a narrow and dirty road. The hurricane had blown the thin silty sand that layered the island onto the street, and the current rainstorm turned it into a sloshy mess. The sailors didn't care as long as they were putting distance between them and their attackers. Krieg was nervous that the houses he passed might have eyes peering at him as his men traversed an unholy enemy land. But the windows to the damp, wood sided houses and shacks stared darkly, unseeing. No light appeared from inside. The power was still out, Krieg thought, but anyone at home would undoubtedly have an oil lamp or candle burning. He had no desire to find out what was inside the houses yet.

Schacht lead the men knowingly down Cemetery Road. Most couldn't read the English on the sign, or the ominous destination would have slowed their progress. Krieg didn't care about the superstitious nature of a cemetery. He merely wanted an open killing field, and some dark woods into which to melt. Schacht had searched the area and found that most of the homes were abandoned from the storm. They may have been used seasonally by visitors, Schacht had thought.

Krieg gathered his men just past the entrance of the cemetery to deploy them.

"*Wie viele der Unmensch hast du lebend verlassen?*" Krieg needed a count of targets.

"*Zwei oder drei. Wir haben sie hinter einer Tür eingeschlossen, aber sie werden aus dem Weg kommen können, wie sie gekommen sind.*" Schacht knew he left zombies still, he thought, *alive?* Not a good description. Functioning. "*Wie viele hast du in der Turnhalle verlassen?*"

"*Zehn oder zwölf.*"

Krieg now had a number of targets. Fifteen, no, he would say twenty so as not to underestimate their numbers. He ordered some of his men to hide behind the nearest row of large grave markers. He then spread them out into the cemetery.

"*Bleib, wo du bist, bis die Teufel auf diese Weise kommen. Wenn du ein Ziel hast, schlag einmal, nur einmal! Beschäftige sie nicht. Töte deinen Schaden und renne dann zum Friedhof. Wenn Sie jemanden laufen sehen, wird es einer unserer eigenen sein.*" Krieg's plan was to whittle the ghouls down, one blow at a time. He would have his first row of men strike at the nearest target, then move five graves back. When the ghouls reached the next row, they would be more damaged and easier to destroy. It also allowed him to protect his men by having them not fight as they had in the gym, but to avoid close hand to hand combat. He was using a military tactic that the British had used in their infantry, only he would slowly retreat as he did damage, as opposed to advancing. He didn't have the advantage of firearms, and his enemy did not feel any fear. These ghouls would fight to the last. They possibly would crawl forward if they were left alive. Krieg didn't plan on leaving them in one piece. His men would be the only living things leaving the cemetery.

Krieg found a place deep within the cemetery, under a twisted scrubby tree, and hid in the darkness. This was the first time he had to stop and think since the attack, or even since they had come ashore. He was able to take in his surroundings, dark as they were. The rain still fell, and there was only the merest strip of color behind the trees to the west as the storm choked out all sunlight. The woods to his back held strange creatures, not dangerous, but numerous, peeping insects or frogs of some sort.

He noticed he was not breathing hard. His body was not tired or sore. He felt some pain, a dull ache in his arm, but his legs were not sore even as they had run all the way from their temporary prison camp. He smelled the rain and dirt, as well as an odd odor, something from the trees, a strange high evergreen citrus sickly sweet scent that he found distinctly unpleasant. He had given strict orders to not make any noise, and now the silence and its resultant tumult from nature was noticeably deafening. Krieg heard an insect fly by his ear. He had to purposefully act not to swat at it, so that his motion would not be noticed, when he realized that even in the warm closure of summer, no bugs were bothering him. He expected a stinging insect to be clinging at his neck, or sucking bug to drink from his eyes. The then realized he didn't smell himself or his men. On a submarine, there is always the odor of confinement. The U-boat had to wait, starving itself of air as it got hotter and hotter inside, until they were finally able to rise and open the hatches for the salty fresh air. The men got sweaty, bearing rags in their hands as they wiped dirt and sweat from their necks. Here on land, all of that was missing. His clothes were soaked, but it was all the cold crystalline water of the rain that fell. It was almost as if they weren't there.

But those ghouls knew where they were. They would find the Germans soon enough, and Krieg would again be ready.

Krieg wondered if his men would grow impatient or worse, complacent, during this time. The waiting was always the hard part. Anticipation and fear ran rampant through any soldier's mind up to and during battle. For Krieg it had been so long since he was able to command. Now he had a goal and a target and a reason. He relished the desire to be back, in charge, controlling his fate and the fates of others. Soon, he would put back to sea, to find a welcoming home somewhere farther south.

Too soon, he thought, too soon to make those plans. Focus on the task.

He waited.

It would take time before the remaining zombies shambled and strolled their way toward the old sandy path to the cemetery. The Germans could hear them first, a shuffling accompanied by a guttural growl. Krieg spied a look from his darkened lair behind a tree. He saw the mass, a group much smaller than the original horde. He smiled a grim devil's smile, satisfied with the damage that he had done. He lost two men, a sacrifice, but one that could be managed, especially when the result was survival.

The ghouls came up into the cemetery in a group; they seemed to sense the location of Krieg's sailors as they marched straight into the middle of the graves. Krieg could see the zombies, piercing red eyes glowing bloodshot in the dim twilight. Hair and faces bedraggled, damaged with bruises and knots, and all they showed were visages of hate.

The first of the ghouls reached the grave markers, and the Nazi line struck. Three men were able to strike out at the heads of the ghouls, smashing in with force, tearing at the wet soggy flesh. One zombie lost an eye, torn from its socket by a sharp metal corner of one of the clubbing weapons the Nazis wielded. Two men, on the far ends of the line, stood up with the others but had no targets. Dutifully, they immediately ran back five rows and hid again, waiting their turn with the diligent expectation of any superman that they would not be needed for a second turn.

The zombies stumbled and regrouped. There were more together now, maybe eight or so, by Krieg's count in the near dark. The zombies moved in a group past the second row. This time the Nazis did not strike but waited until the ghouls were past them, and came up from just behind. Two of the strongest crew members crashed their weapons down upon the heads of the zombies. The force was so great as to cleave the skulls down to the neck. A bloody detritus splattered across the men, who turned away to keep the flying bone and brain out of their mouths. Undeterred and unaffected, the other zombies reached out to the new threats, trying to grab them. More of the Nazi crew sprang into action, smashing away at reaching arms and prying hands. A satisfying crack rang through the cemetery as a forearm fractured and split the decayed muscle. The force pulled the arm out of the shoulder socket of one of the ghouls and the arm hung obviously and grotesquely damaged off the side of the zombie, who showed no affection to the wound. The arm simply hung broken and limp, a sharp splintered stump of bone protruding fully from its arm. Inky black blood dripped down the zombies' coveralls like a gory syrup.

Krieg watched for the third row. His men again had done their duties, strike and escape, but always escape. These *Unmenschen* were no match for him. "*Schacht, Jetzt!*"

Schacht stood up, shining two flashlights into the remnants of the zombie horde. He hoped to blind the ghouls, but the yellow light from the torches didn't bother them, or they were just not fazed by the bright light in the darkness. The lights still helped illuminate and target the remaining monsters standing in the cemetery.

Red eyes glowed out from the zombies torn sallow faces, even as their bodies fell apart. Their wounds were just too much to bear. They moved too slow, their numbers too few now to mount a concentrated attack. Two of the German sailors came from behind the next row of graves. One of the creatures was singled out by the light of Schacht, and the two ratings attacked. They swung their clubs, long thin pipes they had found in the school, both aiming at the head. The strike found contact. With the beam of the flashlight shining, the head of the zombie was crushed between the strikes. The Nazis were not settled. After the sideways strike, a baseball swing to the head, one of the Germans raised his pipe like a battleaxe and brought it down on the remains of the zombie. The blow glanced off the slick bloody remains of the zombie's head, and crashed into its shoulder, shattering the collarbone and tearing into its body. The zombie went down in a heap of its own gore, silently.

The numbers of the zombies fell rapidly, horridly outnumbered by the now overwhelming Nazi crew. When the sailors saw their advantage, the rest of the crew rose to press it. Schacht still held his lights cutting through a wet dirty haze of night. Krieg came out of his shadowed hiding place to stand behind his men. He looked out through the falling mist. There were only five of the ghouls left standing. There may be more, but they would be finished soon enough. Krieg's sailors rose up from the graves en masse, all armed with bludgeons. They were the most simple of weapons, crude, cruel, and personal in a way no other can be. The last of the zombies stood, five of them, not wanting to run, ready to face their fate. Krieg saw them stop and stand still. The zombies stared, stared straight through the cemetery, straight to him. The last of their life, whatever it was that drove them, burned into their eyes, a fire red like hot coals in their sockets.

Krieg's view was blocked by darkness as his men closed to meet the final threat, cudgels raised, then brought down, again and again. Krieg watched as bits of gore flew, torn from the bodies where they lay. The smell of sea water permeated the air. Krieg breathed it in, recognizing the smell. The stench was old, but familiar. It was the same smell of burning diesel oil, fuel, mixed with the salt spray of the ocean, that he remembered from his hunting so long ago. Krieg found great pleasure in the memory of the scent.

31

10:00 P.M.

HYDE COUNTY SHERIFF'S DEPARTMENT

Schacht and his men pushed their way into the offices where they had first been taken captive by the deputy. Now, with clearer skies opening to a full moon, they were able to make their way silently and undetected back to the building in search of arms and ammunition, among other things.

"Hey! Hey!" Eddie Gruber shouted through the holding cell at the Germans. "C'mon. Let me out! What's going on out there?!"

Schacht was not relishing having to deal with Eddie, but the unkempt fisherman had promised them something they desperately needed in exchange for his escape. Delivering on that deal also meant that the Germans could search the only place they knew that probably would have weapons like the shotguns they had used. If they were going to escape, the Nazis would need armament.

Schacht risked a sliver of light to see his way through the rooms. He had secured keys and freed Eddie, but wished he could keep the man quiet. "Where do they keep the weapons like this?" Schacht demanding, leveling the 12 gauge shotgun.

"Probably in the locker room, over there."

The Germans would be rewarded, but disappointed in their haul. The island only had a necessary compliment of four deputies total, and the ones that had left the island in the evacuation had taken their sidearms. A locked cabinet held some sort of weapon, a rifle or shotgun, something long, they knew, but it was behind a locked metal door, inaccessible without a key or extreme force and liberal time, none of which the Nazis had.

They did, however, find a trove of shells for the shotguns, the wonderfully deadly trench sweeper they had used with effect to break the back of the zombies' charge. Four boxes full, and one with fifteen shells left inside. Plenty to do immense damage.

Schacht took the opened box and began loading the shells. Eddie, pushing his way through, grabbed at the shotgun. "Let me see that!" Eddie took the weapon with a glint of glee, the power of a gun in his hands and head, thinking of how people would listen to him when they were at the talking end of this thing.

Schacht had no plans to give Eddie that power. Steeled hands reached back, holding the weapon by the action. Eddie's smile turned into a grimace. He thought he was in charge, he should have the gun. His grip didn't lessen, but he felt the hard grasp of Schacht.

Eddie also noticed that the other sailors stopped what they were doing. He looked around, surrounded with emotionless eyes, all looking at him. "What? Whaaaat?! I was just gonna show you how to load it. I was gonna give it back. Damn…" Eddie shook his head like he couldn't understand the Germans, all the while not realizing how true that was.

Schacht pulled, wrenching the weapon from Eddie's grasp. He turned the weapon, barrel out, not pointed at Eddie, but obviously not pointed at anything else, either.

"Understand this, *Gammler*, you serve us! At our pleasure! You will supply us with fuel and we will aid you in your escape. Do anything else and you will be abandoned to whatever storm you find yourself in! You will follow my orders, always. If you choose to do anything which threatens us, I will beat you until you are dead. It is a simple proposition. You will now say you understand, or I will leave you back in your cell. Most likely unconscious, possibly dead."

Schacht stared into Eddie's eyes, the power of a Nazi officer used to command and unflinching loyalty, with the promise of punishment that most would not imagine. Eddie, now aware of the pact he had made, and his loss of power, tried to find a way out, something that showed that he wasn't as scared as he felt. "Yeah, hey…"

Schacht struck out hard with the back of his right hand, a cold slap of hardened knuckles that turned Eddie, bringing him down to his knees. His head spun cobwebs as his eyes saw bright stars through closed lids. Tear filled, he looked up in the darkened room to see a giant bearing down on him, Schacht ready to strike again.

"You will say you understand. Nothing more."

"…I understand."

It was with the clearing skies of the full moon that the Germans exited out of the sheriff's office. Schacht looked up at the bright moon, a sailor's eye catching the fine veil of the earth's shadow barely creasing its surface. As a submariner, he had both respect and disdain for the light of the moon. It opened up the night sky, making it easier for his U-boat to find blacked out targets on dark seas. But it also shown equally on both hunter and prey. His small party would be easily seen wandering at night. Schacht knew the land fairly well. He knew that the island was mostly empty, and all dark. Any light would be a civilian, and an enemy.

He reconsidered his assessment as he scanned the open road before moving his sailors. To the east he saw them. More of the *Unmenschen*, more of those cursed zombies. He could see the shadows, figures of human form, but so far from human. All blacker than the black shadows, they stood far down the road in a group, an organic aggregation. They looked to Schacht like a thick pool of black oil, oozing its way through water. Only they didn't move. They seemed to be waiting. Schacht could make out pinpricks of devil light, the strange hate filled glare of red, coming from their eyes. And he realized there were more this time.

"*Bewegung!*"

Schacht would not notice three things as he and his men ran away from the horde. His heart, long cold and slow, would begin to beat faster. His feet would start to ache. And he was afraid.

32

10:00 P.M.

OCRACOKE FIRE STATION

Dan Howard awoke with a start. His stomach churned
with an acid emptiness that left a burn deep in his throat. He,
Deputy Tillett, and Chief Stone had all hidden themselves
behind a locked door in the dark of the fire station. Sleep
overcame them, beating out thirst, hunger, and fear. The
tattoo of the storm beating on the roof of the station was
replaced by a cacophonous racket of frogs, all happily
peeping into the night, hunting bugs out in the moonlight.

He shook Chief Stone awake. "Jen... Jen! Wake up!"
Dan spoke in a sibilant whisper.

"We need to get out of here. I gotta go check on my family."

Stone stumbled through her awaking routine, first
groggy and unwilling to give up the rest she so desperately
needed, then waking up with a start, overstimulated. Her
stomach did flips and her brain unscrambled from the mix of

sleep and awakening. She fumbled with getting the immediate needs organized in her head. "We need to find those Nazis," her brain finally kicked in with at least a basic plan. "I would like to get back in that school and see how many of them were killed. They looked like the held their own against those... wraiths, things." Chief Stone replied.

"Like Hell we're going back in there!" Frankie almost yelled, hearing his voice echo in the tall garage, and bringing his words down to a dull whisper. "I'm going back to the office and getting another weapon. We've got a Winchester locked up with another riot gun. I'm not happy about those bastards having my 870 no matter what they were shooting."

Tired, sore, her shoulder stiff and throbbing, Stone thought about just staying where she was, hooking up an IV, and waiting for the Marines to arrive. Even if no one knew they were needed. But she didn't like the idea of "those bastards" walking around with her pistol and her blood on one of their knives. Payback would be in order.

"That's a good idea. We need to rearm ourselves. Maybe get some of the other fellahs in on this. It's gonna be hard sailin' just us three and me with a busted wing. We also don't know where they are, but then, we know the land, and they may not even know we're alive. Maybe we can figure out who would have a hunting rifle or a shotgun around here. I don't like breaking into someone's home, but considering the circumstances..."

Dan thought for a moment. He wasn't armed, never really needed anything more than a fisherman's knife, but... "I think I know where I can get something."

"Alright, meet me over at..." Stone plotted out a location in her head, "How about at the Castle?" The Castle as it was affectionately known was an old shingle sided colonial revival house, a massive building constructed decades earlier that overlooked Silver Lake. "We can get a look across the lake and see if we can find them. If not, we can get over to the base." It was the best plan she could come up with. It wasn't much. Stone began to wonder how they would survive the night against a bunch of Nazis and a swarm of plodding undead sailors. Maybe she should just find a boat and go out in the sound and wait for daylight. Or just keep going til she hit mainland. And find a doctor.

Or she could do what she had to do to take the island back from the Nazis.

"Help me up, will ya?"

33

10:15 P.M.

FIRST AVENUE

Krieg did not take the news of more massing zombies well. He considered what the Coast Guardsman had said, wraiths returning from the sea to seek out vengeance. With all the people he and his fellow captains had put in watery graves, the number of the wraiths would be large. He also had his concerns about the rest of the islanders and how quickly they would respond to both the invading *Unmenchen* and his crew. He had a plan that would, hopefully, account for both issues.

Their alliance with the local sailor didn't alleviate any worry in Krieg's mind. The man had promised fuel, but withheld the location, though Krieg assumed there would be some local depot. He needed to figure out a way to acquire the fuel, store it, and move it to the submarine. Each issue was separate but layered upon the other. Krieg knew he needed to solve the more pressing issue first. He did so with typical Nazi ruthlessness.

"*Trenne die Männer in Gruppen. Wir müssen den Transport sichern, vielleicht den Bus, den sie für uns benutzt haben, um uns zurück zum Ufer zu bringen. Außerdem müssen wir ein Motorboot finden, das groß genug ist, um den Treibstoff rund um die Insel an die Küste zu transportieren.*" Krieg directed his missive to his First Officer and to Schacht, who had done the dirty job of bloodletting and discipline well so far. Securing vehicles and a boat would be fairly simple. Depending upon how well they could trust the American in their midst, he may be of some benefit in acquiring a power boat if there was one on the island.

More difficult and dangerous was the next task.

"*Es wird auch notwendig sein, einige der Einheimischen gefangenzunehmen. Sie können als menschliche Schilde arbeiten, um zu verhindern, dass die Ghule angreifen. Sie werden auch andere Einheimische davon abhalten sich einzumischen. Wir müssen sie an einen großen Ort bringen, an dem wir uns versammeln und beschützen können. Die Schule ist nach dem Angriff nicht mehr lebensfähig. Vielleicht kann der Amerikaner helfen?*" Krieg knew ordering his men to take civilians captive and use them as protection against an attack was clearly against the typical rules of combat, but he saw nothing typical in the events of the night so far. His crew's preservation was paramount.

"*Herr...*" Krieg had heard the man's name, Eddie, but had no idea of his surname. He looked at the greasy man in the darkness, expecting a response.

"Yeah?"

Krieg didn't get the reply he expected. Undaunted, Krieg plowed on. "Do you know of a boat large enough to haul the fuel over to the U-boat?"

"You don't have to worry about that."

Krieg stewed over Eddie's light dismissal of the need. Krieg had to find a way to move fuel, and this man was playing games. The American thought he was being clever, controlling, but he did not know who he was dealing with. Krieg was not the soft American *Polizei*. This American would regret his actions if he did not come through with the promises he made. "Understand, *Amerikaner*, you serve us! At our comfort and suffrage. Do not think you can manipulate me." Krieg grabbed Eddie's shirt, twisted until it tightened around his throat, and turned it some more. Eddie grasped first at the collar, then Krieg's hands, his voice sputtering. Krieg did not loosen his grip; defiantly, he shook Eddie, making his eyes bulge and mouth open. "You will answer my questions or I will kill you and leave you dead in the street."

He released his grip and Eddie gasped for air, rubbing the chafed neck he got from the choking grip. Normally needful of a comeback, Eddie had twice been threatened with death by people who had a hand in the business. These men had no care about ending his life. They may even relish it. Eddie remembered a stupid dog someone had, long ago, back in Alabama. It had barked and whimpered and Eddie had beat it until it stopped. It had learned to not even respond to Eddie's torment. It just took it. Eddie was the dog now.

"Now, *Amerikaner*, I worry about the fuel. Tell me now." Krieg's words left his mouth at a growl.

"It's..." Eddie still had difficulty in speaking. He swallowed over the bruise in his throat. "It's already on a boat. There's a fuel bunker tanker tied up at the docks. They keep fuel here during the storms so that the ferries can be fueled without having to worry about delivering it if the channels get blocked farther north. They gotta keep the ferries running to make sure the island stays connected to the mainland and Hatteras."

Krieg was satisfied with the answer, for now. That would solve one problem. Now another.

"Where can we gather the crew, a large number of people, in a group, that will be safe? We need a defensible location that will allow defense from…" Krieg thought for English words, even as he doubted the man he spoke to had much of a vocabulary, "…boarders." The old term for pirates taking over a ship was fitting, Krieg thought.

"You can use the school," Eddie mentioned. It seemed like the easiest place, go back to where they were before, he thought.

"No, the school is not a viable location anymore. We need another place. A town hall or centre is what we need."

"Well," Eddie thought. There were so few large buildings on the island. Most were small homes. There wasn't even a large hotel. The only large place that could hold a group of sailors was…

"You could use the Coast Guard Station. No one's there now. They all left before the storm."

34

10:30 P.M.

SILVER LAKE

Dan Howard knew what he was looking for. He just wasn't sure where to find it. It had to be on a boat still left in the harbor. And it had to be someone who would not have checked a weapon with him. A lot of sailors kept something on board when they sailed. Most sailors kept a pistol on board, usually a simple revolver. They were easy to operate and easy to keep clean, with few moving parts. A few had bigger chromed semi-automatic pistols, either old .45 caliber weapons similar to what many saw during military service, or newer 9mm glitzy pistols popularized by TV and tropical slick drug runners with fast powerboats. Fewer still held long rifles, meant to reach out across the ocean to scare off any approaching boat before they got too close.

Dan was looking for none of those. All those would be locked, or off the boat, presumably in Dan's own office, and he knew there were none there at this time. Those weapons and their owners had all left. But he knew someone would have the weapon he wanted.

And he found the boat he was looking for.

Tied up tight, the fishing yacht gleamed in yellow and white, with a dark blue hull from gunwale to below the waterline. It was fancy, like its owner, who decided to leave and leave his boat in Ocracoke. Dan had no idea why, more dollars than sense, he guessed. But this was the boat.

Dan jumped on board, going straight to the cockpit. Near the helm, he found the drawer storing the mandatory Very pistol. A flare gun pistol would be almost useless in any fire fight. It was a foolish myth that the flare would fly out at high speed, embedding itself and exploding in an inferno. Any impact at more than twenty feet would probably barely be felt. The Very pistol wasn't what Dan was looking for.

Rolling around, right next to it, was a simple tube, about eight inches long, made of thick metal. The insert would fit snugly into the Very pistol, and allow a .410 caliber shotgun shell to nestle itself into the pistol, turning the flare gun into a very, very short sawed off shotgun. At farther than ten feet, the spread may not do much damage, but close in, it would turn any Nazi's face into soup. Predictably, a box of shells, nearly empty, was in the same drawer. He grabbed couple of shells and a few flares. Dan thought that he would really have to have a talk with this guy. If he got out of this alive.

Running slowly by the light of the late moon, Dan wanted to get to his home to make sure his family was safe. He had no idea how he was going to accomplish that feat. Where would be safer than his house? Take them to the lighthouse? Get the tent out and send them into Springer's Point? Hell, he thought, I might as well put them on a boat and send them into the sound. Stranded on a sandbar would be safer than this.

Dan snuck quietly along the docks, terrified as he crossed the open road by the empty Bluff Shoal Motel. The rooms were quiet and black, all sealed up from the hurricane. The white walls made his dark figure stand out like a bogey man sneaking around in the night. Dan was worried that he didn't know where Krieg and his minions were, or if there were more of those ghouls out on the prowl. He still wasn't sure if they were a threat only to the Nazis or to everyone. They sure seemed threatening when he faced off against one. Then again, they did nothing to him until he and Deputy Tillett attacked. Dan kept seeing ghosts out of the corners of his eyes, and he wondered which side they were on.

It was when he heard the first screams on the island that Dan put himself into a dead run.

As Dan approached his house, he slowed only enough to take in what he saw. A light was on, probably the oil lamp his wife would light, waiting for him to return. Dan could see the fight flicker, going in and out of shadow. Vaguely he heard other sounds from not far off, a neighbor yelling, indistinct banging, and a now familiar guttural bark. Dan looked down the road, darkened in the shadows but lit in the open lane from the moonlight. He saw four indistinct figures moving toward his house from the front as he approached through the back. He was close enough he could hear his wife yell, and an abnormally high pitched scream from his son. There was more motion from the light in the house. People were in there. More than belonged.

Dan didn't care who it was, zombie or Nazi, nobody hurt his family. He drew his only weapon, one shot was all that he could load. He didn't care. One down and he would tear the rest with his teeth if he had to. He saw the ghouls approach from the front of the house as Dan barged in the back door, Very pistol drawn.

The back hall led into his kitchen, tiny and spare but normally neat as any O'cocker would keep it. He heard screaming coming from the hallway to the stairs and bedrooms. They must be near the front door, near the living room. Dan barged through with the cold comfort of knowing his own space.

There, in the front room, three of Krieg's soldiers stood, trying to pull Adam and Michelle Howard out the front door, with the two, terrified and frenzied, fighting and kicking back. Dan didn't wait for any warning. He had no need for restraint now. He raised the cocked Very pistol and pointed it in the direction of the one Nazi farthest away from his family. The distance was a mere six feet.

When the weapon went off, it was less of a cacophonous explosion, and more of a hollow echoing thump. But the weapon did its job well with little precision. The man's face was obliterated.

There is a fact of life in Ocracoke and throughout the islands, that life is less a fact than death. Islanders lived knowing that many of them would not die of old age. Tide and tragedy would take more than time. Locals were dismayed by injury or death, but the days continue for them. So many had lost loved ones or friends, and in sad ways. They had seen the worst of death first hand.

So when Michelle saw the Nazi bastard that tried to pull her and her son away flattened on her rug with his face turned to a morbid gazpacho soup, she may have been repulsed at the carnage, but she lost any compassion when they broke into her home. Her son, younger, more naive, turned away, not able to stomach the torn insides of the man's head. He still was happy his father had come in like a hero to save them.

The other two sailors, however, were frozen in shock. They had spent four decades imprisoned to think of their crimes, but they had never seen what they had done. Submariners like them rarely saw the damage and loss, and even less experienced it. Their spent their time at sea hidden, and went back to France and walked around like heroes. They never experienced damage. Not like that. One of the Nazis looked down at his crewmate, stunned, distraught, unbelieving. The man had his face torn apart from the shotgun shell. A bloody red mass, open holes where his mouth, nose, and eyes were, with a dead and useless unseeing eyeball dangling from a thin strip of muscle. They had never seen a weapon that could do so much destruction. Their grips failed them as they stared in open mouthed shock. For four decades they felt nothing. Now shock and fear poured into their bodies like seawater through an open hatch.

Dan was shocked as well at how functional the Very pistol had been. He stared in wide eyed satisfaction at the damage he caused on the attackers. With a menacing grin, he leveled the short black barreled pistol at the two Nazis. Dan knew he wouldn't be able to open and reload the pistol in time to deliver another shot. He just had to bluff it. The barrel was wide and short, open like the beckoning mouth of Hell itself for the two Nazis. The smell of urine wafted into the air as one of them wet himself from terror.

"Get away from my family."

"*Nicht schießen*," one of the Nazis pleaded. Dan had no idea what he was saying, only that the man was now afraid of something, of him, and all Dan wanted was to get his family to safety. He pointed the Very pistol at the other submariner, still hiding behind his wife. The Nazi ducked behind her, Michelle struggling to get away from him, pushing down on his head, trying to twist his neck and push the man to the floor so she could stomp him to pulp.

That was when the front door crashed in.

Four men, all dressed in thick, drooping uniforms, with thick, drooping eyes, burning red over pale white skin, forced their way into the living room of Dan Howard's home. Unconcerned with any fear, any need for welcome, they moved in a dull charge toward the two remaining Nazis. Terrified, Adam ran away from the clutching hands of one German trying to hold onto the boy to protect himself. Adam ran toward his father, hiding in terror more than any child should ever have to feel. The other Nazi clutched at Michelle in a vice grip, his hands frozen even as she beat mercilessly at the once brave and now pathetic Nazi. Dan moved toward her, wanting to pull her away, unsure what the zombie beasts would do to her. He put up his arm, grasping at her and pulling her, as the Nazi fought to stay behind her.

Two of the ghouls had one Nazi fully in their grasp, and began simply pummeling him. Low loud slaps smashed into his body, like a tenderizer pounding meat. The submariner's screams became garbled as his mouth was filled with the fists of the two ghouls, then freed to let forth a terrified squeak of a scream, before the bludgeons came again.

The other two zombies had no desire to attack Michelle. Dan tried to place himself between the ghouls and his wife, coming closer than he wanted to the things. The intimacy made Dan take in more than he had seen before, when he had been shrouded in fog and rain and fear. The ghoul, man, exuded a single purpose, and didn't seem to care about Dan at all. He merely wanted to get to the Nazi sailor. Hands reached across Dan's body, grasping the arms of the Nazi. The ghoul pried off the tight grip of the Nazi with comparative ease. With Michelle free, Dan pulled her back into the hall.

Dan stopped there. He looked back at the creatures in his home. The husband and father in him, the master of the house, wanted to go back, to push out all the evil from his house and slam the door. It was a natural desire to ban the things that had come into his home and attacked his family. When he looked back, though, all he saw were the four ghouls, holding fast to the two Nazis who tried to attack his wife and child. Two of the zombies dumbly struck repeatedly at one of the Germans, still pummeling him like a piece of meat. The German had stopped whining and moved into a dull whimper after every other strike. Another clutched the German that tried to hide behind Dan's wife, its arm a bent bar, locked in tight around the Nazi's neck. The German submariner had his mouth open, tongue fully out, his arms

198

flailing weakly as he tried to free himself from the death grip. His eyes bulged as he tried to see what was happening to his partner. Fear turned to a morbid and terrifying revelation that he would be next.

The fourth ghoul simply stared back at Dan and his family. The fire was burning softly in his eyes, but he did not move toward the family. He made no threatening motion at all, Dan noted. Dan was stunned when the creature opened his mouth and tried to talk.

"Wuuu..oooo…" the sound was a phlegmatic howl, like seawater washing up and out of its throat.

Dan and Michelle looked on in disbelief. It took the moment for Dan to notice that this was not just a mindless creature. Like Stone had said, it, he, looked like a sailor. Dan looked at the uniform. Waterlogged, sagging, worn and deteriorated, it was still recognizable as something like a naval uniform. Dan recognized it from photos of sailors he had seen from World War II when it had first touched the Outer Banks. He saw the patches on the sleeves and breast of the shirt, opened to the chest, showing the man's pale white skin with black and red bruises across the softened flesh.

"Wh…Who…" the man found his voice; it came out in a croak, "ammm… I?"

It was more a plea than anything else. The other ghouls looked on in earnest. The look on their faces, even as they held fast to the Nazis, was one of a begging desperate need.

"Who… am I?" he said again.

"Dear God…" Dan finally realized what the man was asking. He recognized the patch on his shirt, an eagle screaming down onto a submarine. He was a sailor for the U.S. Navy Armed Guard. During World War II, the Navy armed merchant ships with guns to help protect them from U-boat attacks, with little success. The Armed Guard, and their horrible losses, were well known on Ocracoke. About 2,000 men died at the terrible hands of Nazi U-boats. Many were just young men out of high school, who had never seen the ocean. Many went down shooting. Many died nameless, unremembered.

Dan walked closer to the man, looked at the stitched name on his uniform. The color had gone out, but the letters were there. It was a simple name, strangely plain compared to the unique Christian and surnames of Ocracoke.

"Stevenson... you're Stevenson." Dan said the name reverently, looking into the man's eyes. All the loss, all the death, the uselessness of loss of life, all was seen in Stevenson's eyes. The fire was gone.

"Who is he?" Michelle asked. "How do you know him?"

"He was, is, one of the first victims these Nazis brought here," Dan tried to explain. "He and these men were on ships sunk by Nazi U-boats long ago."

"Oh, God." Michelle looked into the man's eyes. She, too, now just saw a young man, never to live any life, not to marry, not to see children and grandchildren. She knew all the stories of loss from the evil the Nazis did, but now, it was in her home. There was nothing she could do for the man to fix his past, but her maternal instincts held her strong, and she looked past the injuries, past the pallor. She put her arms out to hold the young man. "Thank you. Thank you for everything." Everything. For saving her life. For giving his life. For the fight and struggle that no one would ever know.

The four men turned silently, moving out of the house. They drug one of the Nazis out by his choking neck, the other limply hung as two of the naval guardsmen pulled him by the armpits. The last man, Stevenson, looked down at the mutilated German sailor that Dan had blasted to a bloody mist. With the same distaste a person has at picking up another man's trash, Stevenson leaned down, grabbed the faceless Nazi by the shirt collar, and pulled him unceremoniously out the door.

"How, how are they still alive?" Michelle asked.

"They're not," Dan explained. "I think they're cursed."

Stevenson turned at the doorstep, unused to having air in his lungs and a voice in his throat. He struggled for the words.

"No. We are rewarded."

35

OCRACOKE SCHOOL

Frankie had decided to risk walking over to the school to get his patrol vehicle back. He had locked it out of habit, only hours ago though it seemed a lifetime. He hoped that he could get to it, get in and possibly get back to the sheriff's department, and...

What? Call for help? To who? No one was coming and no one would believe him anyway.

The school was silent and abandoned. No eerie zombies or blood lusting Nazis around, not even bodies. Frankie wondered what the inside looked like. He shook his head to clear the memories of the gore filled abattoir. Those memories weren't coming loose easily.

Frankie skirted the buildings to walk around to the lot where his Blazer sat. Still no sign of anyone, living, dead, or... undead, he thought. He made a dash in the moonlight the last few yards to his truck door, jamming the key in, opening the lock, and piling in. He locked the door back and ducked down. He wasn't happy with what he thought was a slightly cowardly act, but these were strange times indeed. It wasn't a moment to nickpick about bravery.

The Nazis had taken his pistol in the fracas earlier, but like all of his fellow deputies, he kept a personal backup locked in the vehicle. Frankie opened the locked glove box and pulled out the leather holster encasing his personal Smith & Wesson revolver. Frankie removed the pistol, snapping the wheel out and chambering the cartridges. He took two speedloaders from a storage pouch and pocketed them. Reholstering the pistol, he sat in the truck, contemplating his next move. Going to the sheriff's department for more weapons and ammunition seemed the best course. He didn't relish the idea of turning on his headlights in the dark to get there, garnering attention from the good, the bad, and the worst of what was out there.

Frankie started his Blazer with only the parking lights burning at first. He drove around the school itself, avoiding the roads, passing behind the gym and cutting through a yard to get onto the dirt part of Old Pony Road. There were only so many ways to get around Ocracoke. Frankie wanted to avoid the main road of Highway 12 if he could. He took the old beach road east, driving slowly, continually wondering when the boogeyman would jump out at him and land on the hood of his Blazer. "So help me," Frankie swore to himself, and whatever spirits were listening in the nocturnal ether, "if any one of those things says boo to me, I swear I'm gonna conk their head with a brick until it's dust." The stress and lack of sleep made Frankie bitter, angry, and on edge. He slowly felt a boiling temper coming over him. Less scared and more and more mad, he began making himself primed for any action to come his way.

He didn't have to wait long.

As he drove slowly down the road, Frankie glanced at every side street, looking for monsters. He passed an unassuming yet immensely cute home he always liked, screened in but airy, a gingerbread house but built for the beach. It sat at the corner of the erroneously named Ocean View Road, where the ocean could barely be heard, let alone seen. Frankie always admired the immaculate white picket fence and yellow flowers that grew by the gate. It was always a scene of happiness.

Until tonight. The picket fence was down. A faded white and red Ford pickup truck had seen to the fence's destruction. That alone was not the cause of alarm in Frankie's mind. The house belonged to Tina Meekins. Frankie knew the lady well. He knew everyone on the island, but he knew her more closely, due to her tragedy in recent times. She had lost her husband to illness, a strange infection that wouldn't go away or respond to treatment. Islanders were strong in death; they mourn, they feel sad, they move on, because they have to. Tina had to. She also had two daughters. They had pulled together to make it through the toughest of events, and Tina had kept a household together even as it was trying desperately to fall apart. Frankie admired the woman greatly. She was too young to have lost a husband, as were the children, if anyone can ever be old enough to lose a father. He had seen her make life work, doing what she had to do, and if she hadn't made things whole again, she certainly had put a lot of her life back together.

Which is what made Frankie so mad, as he saw three men dragging Tina and her two daughters out of the house in the night.

Frankie flipped on his lights, everything he had. Headlights shone bright into the front yard and his blue rollers flipped in a slow motion dizzying spell, a sign that everyone knew the party was over. He swung the Blazer in behind the pickup, blocking its escape. Looking through the windshield glass, he saw the six people. Three men, now easily recognizable in their uniforms, glared into the headlights. The pale skin and short hair gave them away as members of the U-boat's crew. The blue flashes dazzled them; they had never seen modern police warning lights before. The three men tried to shield their eyes with open hands, while clinging to their potential kidnap victims. Frankie saw Tina, in a long cotton nightgown, along with her two daughters, Susan, fifteen years old, dressed in a worn white t-shirt and some sort of teenage sleeping shorts, and the younger daughter, Frankie didn't remember her name, only about ten years old he guessed. All three were clutched tightly in an arm of each of the Nazis.

Frankie reached for his pistol. He never noticed he was smiling a vicious and ferocious grin.

The deputy jumped out of the Blazer, a mere shadow to the blinded Nazis. He heard one shout, "*Klaus…*" but the rest was unneeded and unintelligible gibberish to Frankie. Klaus, it seemed, was the one holding Tina with one arm. The other arm clutched one of Frankie's shotguns. He tried to level it as Tina struggled to get away from the man and save her daughters. "*Stattlich!*" he cried out, in a more high pitched and boyish sound than Frankie expected, "*Geh runter!*"

Tina elbowed at Klaus' midsection, pushing him away and freeing her. It did three things. Tina was now able to get off the front steps and down toward her daughters to fight for them as the other two Nazis began to duck out of the way of the impending gunfight. Klaus was able to level and stabilize his weapon at the menacing shadow looming up on him and his men.

And Frankie had a clear target.

Frankie opened fire at the only person with a weapon, squeezing off two shots into the center of Klaus's mass, just before the Nazi could fire the shotgun. Frankie could see at first the bullets hit, low but in the center of the body. The blast from the shotgun dazzled his eyes. He felt a whip and sting, like a massive jellyfish had just lashed out at him. He wondered, incredulously, if he had been hit by splinters of the doomed picket fence as it shattered from a near miss of the shotgun. Frankie leveled for a third and fourth shot. His left leg didn't want to hold him up well, but he took better aim, raising his sights to the Nazi's head. His third shot flew well and true, cracking into the sternum of Klaus. Frankie wouldn't know the damage from afar. The bullet, a standard .38 Special round, would mushroom as soon as it hit the bone, cracking and shattering Klaus's chest, splintering the ribs inward, tearing into his heart and turning it into a meat grinding mess of black and red. Frankie tried to fire off another round out of habit, but his grip loosened.

There was something wet running down his leg, and his hip hurt where it catches in the socket. He stopped to look down, trying to figure out how he got water on his uniform. There on his front pocket were rips and holes like it had gone through a cheese grater. Blood had begun to leak out and drip down to his knee. He had only now realized he had been struck by Klaus's shotgun.

"*Klaus!*" one of the other Nazis called as they saw one of their own fall in a bloody mess. Unarmed, the two struggled to contain the girls in their arms. Tina had gone over to the one holding her littlest, and was striking him as the girl stamped and kicked at the Nazi's feet and shins. His head went back as Tina pulled his hair, then jammed her fingers into his eyeballs. He screamed a high pitched yelp, pathetic like a tortured puppy, only more deserving of the punishment.

The other, Frankie looked on, the one Klaus had called Stattlich, held Susan. His arms wrapped around her waist, lifting her shirt and exposing her still childlike abdomen. Susan screamed at the man to let her go. She tried twisting her way out, her head bobbing left and right frantically, but Stattlich held her in a death grip. He planted his other hand over her mouth to stop her shouting and twisting.

It was all too much for Frankie to see. He couldn't shoot either man with the civilians so close. Frankie took his pistol and tossed it onto the passenger seat of his open Blazer. He then began limping forward.

Stattlich saw him coming, nothing but a black on black shadow looming from in front of the strange blue and white lights that dazzled him. The slight limp and the fact that the shadow had been shot but not fallen gave rise to terror in the Nazi's heart. He had no protection except the body of the girl.

"*Nein... Nein!*" he begged, squeezing the poor teenager between himself and the oncoming shadow.

Frankie only saw a coward, touching a little girl. Of all things in life that good men found abhorrent, this was the worst of all.

It only took a few steps to get to Stattlich. The German struggled with holding the girl as she twitched until she could duck out of his grasp. In the same moment, Frankie reached out and grabbed the man by the front of his shirt.

His first punch was all arm. He could get no hip movement into the throw, with his leg being out of whack, but the blow as satisfactory. Frankie landed a left cross that grazed the side of Stattlich's face, punching into the jaw as it opened. Frankie felt the head twist and jaw separate. Frankie wasn't sure if he had broken the jaw, but there definitely were some teeth that would go missing. Stattlich's head turned, spinning with the force, and his neck turned too far. For a brief moment, the punch turned off all the lights in Stattlich's brain and his body went limp in Frankie's still clutching right hand.

Frankie pulled the German away from the house, toward his truck. The Nazi stumbled as he shook off the cobwebs of the massive blow. Frankie looked down to see Stattlich's head loll. The German coughed, and blood came out, then two gray and bent teeth spat on the ground. Frankie grinned at his handiwork.

"You think you can just come here and do what you want to my people?!" Frankie yelled at the weakened German. "You like putting your hands on little girls, huh, Adolph?" Frankie slammed Stattlich's body against the side of the truck. It wasn't hard enough for Frankie, so he did it again. Grasping the man by the back of the head, Frankie pounded Stattlich's face into the hood. "You've caused more pain than anyone's allowed. You decided what you are a long time ago. Now you get what you deserve!"

Frankie picked up Stattlich and pulled him around the door of the deputy's truck, leaning the body half in and half out of the door frame. Frankie slammed the door mercilessly, with all his might, on the ribcage of Stattlich. A sharp intake of air and a gasp as Stattlich felt the tearing pain of his body being damaged. He tried to slip out of the door, to somehow still find a way to escape. Frankie slammed the door again. This time it caught Stattlich in the head. The full weight of Detroit steel and strength of the deputy's arm crushed into Stattlich's skull. The Nazi bellowed a horrid yell, the torment of his body realizing he was going to die, and that it would take a very long time and be exquisitely painful. His head fell from the door to the bottom of the door trim. Stattlich's front jaw crashed straight into the metal frame and he felt his remaining teeth loosen and crack. Frankie slammed to door again.

It took three times to silence the screaming man, and even then Frankie wasn't sure if Stattlich was really dead. He pulled the body off of the bloodstained seat and threw it over the remains of the fence. Frankie then reached back in and retrieved his revolver.

Surprisingly, the other Nazi sailor had just stood there, slack jawed and stunned at the carnage. He had even let go of the little girl he was holding. Eyes wide, he stood in horror watching Frankie deal with Stattlich.

Frankie noticed that both Tina and Susan stared as well, but with much more satisfaction and no apprehension. Only the little one hid her eyes behind Tina's gown.

The last Nazi stammered as he tried to put his hands up or shuffle away or anything that would help him escape the mad man that just butchered two of his cohorts. It was as if the very sand of Ocracoke held him to the spot.

Frankie felt the sudden weight of pain on his side. Now that the adrenaline of action had flowed through him, Frankie felt his injury. There was something seriously wrong with him, he realized. Frankie had little time before the pain hit him like a truck,

He grimaced and grunted, "I don't have time for you." Frankie raised a shaky hand with his pistol and fired directly at the Nazi's face.

Frankie's leg gave out and he fell to the ground about a second after the Nazi did.

36

11:20 P.M.

THE CASTLE

Chief Stone scurried along the side of the giant old house. Not being a native, she knew little of what made the old shingle sided house important. She didn't even know why it was called The Castle. It looked like the old houses built on the shore one hundred years ago by rich vacationers. She made a point to spend some time not caring about any of that later on, if she survived until the morning.

Stone hated that her pistol was gone, when she really needed it. And she felt even worse that it was in the hands of that Nazi, Krieg. She needed to find a replacement on her way to the Castle to meet up with Deputy Tillett and Dan Howard. Since the vast majority of the island was empty, Stone knew it would be easy, though slightly illegal, to find a better replacement. The Winchester Model 70 hung over her shoulder as testament to her success. Islander Bill Bolton was well known for his hunting skills, built on years of patience waiting in the woods for deer to get within his steady range. He had left the island during the evacuation along with everyone else. Not thinking he would be stuck away for long, Bob had only locked his doors and closed his windows.

Stone had no desire to be a cowboy, and didn't want to break into Bob's house more than she had to. The Winchester 70, the Rifleman's Rifle, hung on a rack nearby the door, with a box of shells stored in a drawer just underneath. Stone liked the rifle. It was relatively short and light, so she wouldn't strain her shoulder any more than she already had. The attached hunter's scope which normally allowed for easy work of whitetail deer would allow Stone to reach out and touch someone on this night.

Now if she could figure out what those Nazis were up to.

She already figured out where they were.

She had hidden herself in Bob's house, watching both the Germans and occasionally the shadowy ghouls pass by in the night. The dark house looked like any dark house, and no one sought her out. She heard yelling, some screaming, and saw a few vehicles driving quickly down the main road heading toward the harbor. Stone was quickly able to discern where the Germans were. She was distinctly unhappy with their current location.

The only place with the lights on at the whole island was the Coast Guard station across Silver Lake.

And it was crawling with Nazis.

Stone tucked the butt of the rifle under her arm. Her shoulder was still throbbing so she didn't press it into her body. Not that it mattered to Stone. She needed the scope more than the barrel. Stone felt her wound pull on the fresh dried blood as she bent her arm. Payback would come soon enough. She looked over the sights into the scope. A truck had pulled up, the jerky motion of brakes being applied poorly and clutch popping showed the driver was unfamiliar with its use. Stone saw the Nazis yelling as three people were pushed roughly out. She didn't recognize the people, but could tell they were local by their dress. Or lack thereof. Several were in pajamas or gowns. That made things more difficult.

Stone couldn't simply whittle them down from afar with the rifle. There was a very specific guideline for shooting into innocents, for good reason. Stone wasn't going to put any locals in danger unnecessarily. She was going to have to find another way.

In the relative silence of the night, Stone heard something moving around the other side of the Castle. A moment of panic crossed her sleep deprived mind. Stone had no weapon she could use against either the Germans or the many undead that walked in the shadows incessantly. She could not fire the rifle without fear of being heard, noticed, and hunted by the Nazis. Stone thought for a moment about using it at a club, giving up its primary purpose for a much more elemental use. That was when she heard the voice call her name.

"Chief...?"

There was enough moonlight to see the pale skin of Dan Howard coming around the house.

"Here... Dan..." Stone called. "Over here."

The two met on the old porch of the Castle, looking out across the moonlit water of Silver Lake. The harbor twinkled peacefully with small ripples topped by slivers of light, little knives cutting the tips to a fine edge. The moon's reflection grinned drunkenly as the water undulated. Tonight Silver Lake took on its namesake well. Only where the harbor met the ferry docks to the west was it not a twinkling inky pool. There bright tungsten light spilled like a poison into the water. The light came from the station, now lit in its glory, but tainted into an unholy shelter for the Nazis as they kept prisoners for whatever deed they planned.

"It looks like they have about twelve or fifteen people over there. Holding them hostage," Stone said as she looked through the scope again. "I wonder what they are planning."

"How many of those Nazis are there?" Dan asked.

"I figured all of them. Why?"

"Well," Dan explained, "They definitely are three short. They had a run in with your ghoul friends at my house." Dan took a moment to explain the incident in his front room, showing off his improvised weapon. "It's hard to believe, but I guess you are right that those people are on our side, or maybe we need to be on their side." Dan filled Stone in on who the men were, the Navy Guard uniforms. Stone had suspected as much, but she had noticed that the zombies that started wandering in were in various states of dress. A lot wore the dungarees of a merchant marine or cargo crew member. Some wore uniforms or suits. Others wore dresses. They were all victims of a cruel, merciless, and sweeping set of targets from the sharp end of the metallic sharks the Nazis sent to hunt the Atlantic coast.

"I think they are gonna try to make a run for it. Use us as shields against those wraiths," Dan pondered. He hated to see his people held like that, but he knew he couldn't free them on his own. Not with only a single shot pistol with the effective range of the inside of an elevator. The chief might be able to pick off the Nazis one at a time with the deer rifle, maybe, at a closer range, and with a not so wounded shoulder. It wouldn't take long for the Germans to run for cover, and to endanger the people they held captive. Those Nazis were not going anywhere easily, but Dan still wasn't sure how to dig them out.

Stone worried about them taking more hostages. "We oughta go back and find whoever is left. We can either get some help, or at least get whoever is still here somewhere safe. Take them out to Springer's Point, put'em on a boat, I dunno. I just don't want those guys going back out for more hostages."

Dan *humphed* a soft breath. "I don't think you have to worry about that." Stone looked at Dan for explanation. "Look. Out in the darkness." Dan gestured down the north side of the harbor. The moonlight lit the buildings on the far side of the lake with a clean blue-white color on the side of the shops that lined the waterfront. A silhouette of trees grew up into a twinkling sky. Along the line of the road Stone saw them. A wavering line of bodies, half hidden in the dark, but visible by their glare. Red eyes, now burning with hate, glowed out in the dark. It looked like there were hundreds of them, all waiting in the dark.

"No way those boys are going out into that storm," Dan said assuredly.

"You're right about that," Stone agreed. She didn't want to walk down that road, either, and those wraiths weren't after her.

"I wonder where Frankie got off to. You think he's alright?"

"I dunno right now. If he could, he would be here. I got a bad feeling about this," Stone realized how alone she was starting to feel. She may somehow stop the Nazis from getting off the island, but at what cost. She had no taste for a Pyrrhic victory at this point. "Look, those guys aren't going anywhere tonight, most likely. And if they do, I'm gonna be waiting for them.

"I'm going to make my way over to the channel, by the jetty, just to keep an eye on them if they move. You go see if you can find Frankie. Maybe get you something better than that flamethower," Stone nodded at the Very pistol, "and be ready to stop them if they head down 12." Stone thought the Nazis were either going to find some boats somewhere to take them out or perhaps they were thinking of commandeering the ferry to Hatteras. Where they would go from there, she had no idea. She didn't think they had much of a clue, either.

Anyway, she wasn't planning on letting them off the island alive.

37

Dan had considered his ability to look over the entire island by foot with both zombies and Nazis wandering the land, and decided he would risk getting his truck instead. It didn't take him long to drive the road until he saw the rolling blue lights of Frankie's sheriff's department Blazer. Three pale white faces, drab with rumpled clothes, popped up from around the truck. Dan recognized them immediately, but the two girls and their mother only saw a silhouette dazzled around truck headlights as the harbormaster got out of the cab.

Tina reached down into the darkness and came up armed, the shotgun that had passed from hand to hand, to end up with her, now pointed at Dan.

"Tina, wait!" Dan put up his hands, "It's me, Dan Howard! Where's Frankie?" Dan looked from side to side at the old truck run up Tina's yard, and the big sheriff's Blazer next to it, then the ashen faces of Tina and her daughters.

"Dan!" Tina gushed, almost blubbering at seeing a familiar face. "Jesus, Dan, get over here. Frankie's been shot! Help me," she leaned back down into the darkness.

Dan ran to Tina, looking down at where she knelt. Her daughters stood still, trembling, wanting to be inside, to be hidden, but afraid to leave their mother's side. Tina, in turn, was doing what she could to comfort Frankie, who had saved them from being kidnapped, and possibly worse. Dan looked down at the wounded deputy.

The darkness, even with the moonlight, hid the worst of Frankie's wound. Still burning headlights created dark spots in the shadows on the ground. Dan could tell that the wound was serious. Frankie's hip glistened in the moonlight. Dan couldn't see the color of the blood, but the sticky sanguine mess dripped and pooled in Frankie's trouser leg.

"Frankie, you with us, man?" Dan tried to sound comforting.

All he got back was some ragged breathing. It took a moment for Frankie to gather his voice. "Not so good, Dan." Frankie grimaced, gritting his teeth in the pain as he hissed an intake of breath. "Damn Nazi … got me in the gut I think."

"You just relax. We'll get you fixed up. You'll be fine, okay," Dan tried to calm the deputy, but Frankie was having none of it. He knew there was no way to get treatment on the island, and he wasn't getting off any time soon. Maybe for the rest of his life.

Frankie sighed resolutely. He finally had a chance to realize that he might be done for. His head fell back into the grass and he felt his body start to go cold. Beads of sweat formed on his forehead.

"He's going into shock," Dan said. "Get a blanket." Frankie's lids fluttered as his eyes rolled up, a well of pain pouring out into his back. The deputy groaned as his body tightened before passing out from the pain.

Dan was in difficult straits. He knew without help Frankie was going to suffer and probably die at the wounds from these Nazis, and there was nothing he could do about it. Even if he got Frankie stabilized, somehow alleviated his pain, infection would set in. The only EMT on the island lay dead behind a curtain on the school stage, and no one else around knew the first thing about treating a gunshot wound, let alone a shotgun blast to the abdomen. Dan didn't even know how to move Frankie to a more comfortable place. He wished he could at least get him to a bed. Dying in the cold ground was no way for any person to go.

"You're gonna have to help me. We need to get him inside. He needs to be on a bed or something." he said to Tina as she ran back with a blanket, a stretchy knitted throw made of fluffy scraps. Dan could picture the girls stretching their feet into the blanket while eating popcorn and watching TV. He wondered if it meant anything to them. It would be covered in Frankie's blood soon enough.

Dan threw the blanket over Frankie. "When I pick him up, you gotta help me. He's gonna be dead weight," Dan cringed at the choice of words, "and you need to help support him." Dan nodded at the sisters, "You girls, make sure the door is open and I can get him to the nearest bed." Shocked but at least with something to do, the girls both nodded dumbly, and went ahead to the front door.

Dan picked up Frankie, the deputy's heavy body causing Dan's sleep deprived legs to shake with the weight. He couldn't just throw the man over his shoulder; Dan had to be careful. Straining to lift with his legs, Dan heard Frankie stir, the pain overcoming his unconsciousness, and groan. Dan knew that Frankie's insides were being twisted, little bits of damage probably getting worse. He felt a distinct wetness as Frankie's blood oozed out of the wound, fresh and warm on top of the colder sticky coating of his shirt and pants.

He struggled to even get up the three steps to the porch. Tina lifted the middle of Frankie's body, trying to keep him from falling through Dan's slippery arms and collapsing to the porch. "Take him to the couch," Tina said. Her face was grave. She had dealt with as much as any mom would, alone with her daughters on an island. She fixed problems when they came up, cried when she couldn't, but this... She felt the tears well up in her eyes, unable to wipe them nor hide their effect. She just let them come. Frankie had shown up at the right moment to save her daughters from these strange men, bent on kidnapping them or worse. She shuddered at the thought. A fear that dealt deep down or on the surface for almost all women, Tina knew that she had dodged a bullet, but that Frankie had caught it for her, in the most literal way possible.

Dan spoke up quickly, "No, which one's the nearest bedroom? Take him there." He didn't want to explain or tell Tina why, but he needed Frankie behind a door. The last thing Frankie would need is for someone to gawk at him in his final moments. Those girls deserved something better than to see that, too. "The bed will be better for him," he said simply.

Dan carried Frankie into the front bedroom. It was Tina's bedroom, Dan assumed, as he considered the plain furniture and fairly spartan decorations. There was no pink and white or doll figures strewn about. No clothing or delicates set haphazardly as he would guess a teen girl would have in her room. It was all to the good for Dan. He didn't think the girls would sleep well for a while anyway; having a bleeding dying man in their bed would probably send them into years of sleepless nights.

Dan wondered if he would ever sleep again.

Frankie got closer to his final sleep as every minute passed. Dan had to find some way to treat those wounds. All of this was his fault. He had let the Nazis in, he had assumed they would be sailors like him, respectful, or if not, at least predictable. Chief Stone had known the truth, knew it from the beginning. And now this is what we got. A good man killed. Or at least half killed.

Dan called to Tina. "You got any bandages? Clean cloths? We're going to put something over this wound. I don't know what will help, but maybe we can stop the blood loss. This pepper sure tore him up, but the holes are small."

Tina came back with some pillowcases. The material was cheap, thick and stiff. If Dan wasn't overwhelmed with the scent of blood, he was sure they would smell of sea breezes and ocean sands, just like everything else did. As it was, all he smelled was sickness.

"Get some gauze pads, put them on and place this over the wound," he pointed to the pillowcase. "We gotta keep his legs straight and down. You don't want the blood to pool in his abdomen."

Tina did as she was told. "Can't we get him a doctor? Call the ambulance?"

"No. No doctors on the island. And we can't get the ambulance," Dan didn't want to get into that, either, by having to explain that the only man on he island that could do an IV was throttled to death by Nazis. "You got any pain killers on hand?" It was an understood and open secret that most people kept something in their spares just in case they had an injury and couldn't get to the doctor until the next day. Most households had some Tylenol 3 or something hidden in the back of the medicine cabinet. Cuts, sprains, aches and pains, a fishhook to the finger, all those things could be fixed with enough band aids and Tylenol. But none of those things would fix Frankie's problems.

Nothing was going to fix this.

Dan waited, sitting silently while Frankie moaned softly in his unconscious state. Tina finally came in with a brown bottle and spoon. "This'll work?" she asked. "How much do you think I should give him?"

"The whole bottle," Dan thought. An overdose wouldn't hurt him now. "Give him enough to let him sleep. No water."

He stood up and pulled Tina from the doorway to talk quietly. Discretion didn't matter where Frankie was concerned, but Dan still worried about the girls. "Listen, I can't stay here, but neither can you. I'm gonna move those trucks out of the way so no one sees them. You need to take the girls somewhere safe. Go over to the Loop Shack, go anywhere that you know that they won't look for you. Take the girls, go over there, head north in the morning. Go to the ferry docks. There should be someone coming over by then. Get the girls off he island."

"But who are they? They aren't those boys they found on the beach?" Tina was still unsure of what was even happening.

Dan explained. He explained everything. The darkness and his sleeplessness gave him an air of desperation. He felt the futility of all the actions he had taken so far. He described how he had brought the men in, gave them shelter, all without realizing how horrid they would become. Stone had seen it, Frankie was dying for it, and now Dan was paying for it.

"Now we think they are going to try to escape. They are kidnapping islanders to use as hostages. But I don't think they will do that any more. They can't afford to lose any lives." Neither can we he thought. The number of people on the island was finite, he realized. Except for those wraiths that showed up. They seemed to be multiplying exponentially.

"Chief Stone thinks they are the victims of all those Nazi sub attacks, and they are after these guys, the last submarine left in the damned Third Reich.

"I saw some of them. They are all sailors, it looks like, soldiers in the old Navy Guard that armed the merchant ships."

"You mean..." Tina was dumb-stuck by the idea, "that they are, like, zombies or something?"

"Stone called them wraiths, more like ghosts, with bodies, I guess, come back to seek revenge, or avenge their deaths, more like it. All I know, they saved my family's life." Dan went on to tell his tale of the men coming in to drag out the Nazis that attacked his wife and son.

"And they tried to do the same thing to my girls," Tina looked away into the darkened hall where her two daughters waited. As scared as she was, Tina was angry as well. She thought back to when those monsters were trying to take her girls, seeing her younger crying and petrified, her older being picked up and carried away. She is only fifteen, Tina thought. Tina pictured her girl, that... Nazi with his arm around her waist, her bare skin showing as he pulled on her, lifting the cheap faded t-shirt she wore to bed. The thoughts of what they would have done to them. Tina shook her head to clear the memory, but it wasn't going anywhere.

"I'm going to take them over to Harbor Cove. I got keys to a rental over here. They got a boat. If I have to, I'll put 'em on a boat and take them out in the sound."

She wasn't going to just put her children away in a house and let those Nazi monsters run over her island, doing the same thing to other people that they tried to do to her family.

"Then I'm coming back," she stated firmly.

38

MIDNIGHT

SILVER LAKE INLET

Stone nestled herself uncomfortably into the rough stone jetty that created the edge of the inlet to Silver Lake. Large boulders had been placed around the short canal that was the only way in and out for any boat or ferry that used the old harbor. Dredged and deep, normally the ferries that went to Swan Quarter and Cedar Island ran out of the inlet. Tonight the lake and inlet were quiet and lonely, the water still like glass after the two storms that had rolled through over the past several days.

A storm still boiled in Stone's head. Her body ached with injuries and lack of sleep. She could feel her heart beating in her teeth. Her shoulder had moved from a dull throbbing to a crusty tight burn. She wasn't even going to try to lift it over her head to see how far she could move it. She would save that for when she had to. She might even get out of this alive.

Others might not be so lucky.

Stone looked over her scope into her former base. The Nazis had possession of it now. She watched as they began to push several locals out of trucks and into the building. The darkness made it difficult to determine who was who, officer or enlisted, and she couldn't risk a shot. Not yet, not until she had a target. Those Nazis wouldn't care if they took a truck and drove it through every living person on the island. Every dead person, too, in this case, Stone thought. She, on the other hand, couldn't take a chance on hitting a civilian. Only if she had a target and they were a threat would she take that risk.

Stone tried to count the number of people being herded into the building. The Nazis were standing them on the porch facing the lake. She could tell some of the Nazis were armed. Rifles at arms or pointed at the civilians posed a threat she wasn't able to counter. Stone understood why they were circling the base. Out in the darkness a sea of black shapes and red eyes waited. The light of the base, generators humming full bore to keep the black away, created an imagined shield for the Nazis, as they always glanced into the night to see if the wraiths were still waiting.

Stone kept looking for someone giving orders. She hoped to at least find Krieg. If she could get her scope on the captain, she might find a chance to end this. Without the leader, the rest might just give up. Or they might go nuts and kill every living person in a mad dash to get off the island.

"What are you planning, Krieg?" Stone wondered out loud.

Over the line of water Stone could hear snippets of language. She was too far away to determine if it was German or English, though she knew it likely to be the former. They certainly weren't too concerned with being spotted, now that they had hostages.

The Nazis were fewer in number than before. She thought of what Dan had told her, of killing the three Nazis

226

in his home, how they were attacked by the wraiths. Stone wondered how many more had fallen. Who would Krieg be willing to sacrifice? How loyal was he to his crew? How loyal were they to him? They seemed ready and willing to follow his orders, but then, in this circumstance, they may see his way as the only way out. After being locked up in darkness for decades, Stone was willing to bet they would do just about anything to stay alive.

Stone saw two men silhouetted in the tungsten yellow light of the base. A tall muscular man was arguing with a shorter man, long hair,... "Eddie..." Stone recognized the short greasy haired man even in the poor light. "You were locked up, with..." Stone realized that Eddie must have made some deal with the Nazis. That seemed about right for the little toad. He had no idea what he was getting into. Eddie could have helped arm the Nazis. They could have gotten the weapons from the sheriff's department. Stone hoped that they hadn't caught Frankie heading that way, but the circumstances didn't seem too promising. She hadn't seen the deputy since the three of them had split up. "What *are* you doing?"

Eddie was gesturing out into the lake, somewhere. Was he going to put them on a boat or something? His little fishing boat was pumped out and moved, but nowhere near seaworthy. None of the other few boats that were left were able to carry that many men away quickly. They would need something big, fast, or easily hidden. The only thing to take that many people off the island really was their submarine. And that wasn't going anywhere, Stone thought, as she followed Eddie's gestures toward the ferry docks.

Right to the bunker tanker tied up, ready to deliver fuel to the first big craft that needed it.

"So, that's your plan, huh?" She thought back to the time she went on board the U-boat. Considering it had been under water for so long, it was remarkably shipshape. No leaks, no corrosion, just some damage to the fantail. She never saw the entire stern or screws. If that thing was operational, they could get to deep water and disappear. Stone knew exactly how hard it was to find a boat on the open seas. Finding one that could sink on purpose would be almost impossible.

She had to separate Krieg from the hostages. Stone couldn't risk them getting caught in the crossfire. But she doubted that the U-boat captain was just going to let them go.

Stone looked back through her scope, scanning for the captain, any officers, any way to get the islanders away without turning the whole thing into a butcher shop.

One of the Nazis was doing his best to be a master race by pushing one of the locals in the back. Stone watched, knowing she could put a bullet in the Nazi's head easily, if it would help the local escape. Stone tried to recognize the man, but all she could see were hazy silhouettes; the fit of clothes and demeanor were obvious enough to distinguish the two. The local pushed back. Some of these local guys, well, Stone thought, they sometimes didn't know when to quit. It was impressive if it didn't get the man killed there on the docks.

The Nazi raised his hand to slash down on the man, but the islander was as much a fighter as the German. If it was a fair fight, they might be evenly matched.

But the Nazis weren't known for being fair, or honest, or compassionate. Another black shape came over and smashed the man in his upper back. Stone watched his head flop with the whiplash movement. Stone felt the hit in her own back. She was a big football fan, and knew the numbing pain of a clip in the back, feeling the body fold in a way it shouldn't, so shocking and painful. And all you wanted to do was just clobber the person who did it to you.

Which is exactly what the islander did. He turned around, hand to back where the pain was felt, and swung hard with his other fist, catching the Nazi sailor on the edge of the jaw. Stone saw the head turn, even in the dim light through the scope, as the Nazi twisted and crumpled.

228

That was a good shot, Stone thought.

Stone kept her eye in the scope, finger itching for a target, anything that might give the hostages a chance. The big Nazi was bearing down the islander, who seemed like he had finally gotten a good idea in his head, and turned to run into the darkness. Terror had a way of propelling the body faster than sheer power, and the islander was several steps away before the Nazi was able to think to give chase. Stone felt time slow, though the next few events happened in an instant.

The Nazi stopped, giving up the chase, it seemed, before Stone saw him draw forth a pistol. Distantly, she heard shouting, but the narrow vision of her eye only showed her a small portion of what was happening. Stone saw the Nazi start to lower the barrel. She now had her target. There was no time to account for distance. At least there was almost no wind, Stone said to herself. She raised the scope to just above the top of the Nazi's head, hoping the bullet would have little if any drop. It was a good quality hunting rifle, but not one she was experienced with. She just hoped the bullet would fly flat. Letting out a soft sigh, she then squeezed the trigger back into its guard.

The Nazi fell out of Stone's sight, and over at the Coast Guard base, all hell broke loose.

39

12:04 A.M.

OCRACOKE COAST GUARD STATION

Krieg only vaguely noticed the argument between Brandt and one of the locals. It wasn't until the shouting started that he turned his head away from the darkness of the harbor toward the light of the Coast Guard station and the figures caught in a brawl that he became aware of the events that would take place. One of his men was down from a punch to the jaw. This alone surprised Krieg, as they had barely felt any notion of pain, or any other feeling, for the entire time they were on board the sunken U-boat. Now they were attacked, wounded, some killed by those *Unmenschen* during the assault on the school, and one of his sailors lay unconscious on the concrete pad by the station. He almost felt sorry for what Brandt was going to do when he caught the civilian.

That was when the shot rang out.

231

Krieg saw his man crumple as a puff of blood and bone whiffed out of his leg. The shot lifted Brandt's entire left leg off the ground, the impetus flinging his calf forward, locking his knee and bending in the thigh. Brandt's body was flung backwards, as if an invisible wire had pulled his legs out forward from him. He went down in a thump, landing first on his hips, then careening back to have his head crash onto the hard pebbled concrete. It took a moment for him to even begin screaming, it all happened so fast.

Krieg realized that someone had shot Brandt, but where it had come from he had no idea. The darkness, even with the clear night sky and full moon, hid anything that wanted to be hidden in perfect black shadow. Somewhere, someone had reached out from across the lake to shoot one of his men. It wasn't one of those *Unmenschen*, he knew that much. They showed no proclivity to weapons, preferring to use bare hands. No, this was a... human, a man.

Or a woman...

"*Stoppen Sie diesen Mann*," Krieg yelled, moving forward and ducking his head. Someone was out sniping at his crew, and would like to find him, he was sure. About five or six of the fifteen civilians they had rounded up took the confusion as a chance to run, and the sailors were having a hard time keeping the ones that remained in place while tracking down the ones that ran off into the darkness of the nearby parking lot. "*Nein! Nein! Holen Sie sich das, den Mann, der bei Brandt war!*" He was the one they needed. Krieg had a good idea who was shooting at him. It was impressive to shoot so well, in the darkness, and with a wounded shoulder, no less.

"*Oberbootsmann* Stone!" Krieg called out. He was going to make sure that the shooter knew who was in charge. He had to show no fear even out in the open, in the dark. Krieg looked out over the water, toward the far end of the harbor. He didn't know where Stone was, but he knew she had to be out there. Anyone else would have just started shooting. They may be on the coast, but the Americans were all cowboys. Except for that Stone. She was different. She was a sailor, but she had rules to follow. She wouldn't risk the lives of the civilians, which was what Krieg was counting upon.

It was a problem Krieg did not have.

He called out in the dark. He was naturally used to using his voice to carry over the water, as well as giving command. The open stillness of Silver Lake was symphony hall for his commanding voice.

"You may think you can reach out from your hiding place in the dark, but you will regret your actions. Do not think that I can't find you, that I can't find your weakness." Krieg deliberately faced outward, alone, as he listened behind him to his men following his orders. They had captured the man that tried to escape. Krieg needed him.

"We will be leaving tomorrow. That you cannot stop. You make it worse for us. You may kill some of us. But mark my words, we will make you pay in kind."

Krieg turned, his timing impeccable as two of his sailors brought the civilian to him, arms locked as he struggled vainly. His men fought to hold the man. The struggles stopped as Krieg drew out Stone's pistol.

40

12:05 A.M.

SILVER LAKE INLET

Stone was listening to Krieg rant. She watched as Krieg
strutted around, not knowing where to speak, and seeing the
local being drug back to the Nazi captain. Stone could hear
Krieg clearly.

"If you continue your actions, all of these people will
face this fate, or possibly worse."

Stone watched as Krieg lowered the pistol and shot the
man in the leg.

As tough as the man was, no one could take a shot like
that. Stone saw the knee split and buckle. The man fell
before he even realized what had happened. It took a few
seconds for the pain to move out of shock, and into
realization. Stone had seen it before with broken bones and
other injuries on the decks of ships, though never caused by a
shooting injury.

Then the screaming started.

The man bellowed a scream of sheer terror, a horrendous and indescribable sound of pain, which carried across the harbor and echoed across the darkened buildings. Stone almost thought she could hear the heavy intake of breath so that the man could scream again, which mirrored the first sound still echoing across the island. Stone knew what would happen next. Her finger itched to shoot, to put a bullet in Krieg's head, but she couldn't trust her body now, and couldn't endanger all the others.

The third scream was the worst. It always was the worst. The lungs put everything into this one, his mouth opened with the sharpest intake of air, and what started as a scream became a palpable ululation as the man's head went back, eyes rolled into the back of his head, and his tongue stuck out and waved, with a scream of horror so loud and long that Stone was sure the whole village could hear the yell.

41

12:06 A.M.

OCRACOKE COAST GUARD STATION

"If you try anything, this is what you get."
Krieg left the man on the concrete to writhe in pain.
"*Lassen Sie ihn zur Erinnerung.*"

42

Stone awoke from a fitful sleep. She had no way to cross the lake and save the islanders held prisoner or approach from the road, nor could she do anything for the man that lay shot on the docks. Stone had slipped back to the Castle to find some shelter for the night. She was afraid of falling asleep and not waking up until midday, but her mind wouldn't let her rest. She awoke long before sunrise.

The old home had long been empty and there were no provisions in the kitchen. With no power, Stone had no way to make coffee or cook breakfast. She wasn't hungry anyway. Her stomach sat heavy in her gut, churning acid she wished she could spit out.

She thought over her next move. With the deputy and Dan Howard, all well armed, she may somehow be able to storm the station and free the hostages, likely losing her life

239

and others, too, in the process. Since she hadn't heard from either person, she wondered if they had been killed, or captured, or maybe had just gone into hiding like her.

That might be a wise option, Stone thought. Just stay here, wait for them to leave. Stone had no inkling of what the Nazis would do with the hostages. Would they take them on board the submarine? Or kill them where they stood? Krieg showed a penchant for killing. He made a good Nazi U-boat commander, no sense of remorse, a delight in hurting others, and a narrow focus. Krieg would do what he thought necessary and he would, without compunction, kill anyone in his way.

Stone picked up the Remington, forgetting her injury for a moment as she raised the scoped sight to her eye. Her shoulder wound stretched and began to throb. "Aaahhhcchhh!" she cried out softly. Even from within the interior of the old house Stone worried that she might be heard. Sound traveled so well in the silence of the stranded island.

More gently this time, she raised the sight, bending her eye to meet it. Stone tried not to look, but couldn't help herself. The man that had been shot was still there. He had moved some in the night, and Stone could just make out the pool of blood behind his knee. Stone hoped he was only passed out. Shock can do some horrible things to a body, but the wound to the knee would be survivable, if they could get him to a doctor, and the blood loss wasn't too severe. He would probably lose a leg. Yet another victim to be chalked up to Nazi cruelty, Stone thought.

Further up by the station, a group of six locals looked huddled on the porch, just under the windows to the mess hall. The blinds were drawn, and not even a hint of movement was given away behind the panels. They could be anywhere in the base right now. Stone was able to spot two guards, at least one armed with a shotgun, standing over the hostages. Stone didn't know how many, if any, had gotten away in the night. There could be more inside.

Pulling the rifle down, Stone double checked to make sure there was no bullet chambered in the action. Until she knew how they were all going to leave, she was unable to respond. She pulled the scope back up.

The station was on a cleared off promontory, surrounded mostly by water, and a large parking lot for summertime visitors on the ferries and spots for boaters to park their trailers. Past that the Carolina pines grew up over the shorter scrub brush and twisted oaks that dotted the land. They were a very visible barrier between the village and the natural soundside shoreline. Just along that line stood the wraiths. They hadn't moved any since the night before. Neither close nor distant, they just waited in their own time. Stone wondered what Krieg's plan was to get past them. He certainly wasn't going to fight his way through that mass. Those wraiths may not stand up to bullets and shotgun shells, but they would never tire, and never give up.

A noise startled Stone off her search of the station and its temporary inhabitants. Clunky footsteps thumped along the side of the building, creaking the wood with every tread. Stone cringed as she pulled the rifle down, her shoulder permanently reminding her of its injury.

"Stone…" came the hissed call to the chief.

"In here," she whispered back. Dan Howard walked across the porch to the double doors to come in. Even with the morning still dark, Stone worried that the motion would be spotted. Those Nazis had to have sentries posted. She wondered if they were getting tired by now.

Dan stepped in as Stone pulled the harbormaster deep into the shadows of the main room, away from the doors and windows. "You alone?" Stone asked, her nerves now permanently worried about being found. "No one saw you, right?"

Dan took the question more somberly than it was meant. "Yeah, I'm alone. I got bad news. Frankie's dead. Those bastards shot him last night trying to take Tina Meekins' kids hostage. He got 'em, but he died this morning," Dan looked down, his thoughts on what, if anything, he could have done to stop Frankie's death.

"Dammit!" Stone cursed. She had seen death before, lost people she cared about, but there was no bandage for it. Friend, colleague, or acquaintance, it always hurt. Frankie may not be the last one.

Dan went on to explain what happened. Stone listened with cold indifference, one eye always on the station, waiting for the first light to illuminate it and see what happens next.

"What do you think they are going to do next?" Dan joined Stone in watching the station. There still seemed to be no movement from the Nazis.

"They are going to take the bunker tanker and fill the U-boat."

Dan looked incredulous. "You mean that thing still works?! There's no way that sub is functional."

Stone looked at Dan, a simple shrug and gesture across the water at a base full of 65 year old Nazi sailors that all looked like kids. "Think about it. When we went on, that thing was completely shipshape, not even a mark of corrosion or blemish. No marks on the deck or hull. The wood wasn't even rotted. Whatever preserved those guys did the same thing to that boat. I don't know if it will sail, but I can tell you that's their plan, at least."

"Where will they go? They can't escape."

"Escape from whom? It will take days until we can contact anyone, and who's going to believe us? They will go to Argentina or Panama, or heck a beach in Mexico and just walk ashore. They may not blend in, but they will disappear before anyone else knows they ever were here.

"And I for one am not interested in letting the last of Hitler's fucking cherubs get away after killing Americans."

Stone made the declaration she had been hearing in her head for a day now. They weren't getting away, if she had to plug every one of them by herself one at a time.

"So, how are they getting there? Are they getting on the tanker and riding out to the sub? Heck, they'll hit the first sandbar they can't see. Even Blackbeard knew that." Dan scoffed at any stranger's plan on navigating the infamously mysterious and fickle channels of Ocracoke inlet.

"Well, first of all, I think they got some help for that." Stone shook her head. "Eddie's over there with them."

"You mean that greasy little asshole went over to the other side?" Dan wished he had punched Eddie when he had the chance.

"Yeah, and that's not all. They have at least seven hostages over there. One's wounded." Stone didn't bother going into detail of how it happened.

"I'm guessing they will put everyone they can on the bunker and try to get out to the sub from here. God knows what's gonna happen to them after that.

"And I wonder what our friends are going to do once the Nazis try to escape." Stone thought about how much empathy a hundred long dead ghouls would have for a few hostages. Would anything like that stop them? Even slow them down? It wasn't like the Nazis could reason with them.

"We could pin them in. Wait for them to leave and take them out as they cross through the opening to the channel. That tanker's slow as hell, we could just shoot them off one by one." Dan wanted to find some way to stop them.

Stone shook her head. Even that hurt her shoulder. "With what? This one rifle? Your zippo gun there?" She nodded at Dan's Very pistol. "Nah, they will just hide and put the locals up as shields. I could get one, maybe two. Maybe even Krieg and Eddie, that would cause problems. But no way we get them all." Stone sighed, the life going out of her tired and wounded body. "No, we may be best off just letting them go. A least we can see what they got planned. Maybe our pals out there got an idea."

Dan merely *humphed* at the lack of action. Stone was right. Dan didn't like it, but Stone was right. The two settled in to a silent staring contest across the water with people who didn't know where to look. They would have to wait.

43

6:30 A.M.

THE CASTLE

Stone had found a way to sleep deeply for all of a half hour, only to awake, sickened, tired, and aching from her wound. Her mouth was dry and pasty, and her head throbbed, most likely from the lack of coffee that drove almost all the Coast Guard to get up in the morning. Coffee wouldn't come today, and it wasn't high on her priorities. If anything, she would like to get some penicillin. Or Tylenol.

Dan was asleep leaning on the windowsill. His mouth was open, a thin layer of drool pouring out of his mouth onto the wood. Stone understood. Sailors had always found a way to sleep in the most uncomfortable of conditions. Fatigue made sleep come on like a ship in the fog, unable to answer to the helm's commands.

"Dan, wake up," Stone nudged the man. "Take a look and see if those guys are moving."

It was still about a half hour to sunrise, and the milky night hung heavy over the harbor. The first rays of orange and red caressed the side of the Coast Guard station, but kept the harbor side of the castle still full in shadow.

There was going to be a storm today, Stone thought. She wondered if the Nazis had the same rhyme as every American boy learned before going out in the water. Red sky at night, sailor's delight. Red sky at morning, sailor take warning. If she had anything to do with it, there would be a storm so bad that the devil himself couldn't summon anything worse. Stone hoped the sky wouldn't be the only thing red this morning.

Dan was in no mood for ancient rhymes.

He spied through the sight of the hunting rifle. "Looks like they are getting ready to move." He squinted and grimaced through the weapon's sight, his eyes still trying to wake up and focus. Dan wiped the sleep from the corners of his eyes. "Dammit!" he cursed.

"What?!" Stone was quickly alert.

"We got problems," Dan said.

44

6:35 A.M.

OCRACOKE COAST GUARD BASE

"*Nimm diese Leute die zwei Lastwagen,*" Krieg ordered his men to the two large pickup trucks they had stolen the night before. The Germans had been stunned at the comfort and ease of shifting gears in the new American vehicles. This morning there was no wide eyed curiosity. The U-boat crew only had wary eyes for the mass of *Unmenschen* that stood about two hundred meters away.

He watched as Schacht marched six of his captives out of the building toward the trucks. Of the twelve people his crew had been able to capture, only eight remained. Three had escaped into the night, their whereabouts unknown. Krieg had no desire nor concern to search the dark pine forest for them. If they escaped or were attacked by the *Unmenschen*, it made no difference. He merely needed shields to protect his men from both the ghouls that awaited, and any overzealous islander attempting to stop them from their exodus. Krieg didn't even bother to glance over his shoulder at the man he had shot the night before.

Krieg would have been happier if he was better armed. In addition to the remaining shotgun he had taken from the *Polizei*, his crew had to their credit a double barreled shotgun and a long barrel duck hunting 12 gauge that had been liberated from a home. Krieg was personally armed with the semi automatic pistol he had taken from the Coast Guardsman. One of his officers was armed with the other police pistol, and they had acquired a poorly cared for revolver from the American traitor, and another six shooter cowboy weapon from a home. The Coast Guard station had been a surprising dearth of weaponry. Krieg assumed the weapons had remained on board the absent ship.

"Platziere alle außer den beiden Frauen in den Lastwagen. Wir nehmen sie mit auf das Schiff." Krieg didn't need much to screen himself from any attack on the boat. The *Oberbootsmann* would not think to shoot while two women were held at gunpoint. *"Platziere eine Person in jede Kabine und bewaffne das erste Fahrzeug mit dem Großteil der Waffen. Behalten Sie die meisten Gefangenen im hinteren LKW. Verwenden Sie die Pistolen, um die Gefangenen unter Kontrolle zu halten."*

Schacht gleamed with delight at being back in a fight. *"Ich bezweifle, dass diese Unmenschen gegen diese Lastwagen bestehen können. Wir können die Gefangenen als Köder benutzen, wenn wir müssen."*

Krieg was less sure how the *Unmenschen* would respond to the islanders as bait. He was more worried about losing any more of his crew. His number had been whittled down by ten, which would mean less down time for his sailors, but the crew was still functional. No matter what, he needed something to stop those ghouls from attacking him. Part of his crew would lure the *Unmenchen* away, then speed to the U-boat once he was clear and had crossed through the

248

inlet to the Atlantic. Once free to the ocean, he should have time to safely fuel and free his boat away from both the threat of the islanders and the ghouls that clogged the predawn roads.

"*Nehmen Sie ... sieben Männer und den Großteil der Waffen in den Lastwagen. Wir werden die beiden Frauen an Bord des Tankers nehmen. Es gibt weniger Bedrohung, wenn wir einmal da sind. Etwa dreißig Minuten nach dem Verlassen. Sie müssen an Bord sein, wenn wir mitkommen, um den Tankvorgang zu beginnen. Wir werden den Tanker benutzen, um das U-Boot von der Sandbank zu befreien, sobald die Flut steigt.*" Krieg did not like the amount of time it would take both to get the tanker around the promontory, nor was he happy with separating his crew, but it must be done. Krieg was desperate, and this was his final move. He hoped to disappear into the sea, but if he had to, he would shell the island to bits to get away.

"*Beginnen Sie mit dem Laden.*"

45

"Damn it all," Stone winced as she whispered her oath, while lowering the scoped rifle down. "He's separating the hostages."

"Is he gonna take them on board the submarine?" Dan felt an icy chill pour down his back; his legs weakened. He put himself in the place of those people over there, captured and in fear, trapped until the whims of those Nazis decided to free them, or just throw them overboard. "We gotta stop them!"

Stone thought. There were only two of them to stop an entire armed crew, with hostages. There was no way, she thought.

"Maybe we can slow them down, at least. Give those people another chance to escape," Stone thought back to her last attempt to help free one of the captives. She couldn't

251

trade a life for a life. "Go back to the main road. See if you can set a roadblock or something. Maybe you can slow them down enough that some of them can get out of the trucks. Maybe our friends out there will help." Stone didn't believe her own words, but she was ready to make any last attempt.

"Me?" Dan was incredulous. Armed with only a shotgun and his one shot Very pistol, he could do little to slow down the trucks, much less stop an armed gang. "What are you going to do?"

Stone was grim. "I'm going to try to cut off the head."

46

SILVER LAKE INLET

Stone was able to move slowly and stealthily enough to find a spot along the rocky seawall that framed the inlet to Silver Lake. She planned to settle in before the bunker tanker left, and then shoot that Nazi Krieg right through his fucking nose. Stone hoped it would hurt for the instant before he died.

It took her longer than she planned, and she heard the unmistakable burble of diesel engines cut through the silence of the early morning. She was able to find an uncomfortable but straight on sight for her rifle. She rested it upon a scrap of blanket she recovered from the Castle, just to allow for a softer, more insulated shooting platform. She forced herself to take her time, trying hard not to increase her heart rate and breathing. Even at this fairly close distance, she didn't want anything to throw off her aim. Stone chambered a new round into the top loading internal magazine. The bolt was heavy, firm, and quiet, a solid and stoic piece of machinery. It felt good in her hand. Even the stock nestled comfortably into the crook of her shoulder. It would hurt like hell when she fired it, so she needed the first shot to work. But she would fire off every shell, then wade out to the tanker and use the damn rifle as a club if she had to. Stone nestled into her firing position, her eye going to the scope just as the bunker tanker sailed around the small promontory by the station. Her finger rested on the trigger guard, ready to climb inside and squeeze off a round as soon as she found her target.

Through the scope she saw Eddie, useless traitor, nervously piloting the big tanker out the channel. Time would come for him, but not now, Stone promised. She let the bunker tanker do the work of coming around into her sights. Her finger itched. Stone saw her sights move to the target she wanted.

Then it was blocked.

In front of Krieg was a woman. Stone recognized her as one of the locals, sandy blonde hair long and bedraggled, still in some form of sleepwear, sweats and a shirt. Fear covered her face like cheap makeup. Stone saw why. Behind her Krieg stood with a pistol drawn. The morning haze and distance disallowed Stone from making any determination of the weapon, but it didn't matter. Stone knew it would be her pistol, the one taken from her when she had been stabbed.

Stone looked for other targets, especially Schacht, the one who stabbed her. She saw nameless Nazis, and another woman, younger, near the bow.

Stone removed her finger from the guard, pulling the bolt to make sure the rifle wouldn't go off. The bunker tanker was passing by her now, and there was nothing she could do.

Stone stood up, full in view of the passing Nazis. She was going to make sure they knew how close to death they were. It would have been easy to do. She needed to show them at least something, to show them how Americans were better than them. No hostages, no cowards hiding behind prisoners, no propaganda. Stone stood up, shoulder aching but her body didn't flinch this time. She kept the rifle in front of her, as a visible promise.

Some of the sailors, officers or non-coms, began to point and shout in German. Stone saw Eddie, giving a mock salute as he escaped into the sound. "Better learn a different one, Eddie," Stone thought about the salute. "Good riddance, you won't get far with those bastards."

Krieg only looked over the hostage's shoulder. He moved his feet slightly, just to be behind her body as they passed. Krieg took no chances, Stone saw. The Nazi captain waved the pistol slightly, a hint of the threat he made with the woman above deck. Krieg also showed what he really was. Stone stood out the open. Krieg could take a shot if he wanted. At that distance, the pistol wouldn't even come close, and Stone could return fire at will. But Krieg hid behind a captive.

Stone looked straight into Krieg's eyes, then turned away and spat.

47

Dan Howard had driven the stolen pickup the Nazis had rammed up into Tina Meekins' house into the middle of the road, near the intersection of Old Beach Road and Highway 12. It was a narrow point, relatively narrow, Dan thought. It may help become a choke point to slow the two trucks down, just long enough to do... something.

Dan stood in a tall copse of trees, a mix of yaupon and twisted oak. He didn't have much of a plan. He was armed with his one shot Very pistol, which had proven to be very effective within a few feet, and he had Frankie Tillett's service revolver, taken from the late deputy, which would have only a slightly longer range, but a much greater capacity. The fact that Dan didn't think he would live long enough to fire all six shots was tucked away, deep inside his brain, nestled darkly behind the idea of saving the lives of the other islanders held hostage on the trucks.

Dan was resolved that he wouldn't live through the assault. He only hoped that he didn't get killed before even firing a shot. There was one small hope, one bit of comfort that made him think that he may at least have a measure of partial success in his rescue attempt. Tina Meekins knelt beside him, leaning upon the black shotgun taken back from the Nazis in their attack on her and her daughters. Tina had insisted. Anyone would take it personally if someone had attacked their own children. Tina had secured her girls away hidden within newer condominiums somewhere on the north side of the island, then had come back. She was cold, staring out, and comfortably ready to deal back on the dirty deeds that the Nazis had tried to act out on her family. Deputy Tillett had given his life to save her daughters. She swore to pay back that loss.

Dan, tired, and with a dark resolve in his own heart, had not bothered to argue. He didn't relish the idea of putting a mother out into battle to make orphans of her daughters, and he had told her in so many words to do what she could, but don't risk her life unnecessarily. Running out to face a horde of cold blooded Nazi killers was just that, Dan considered. But if he and Tina didn't do anything, all the people on those trucks, well, he was just signing their death certificates. Again.

The first time was when he let those monsters on his island.

The morning breeze blew in as the land warmed, sending the sweet smell of yaupon into Dan's nose. The indescribable dusty sweet scent and cooler air was a reminder of the coming of Fall, no matter how warm it got during the days, the cool breezes would come. Dan hoped he would survive to experience one more season.

One more day.

He heard the roar of the pickups come from far away along the otherwise silent roads.

One more hour.

A strange hum came from along the road, and Dan noticed that the sides became littered sporadically with the darkened shapes of the wraiths.

One more minute.

Please God, one more minute.

Then the trucks were upon them. The roadblock confused the drivers, with the truck in the middle of the road. Indecision on which way to go around made the trucks slow. Dan saw the submariners all standing, while the captives cowered in the beds. "Lucky me," Dan thought. It made picking targets easier as he ran out.

The lead truck peeled to the left, into a wider, more open path around the abandoned pickup in the middle of the street. The rear truck slowed, skewing unsurely as to which way to go, until committing to the right, splitting the vehicles.

Dan and Tina ran out together, Tina skirting along the front of the roadblocked truck, using it and Dan as a shield. Dan fired his pistol indiscriminately from his good hand. He didn't care about hitting anything; he merely needed to keep from getting shot before getting around to the driver's side of the truck. A German screamed his guttural gibberish, something Dan didn't understand and didn't care. He simply fired up at the sailor's head to keep him down.

The driver instinctively slammed on brakes from his slow roll through the blocked intersection. That would be his last mistake, thought Dan.

Tina had crossed to the other truck, which had stopped to help the fellow sailors from the ambush. Tina lowered the shotgun to her hips and leaned in. She fired a blast straight into the grill of the truck, hoping to tear the engine apart. She was rewarded with the explosive hissing steam of a shattered radiator as her body shook from the blast. Tina took three steps back to balance and recompose herself from the force of the 12 gauge riot gun.

Dan had more personal plans. Now within reach of the driver's door, he dropped the pistol on the hood of the truck and reached in to grab the driver. He was just a swab, with a mix of anger and terror on his face. In the passenger seat sat one of the captives. Dan recognized the old man, and regretted what would happen next, but it would be better than the alternatives. Dan grabbed the driver by the shirt collar with his right hand and pulled him close through the window. Accuracy wouldn't matter at this range, even with an unsteady left hand holding the Very pistol. Dan jammed the short metal barrel into the swab's eye, pulled it back six inches, and fired.

The cab of the old Chevy pickup turned crimson as blood, brains, and bony bits scattered onto the back window. The glass cracked from skull fragments, forming a spindly spider's web painted roughly with the swab's gore.

The old man in the passenger seat had been struggling to get out of the door. It was a difficult task with tied hands. Now the man became frantic, covered in blood. He tugged mercilessly at the handle, banging on the door to be free. The door sprung open, and the old man fell to the asphalt, but popped up immediately and ran into the woods.

Dan stepped back, trying to reach for the pistol on the hood. He heard a banging on the roof of the truck, a dim echo hidden in the hollow ring of his ears from the pistol blast. One of the Germans was pounding on the truck, trying to get the driver to go. Dan saw him look through the blood stained and cracked glass. The Nazi stood up. Dan remembered him as one of the non-commissioned officers. A look of sickness mixed with awe and pure hatred rolled over the Nazi's face. His teeth gritted, the Nazi showed anger past the point of comprehension at the death of his man. In cold rage, he stood himself up to his full height, swinging his weapon, a double barreled shotgun, to bare down on Dan.

Dan realized that this was the end for him. His feet tried to step back, but he could only make a feeble stumble. The movements were so slow. He couldn't react quickly, and the Nazi seemed to be baring down at a deliberate pace. The barrel was half way down when Dan was awakened by a tremendous explosion. The Nazi turned, looked up at the sky. In the plethora of sound and motion, Dan heard the distinctive hollow *pumpht* the double barrel shotgun made as it went off harmlessly pointed to the sky. Dan looked up to see what the Nazi saw and feared, but only saw a small puff of pink mist.

Dan realized it was the top of the non-com's head coming off.

He looked behind him to find Tina, falling down. She landed flat on her buttocks. She held the shotgun high, keeping the barrel pointed away from Dan even as she had just shot over his head to save his life.

Dan ran over to her, helping Tina up. The truck she shot was steaming and the driver was trying to get moving. In the pandemonium, the captive islanders had jumped off the trucks. Dan saw the Nazis trying to pull two people back into the bed when he noticed that they were no longer alone in the assault. Several of the wraiths had approached from both the village and from the beach side, appearing out of the island ether. It had an immediate effect upon the Nazi sailors. Panic stricken, they let go of their hostages and began screaming. The deep Germanic tones were gone as the young swabs began to screech in terror. One sailor leveled a weapon at the approaching wraiths and fired. The blast was at too great a distance to do much except knock one back. He showed no sense of pain, and joined his inexorable parade toward the Nazis.

Tina shook off Dan's help once up. She was okay. The truck she shot was moving again. Tina took the shotgun in her arms and pointed, from the hip, at the rear axle, aiming vaguely at the rear tire. She fired low, the blast crashing into and through the thin metal, but the pellets were too small to penetrate the tread.

The wraiths closed on the second truck, now driverless and stalled. The remaining crew abandoned the truck for fear of being overrun by the approaching ghouls. Rather than fighting, they panicked and ran, shrugging away the grabbing hands.

Tina looked at Dan in concern and fear. She began to level her shotgun, but Dan stilled her hand. "No," he said, "no, let them be. Go help the others." The former captives were running in terror. After being held by the Nazis, it was an unpleasant move to now be surrounded by the horrid waterlogged ghouls.

"This way!" Tina yelled. She held the shotgun high, keeping the barrel away from the others. She had only one shell left in the action. She had planned to fire her shots and run back into the woods to reload, hopefully finding shelter for a moment. Now she moved away, taking her fellow islanders away from danger. She didn't know where she would go, but she would just keep moving until there wasn't a threat.

Dan stood in the middle of the street. He had survived for another minute. He didn't even care or notice the horde of wraiths moving past him, unaware of his presence. They pursued deliberately the receding Nazis. Some ran while the truck, still steaming, drove on toward he beach and their last salvation, the U-boat.

Dan felt his legs go out from under him. He had escaped certain death. His body was operating solely on adrenaline, and it just gave out. He looked at his hands, shaking while holding his pistol and flare gun. He struggled to break the Very pistol and take out the spent shell. He had fired two shells and couldn't find or remember how many he had taken. His pockets held the last of his ammunition, a few of the flares he had taken from the boat. It wasn't going to do any good, he thought. A flare wouldn't do much more than burn a hole in a shirt. He tried to tell himself it was better than nothing, but he couldn't even convince himself of that.

Dan sat on the dirty asphalt, which was still dusted with silt, sheltered unceremoniously by two pickups. The old Ford the Nazis stole to get to the shore towered above him. Dan looked up into the cab, with the back window dripping in blood and the steering wheel propping up the remains of the head of the sailor he had shot. He wasn't getting in that thing.

In the distance, a roaring sound radiated from the road toward the village. Another truck was coming down the highway. Dan pried himself up off the ground, hoisting the pistol and flare gun toward the sound. He thought about just heading away, to find Tina and just run away. His body told him he was done, but the invaders weren't going to let him. Dan didn't have any fight left in him, but he wasn't going down easy.

He leaned over the back of the truck and leveled the pistol. He figured he had two, maybe three shots left. The truck bared down toward him, honking its horn. He wasn't about to get out of its way.

Dan lifted the short barrel of the pistol as he recognized the white Ford Bronco coming down Highway 12. The last time he had seen the truck was when it was parked at the school. It seemed so long ago. The large orange stripe marked the unmistakable livery of the US Coast Guard. Chief Stone slid the large truck sideways as she slammed on brakes.

Dan looked in the cabin of the open window. Stone looked back, her eyes red, bloodshot, rimmed in pink and sagging. "Did they get away?" she pointed down the road at a slow moving horde of the wraiths inexorably walking down the disappearing remnants of the Nazi escapees.

"We got everyone away. Tina took them, uhhh..." Dan felt his brain slipping. He had no clue where they went. "That way," pointing vaguely up the road to the north. Right now, it was good enough fro him. "You get Krieg?"

"No," Stone sighed, looking like a little life was leaving her body with every breath. "He had two hostages on the boat. I couldn't risk taking a shot.

"Bastard," the oath came out under her breath. Stone wanted it saved for Krieg only.

"You don't look so good," Dan stared at Stone's face and bloodied shoulder. Stone looked like she was just beginning to feel the effects of infection along with sleep deprivation.

"I still got a little in me," again Stone made the statement as a promise to Krieg more than anyone else. "Get in. We're gonna meet him at the beach."

48

7:35 A.M.

OCRACOKE BEACH

U-857 floundered in a deep well just offshore, rocking in the waves as it bobbed slightly at high tide. He had to hurry to fuel his boat and pull it off before the tide went out completely.

"*Beginnen Sie sofort mit dem Tanken. Lassen Sie den Amerikaner an den Pumpen arbeiten.*" Krieg wanted to get the bunker tanker tied to his U-boat and begin towing the craft into deeper water while filling the engines. His engineer gave a muffled "*who!*" and went to work.

"*Was ist mit den beiden Frauen?*" Schacht came up to the captain as orders were given to the sailors. Krieg stared at the shore, still too close by far for the submariner. He should have been much farther away.

His thoughts rested more on getting away quickly. It was the captain's drive, and fear, to be out of the shallows and able to find deep water where he could hide. No one was looking for him, no American planes searching with torpedoes, no destroyers with their deck guns seeking him out. Yet, the beach was much too close, the sandy bottom much too shallow. *"Werfen wir sie über Bord, sobald wir unterwegs sind."* The women he used as shields could swim or float to shore. He assumed the locals all knew how to swim.

"Und der amerikanische Verräter?"

"Ihm auch. Wenn er fertig ist. Ich will ihn nicht auf meinem Boot haben." Krieg didn't care if Eddie could swim. His usefulness was nearing an end.

The first whiff of a sea breeze was just beginning to blow. It carried a salty fish smell, clean and unique. Krieg was used to a more mechanical smell. Diesel, the burn of oil, creosote and the sandy grind of concrete were all the scents of the U-boat base, now long gone. Krieg looked on at the shore, a hopeful last view for some time until he could find more friendly ports.

He squinted, a poor habit of most sailors.

"Laden Sie die Deckgeschütze."

49

8:00 A.M.

OCRACOKE BEACH

Stone didn't want to get out of the truck.

"Ugh…" she and Dan sat in the front seat of the Bronco, which was jammed severely into the soft wet bank of sand that had piled up over the past days. She had driven hard, hurrying to get to the shore before Krieg and his goons had gotten away. In her haste, neither she nor Dan had bothered to put on their seat belts. The thick sand had caught the tires of the Bronco and held, slowing the vehicle to a halt, but sending Stone into the steering wheel and Dan banging his head into the windshield. Neither was seriously injured, but it did nothing to help the aches already coursing through their bodies.

And adding to their concerns, the dunes seemed to be slowly filling with the wraiths that had risen from the sea to come after the Nazis freed from their own trap only a few days ago. There looked like hundreds of them.

"Dear God, how many people did they kill?" Dan was in awe at the plodding dark figures, all but oblivious to the two people in the truck. They had only one goal on their limited minds now.

"About three thousand, around here. At least." Stone said matter-of-factly. "C'mon. I'm not letting these guys have all the glory."

"You sure we should even get out?" Dan was not at all sure about being on the same beach with potentially thousands of angry undead ghouls all hunting for blood.

"Just give me long enough for one good shot. After that, I don't care, cut and run, swim for the mainland, whatever, I just want to put one in Krieg."

The door creaked as Stone opened it. She left it open and removed the big Remington. The box of shells rattled as she picked it up. One of them had Krieg's name on it. Her shoulder screamed as she moved her arm. Maybe one for the guy that got her there, too.

The two trundled up the dune, Stone lugging the rifle in one hand, favoring her weak shoulder as bolts of pain shot through her with every stumbling step through the sand. Dan carried a worn itchy blanket, handed to him by Stone. He laid it out across the sea oats and sharp grass, still wet from the storms. The view they saw was a strange battle between World War II butchery and the savagery of a Dark Ages melee.

A small group of Nazis had deployed a large rubber raft to the beach to retrieve the remaining survivors of Dan's ambush. The wraiths had closed in with the desire of hand to hand savagery, but had been fended off by the last of the weapons the Nazis had stolen. Stone watched a familiar form rise up into the shallows from the rubber raft. Schacht began firing small arms into the crowd of ghouls. The bullets ripped through the wraiths' dead arms, tearing the soft flesh off, but only slowing the inexorable approach, staving off attack for only moments while the last of the sailors ran into the breakers and began swimming toward the submarine.

For every wraith that fell, twenty took their place. The beach swelled, and the ocean color changed from the frothy green to dark blue in patches. More of the wraiths rose up from the dunes, hidden in the salt grasses and shadows of the shrubby hills. They were only waiting for a target. Now they had found the cause of their torment, and nothing would stop them.

Stone watched as the men swam for their lives. At that moment, she heard the phlegmatic cough of a giant, and the U-boat belched smoke. Krieg was trying to start up his boat. Stone nestled herself into the blanket. She felt the tiny spikes of dried sea oats poking through, and the itchy wool radiating a familiar warmth. She wiggled her hip as she felt a stem break under her weight. Her shoulder settled into a slow warm burn. Stone had removed herself from the pain and discomfort. It was now just a reminder for her as she delivered penance. She nestled her eye into the scope and looked for Krieg.

50

8:01 A.M.

U-857

Krieg had moved to the conning tower to have a better view of his crew and the approaching U*nmenchen*. There were hundreds now. He looked down at his crew, manning the anti aircraft gun. They awaited his order once the beach was cleared of the men swimming from the shore. Krieg's feet spread apart as he felt his boat move. It was already becoming free, losing the same curse as its crew. Once the engine fired, he would be able to use the tanker to aid in pulling the U-boat to deeper water. Looking to his right at the flak gun, he simply gave that comforting order to stand by, "*Bereithalten.*" The bigger 8,8 gun on the main deck to his left sat untended. He didn't have enough crew to man it, and Krieg wondered if the heavier gun would be of much more use as an anti-personnel weapon.

The fuel loaded unabated, even as his engineer began the laborious process of firing the engines. The gurgling cough of the engine firing was normal to Krieg, no matter how loud it was in his ears. He almost missed the whining crack that seemed to ping somewhere aft of the ship. It could have been the two boats rubbing, or the clank of a tool, or...

The bullet ripped across the conning tower, followed instantly by the echoing cough of a rifle being fired. Instinctively, Krieg ducked behind the conning tower wall, and yelled at his flak crew.

"*Finde mich ein Ziel*! *Feuer*!" Krieg pointed toward the shore. Someone was firing a rifle a him. It was a more direct threat than the gathering horde chasing his men into the sea. Krieg gathered binoculars from a sealed storage box just below the main hatch, and waited. He wondered if the conning tower steel would even stop a bullet when he heard the whine-crack sound of a third shot. Ignoring the shouting, vaguely recognizing the voices were in English and German, Krieg looked over the gunwale. "Where would you be, *Fräulein Stone?*" he thought in English. American, he corrected himself.

Futilely scanning the beach, Krieg counted to himself. When he got to four, he ducked back down. The bullet came at five. Krieg was back up in a surprisingly rapid heartbeat. His eyes scanned the beach again. It crawled with the fetid ghouls all looking to find a way to his submarine and his crew. Then he saw it. The barrel waved upward slightly, the rigid line a telltale giveaway compared to the gentle swaying of the sea oats.

"*Dort*! *Dreißig Meter nördlich auf den Dünen. Feuer dort!*" Krieg pointed toward his target. The gun crew searched out for a target that only Krieg had seen, but began cranking the antiaircraft weapon toward the dunes to their right.

"*Feuer!*" Krieg was adamant. The gun aimed at the embankment near where the captain had pointed and fired.

51

8:06 A.M.

OCRACOKE BEACH

Stone struggled to drop four more shells into the top magazine of the Remington. The scope made loading difficult as she tried to keep muzzle control with her stiff and sore arm. In a flash of recognition, she heard the hollow kicking sound and a whistling scream. Her brain, without the aid of any processing, recognized the sound, similar to the big guns used on the large cutters. Immediately, her arm went out and smashed Dan's head straight into the blanket, her own face buried into the scratchy surface. She didn't even have time to wonder if this was her last moment on earth before the shell hit.

The shot impacted low on the dune, about forty feet from them. It exploded more with a deep *whump* than a cracking explosion, but the blast sent waves rolling through the dune. Stone felt the whole hill shake. Her stomach churned and she felt like she was going to be turned inside out.

But she was alive.

Sand rained down on them, mixed with shredded bits of organic matter, reeds, sheared and burned grass, and bits of sea oat seed. The smell of explosive, burned metal, and sickly sweet sand gave a mix of odors, all bad, to Stone's nostrils. It smelled like rancid bacon; Stone's stomach rolled again.

She rolled over onto Dan Howard, hugging him full body, and pulled herself along with the harbormaster down the back of the hill. A second impact came, higher up the hill. But now the dune was between them and the threat. The dune was being torn by the submarine's gun. It was firing a shot every two or three seconds.

Then it stopped.

Stone had already been shot at and stabbed, so getting shelled on her own home island by an enemy of her country was so beyond the pale, she no longer even cared for her safety. She gathered her rifle and ran over the hill to the beach, with Dan Howard in tow. She sighted down the scope at the sub.

52

Krieg stared at the gun, silent and smoking. The crew was not silent, as they swore while trying to clear the jam. Krieg climbed down the tower, past the non-functioning gun, and toward the fueling lines. He gave little interest in the flak weapon. It would often jam. Most sailors feared using the weapon more than relished it. It usually meant that an aircraft had found them on the surface. He was more concerned with what happened behind him. The yelling was more frantic, and Krieg distinctly recognized the mix of a rancid English and desperate German. An oily smell permeated the air, more than the usual background aromas of diesel and body odor. He struggled to take his eyes off of the shore, with its unknown threat and massing undead enemy.

Glancing back toward the bunker tanker, he saw the cause of his problems. The American was screaming with one of his engineers, who was trying to continue to fill the fuel tanks. A fine mist was pumping out onto both decks while the fuel still flowed into the U-boat. The greasy American was yelling at the engineer, "You gotta stop pumping and seal that!" and the engineer answered in his native language, "*Wir haben keine Zeit zu stoppen. Wir müssen weiter tanken! Ausweichen!*"

Krieg used the makeshift gangplank to run over the now rolling decks to the fueling tanker. "What are you doing?! Leave that man alone! You, keep this craft stable in the current, nothing else!"

Eddie was adamant, and terrified. "You can't have that marine fuel spraying on a hot deck, you asshole! It's not safe! Uncouple and let's get out of here before those things come for us!"

"The diesel is safe," Krieg contradicted the American. "You do what I say." Krieg tried to keep from reaching for the pistol to emphasize his threat.

"No way, you gotta get me outta here!" Eddie was in a full panic now. He had just seen the Nazis shell his home. There was no going back, and this was the only way out. He tried to push past the captain to cross over to the submarine. He hadn't expected shooting and cannons and those strange creatures flooding the beach to come after him.

Krieg struck out with his hand, a full force blow to Eddie's chest, knocking the American to the pitching deck. Eddie screamed, high pitched and terrified, "You can't do this! We had a deal! You have to get me out of here!" Eddie's eyes welled up with tears. His rational decision making skills, never a strong point with him, had given way to full on terror. He jumped up from the deck. Even with the painful imprint of Krieg's hand still on his chest, Eddie bared down on the captain. Eddie's hands balled into fists, but he couldn't bring himself to raise them. He merely squealed, "Let me go! You gotta uncouple and go!" He barged into the captain, full body, unsure of his own strength against the Nazi. Eddie had always hoped that he could goad someone else into a fight. This time he hoped that by not striking the captain, he couldn't be blamed for hitting the man. Eddie was trying to run to the submarine. The captain was just in the way. Eddie's mind said it was the captain's fault for being there in the first place. It was a first grader's rationale, and Eddie didn't realize that he was not dealing with someone who needed to show restraint.

Eddie barged into the captain and kept running. He made it to the submarine deck and tried to uncouple the fuel hose. He would make them leave. Now.

"*Halt!*" Krieg yelled at the maniacal American. Eddie was trying to unhook the fuel nozzle. Krieg had no more patience to use with this man. He pulled the pistol he had stolen and began to level it at Eddie.

Eddie stood up, exposed and realizing he had nowhere to hide. He tried to raise his hands, but his body wouldn't let him, as it tightened to hold his bladder and bowels.

Krieg didn't bother aiming. The decks rolled with the waves, so he simply pointed toward the center of Eddie's body and fired once. The bullet embedded in Eddie's gut. A small leak of dark red blood came out as

Eddie tried to hold back the bleeding. It took a moment for the pain and shock to hit him, only to have him double over, screaming.

"*Wirf ihn rüber,*" Krieg commanded, as if he was tossing out the rubbish from a day voyage. "*Sichern Sie die Kraftstoffleitungen.*" The diesel fuel where Eddie attempted to disengage the lines spilled onto the deck and down the open hatches.

Two crewmen unceremoniously tossed Eddie Gruber into the deepening water. He would drown before the wound killed him, thought Krieg. He then never gave another thought about it, as he turned to finishing the refueling.

"*Holen Sie sich die Motoren an.*"

53

8:08 A.M.

OCRACOKE BEACH

Stone witnessed all this through the scope of her rifle. She was almost too entranced to remember she held a rifle in her hands.

"Chief..."

Stone watched as Captain Krieg moved from boat to boat, the argument with Eddie increasing as the greasy little toad became manic on the ship. He looked like he was trying to untie the two craft and strand Krieg on the tanker.

"Chief."

Krieg was shielded, by Eddie, by several other sailors, and various objects along the two ships, but Stone was too fascinated by the strange and surreal play going on board the two boats. She almost missed the moment Krieg drew and fired, as Eddie didn't fall over immediately.It wasn't until the sailors unceremoniously tossed his body into the ocean that Stone realized what had happened.

"CHIEF!"

Stone was pulled away from the bloody macabre death she just watched. She pulled the scope from her eyes to see why Dan was so adamant, pulling at her good shoulder. She tried to shake off the grip, when she realized Dan was on her other side.

A wet and clammy hand had a grasp of her arm, pulling down the rifle, keeping her from getting a shot. Next to her stood a group of the wraiths, each as ugly and mutilated by time and tide as the next. A white hand, covered in black bruises and small pink scratches, bloodless and fleshy, pulled at her. It was attached to a long and previously muscular arm that led to a barrel chest, a tall figure with a face to match the hand. His eyes were sunk in, the flesh sagging down revealing the underside of his lids. The eyes glowed red with hate, even in the morning light.

Black lips and a black tongue tried to find a function. Stone tried to pull away, but the wraith held her tight. Then she heard the sounds.

The man was trying to speak. Water bubbled from his throat, and the first sound was nothing more than a horrid gurgle, as salt water, mixed with whatever ancient horrors had been cooking in the man's cold stomach for decades under the sea, spit up past rotted teeth. But the man made no move to strike or harm Stone.

"What?" Dan spoke up. He had heard them speak before. He saw past the horrors. "What do you want to say?"

The sounds came, horrid choking gurgles of salty phlegm caught and stuck in the lungs, then flew up and out, and the sounds came. "Chreee…

"He…

"He ish oursh."

Stone was dumbstruck. But Dan understood. He spoke up again. "Who do you want?"

The man/thing let go of Stone, and looked at Dan. Finally relieved of the horrid cursed stare of the wraith, Stone was able to look at him. He was big, muscular, but tall. His hair was dark, and a mess. It hadn't grown since he died long ago, and Stone could still see the short crew cut style, hidden in all the pain and gore on the man. Stone realized, he probably was a handsome man before the Nazis got him. His uniform made him out to be a civilian crewman, or maybe merchant marine. Stone took in that he used to be a real person, with a life to live at some time long ago. Stone had more empathy for the man in a moment than those Nazis ever did when they sank the ships during and before the war.

"He is...ours." It was the best he could say, the first words in over forty years. Stone looked at the man, then out to the submarine. All that pain, all the time trapped in a worse curse than anything brought upon the Nazis entombed in a submarine. The wraith pushed the barrel of the rifle down. Stone didn't want to acquiesce, but she knew they deserved it more.

"I want him so bad. For what he did to us. But, yeah, you got him.

"Who can I have?"

The wraith looked at Stone, then her shoulder, then out to sea.

Stone followed his gaze. Not to the submarine, but to the rubber skiff, still plodding through the waves, carrying the remainder of the sailors that tried to run through the island to the beach. They were as nameless as the wraiths to Stone. Then she saw one, shouting and waving. Schacht.

Stone's shoulder ached.

That one will do, thought Stone.

She couldn't kneel to brace herself; the waves and low coast made even a standing level shot difficult. She raised the rifle quickly. Stone felt the wound tear open again, but she had become accustomed to the pain. It had stopped bleeding by now. Mostly. The wind blew straight in, a mild

281

onshore morning breeze. She had little to worry about with her aim, except her own shaking body, rapid heartbeat, and a rapidly receding target bouncing in the waves. Stone took a deep breath, and sighted her target.

Schacht was yelling, though Stone couldn't hear anything with the wind in her ears. The big Nazi's head bobbed up and down in low rolls. Stone recognized the easy motion of the rolling waves, and the frequency and duration. She counted silently, in her head, to attune herself to the waves. When she found the pattern, Stone rested her finger inside the guard and firmly pulled on the trigger, to no effect.

"Damn!" she had reloaded but in the chaos of the shelling, she had not chambered a round. She pulled the bolt to load a shell, and began her ritual anew. Stone noticed how the ocean was now being flooded with dark bodies, the zombies slowly fighting their way past the breakers toward the sandbar that was slowly sinking in the oncoming tide. She had to hurry.

Stone found Schacht's head, again, and watched the rhythm of the waves. She waited until she had the Nazi sighted, and balanced her aim so that Schacht's head dropped just to the bottom of the scope as the little rubber raft bobbed in the waves. Stone was counting on the natural drop of the bullet, even at this close range, and the rise of the boat, to hopefully meet the bullet. Right between the bastard's eyes.

Stone inhaled, let out half the breath, and squeezed the trigger. Her eye blurred, her sight marred by something. She scanned the boat and discovered a sailor had caught her first shot. The boy must have stood in the way and caught the bullet. The body twisted in a macabre dance, flinging blood from a torn shoulder blade. The other sailors were shocked and repulsed. Stone was only mad that she missed. She resighted as she pulled back the bolt for another shell.

Stone saw only a microcosm of the entire events happening around her. Dan Howard may have been nearby, or he may have run off. Stone may be surrounded by wraiths

282

ready to attack her. But all she saw was Schacht, his face a mix of surprise and disgust at the bloody carnage on his little boat. "Too late, you bastard," thought Stone. "You shoulda realized what you were doing to others before you started." And Stone squeezed the trigger.

This time the bullet flew true. All the remaining sailors had ducked down, in fear of being shot, or in disgust at being covered in blood and bone. Schacht alone stood out, looking at the beach for whoever was shooting. It made an easy shot. The Nazi's face was one of anger, plotting retribution. Then it wasn't there. The bullet dropped only a few inches, hitting Schacht in the face, just left of his nose. The soft cartilage and bit of flat bone did nothing to stop the bullet, nor did the Nazi's brain, as the slug mushroomed and blew out the back of his head. Stone watched, time slowing, as the tiny hole first formed on Schacht's face, and then the puff of pink from behind as his brain and skull expanded out the back. His body was still for a moment, then tumbled backwards into the ocean.

Stone lowered the rifle. Her body finally gave out. She felt her legs go out from under her and she sagged down into the damp sand of the shore. Her forehead began to sweat, a cold flood of perspiration that poured into her eyes. Stone waited for the chills and shakes to come; she knew she was going into a mild shock, and just let her body give way to the stress. She was done. The death of Schacht, seeing his head come apart, had released the greater demons in her own head. Krieg was still there, but the Nazi captain was someone else's troubles now.

Just then she heard the engines fire, and saw the ocean churn.

54

8:09 A.M.

U-857

Krieg saw Schacht go down. The back of his head simply exploded into the water, and the body fell over backwards into the morning waves of the Atlantic. He watched the body float there. It was a perverse and discomforting sight. The corpse floated, face up, as if Schacht were merely a swimmer enjoying the sun on the waves, until one of the rolling shore breaks caught his body and sent it tumbling as if in a washing machine. The sea had no respect for the dead.

The engine fired again, and this time the carbon rich smoke of marine diesel choked out the exhaust, and the once familiar hum of his U-boat's engine vibrated under his feet. He scanned the shore again. He was still worried about someone out there, Stone, probably, maybe anyone, shooting at him, as he peeked behind the side of the tower. He yelled again at his gun crew.

"*Holen Sie sich diese verdammte Waffe! Auf das Ufer!*" The mass of U*nmenchen* had grown, and was walking into the water toward him, oblivious to the waves pushing them back. He had to leave, now.

The U-boat was still partly grounded on the bow, but the sand bar was soft, and the tide was high. He gave orders, expecting them to be followed before he was done speaking.

"*Flut die strengen Ballasttanks. Pump alles vom Bug.*" Krieg needed to get the U-boat free, and hoped to pivot it on the balance point by using the bunker tanker and his own engines. The stern was damaged, but the screws still worked. His boat had life again.

"*Vollgas achtern, Notfall.*" Krieg called into his communications equipment. It took a moment to transfer the command to the engines, but within moments, the stern of the U-boat was a churning froth as the screws got up to top speed.

They were still pumping fuel, and would need to as the emergency full power would drink the diesel rapidly. Krieg didn't like the setup he had with the lines running over his deck, but he had little choice. The ghouls were getting closer.

55

8:10 A.M.

OCRACOKE BEACH

"I'm done, Dan. I got nothing left."

Stone took several deep breaths, but couldn't find one to satisfy her. She just needed to fall back into the sand and let the weight of the world crush her. Dan looked at the Coast Guardsman, bloodied down to her waist, eyes almost as red as the demons around them, all storming into the water.

Dan felt his own weight on his soul as well. He hadn't done even as much as Stone had. Forgotten in his right hand was the Very pistol, its light frame drooping and useless. Even with a shotgun shell, it would not have the range to do any damage. He thought about firing off the flare tucked in the barrel. Maybe it would frighten the Nazis. Maybe it would signal for help.

He just dropped it instead.

As he sat down next to Stone on the sand, the same wraith, thing, man, walked by him, and picked up the flare gun. Wordless, he waded into the water with the rest of the ghouls.

"Uhhh… Chiefy? I think we better find a little bit better place to sit on the beach."

56

8:20 A.M.

U-857

"Bereiten Sie sich darauf vor, die Angreifer abzuwehren."

They were words Krieg never thought he would have to utter.

Having to give the order to repel boarders was something an Englishman would do when fighting pirates in the tropics. They were words for tales of little boys playing with swords, not sailors of the twentieth century. The boat moved agonizingly slow, as the waves pushed against the hull, and the engines tugged relentlessly against the sandbar. He would have gotten out and pushed on the side of the hull, if he had thought it would help.

There was no way he was climbing off his boat, though. The ocean teemed with *Unmenchen.*

The U-boat shifted, an unearthly shrug as if a giant had finally given them a push. The submarine dropped, and bobbed, off the sandbar and into slightly deeper water. It was almost enough. They could be free soon, Krieg thought.

"*Blasen Sie alle Ballasttanks.*"

The last of the seawater was blasted from the ballast tanks. Krieg could feel the ship give way.

"*Entkuppeln Sie die Kraftstoffleitungen. Löse die Hecklinien. Benutze den Tanker, um uns zu tieferem Wasser zu ziehen.*" Krieg hated to disconnect the fuel lines, but he needed to pull his boat to deeper water. His men stood on the deck, looking anxiously at the bunker tanker as it freed itself. Of the two craft, the tanker was more seaworthy at the moment. Some wanted to be on it just to get to sea, to be away from the ghouls still creeping closer and closer. The men waited on deck, armed with MP-40s and a few of the bigger MG-34 machine guns and pistols. He had enough firepower and ammunition, but there were fewer men. He had lost too many, and others were still doing their duty of running the boat.

Krieg had no other duty than to order others. He walked around the conning tower to the bow, taking an MP-40 from a sailor and ordering him to acquire another weapon.

The remaining men in the raft had beaten the waves and almost reached the U-boat, when the submarine was finally freed, which put them again just out of reach. The men in the raft were becoming desperate, as they saw the ghouls flooding the shore break and turning the green water black. Only three were using their paddles, and the others, in terror, reached into the water to push with their hands.

Krieg saw the first one get pulled under when a white slimy hand reached up from the water to grab the sailor's arm. He screamed, an ululation of terror that was drowned out as the Nazi hit the water. Salt brine flooded his throat, but he was unable to cough, as the water surrounded him. His body spasmed as paroxysms shook him. The wraith held him under water, waiting until the first bubbles poured out of the Nazi's nose. His grip got only stronger, holding the terrified German under. Fighting was useless. The current moved them, but there was no freeing the Nazi from a guilty watery grave.

The others stopped. They were terrified to stick a finger in the water, let alone a paddle. One began screaming, "*Komm, hol uns!*" That was when the other hands came up.

Krieg wasn't about to move the U-boat any closer to shore. Not closer to the sand bar. Not closer to the ghouls.

He primed his MP-40 and began firing into the water near the raft. The men were dead if they didn't kill the U*nmenchen*, even if they could be killed. "*Schieß ins Wasser!*" The bullets flew, one striking a sailor, while many tore at the waterline. Still the hands came up. The sailors began slashing at the water with their paddles. More of the ghouls reached up. Bullets tore into the bodies, ripping fleshy holes into wet waterlogged skin. Some bodies went down with their backs pocked with holes, but more came up.

The small boat began to collapse. Stray bullets had already pierced the rubber, and the boat started to fold in the middle. The screams became shrieks, terrified and shrill. It would only take moments for the churning waters and groping beasts to finish the men off. If Krieg had ever listened, he would have recognized the sound as the same that men made long ago as they drowned and burned from his torpedo attacks.

He could only imagine what was happening to the men being pulled under by the revenging ghouls. The perpetually young Nazis on the raft had a more intimate reception. The ghouls held them under the water, slowly drowning the U-boat sailors. At first the Nazis tried to fight back, but the waves and water made it difficult to do anything more than flail and pull weakly. Finally, with their bodies desperate for the air that they only recently were able to breathe anew, they threw all their energy into reaching back to the surface.

Some were pinned under the floundering raft as it sank into the waves. One young sailor made it barely to the top, his mouth frothing as he had breathed in seawater. It only made him choke on the horrid bilious fluid as he coughed, trying and failing to clear his lungs. He was able to partially exhale when he was pulled back under. His lungs involuntarily expanded as he inhaled a lungful of salt water. His throat burned down to his chest as the weight pulled him down to the ocean floor.

Another sailor thought he may escape the torment, as he held on valiantly with one arm to the rapidly deflating raft. Even with little air in the chambers, it still floated, just barely. He watched as heads bobbed under the rubber flooring, his friends trapped under the water without hope of escape. He held with a death grip with one hand while he bashed uselessly at the ghouls just under the water. It took several swats until one of the ghouls got a slimy hand to grip the free arm of the Nazi. He still jerked madly, terrified of being pulled under. Instead, one of the ghouls used it to pull himself up to the raft, and to the man's face.

Staring sightless into the Nazi's eyes, the ghoul came above the water, black eyes tinged with red glow, its face a horrid pockmarked moonscape, dripping with weeping seawater and white puss from his ancient wounds. The ghoul had been burned long ago, and the seawater and his curse had kept the wounds soft and fleshy. Its mouth opened, a gurgling oath coming out only as a horrific moan, right into the Nazi boy's face. The rotten stink of a death at sea permeated the ghoul's breath.

Black teeth, rotten and matte with the loss of enamel, stood out over the torn cracked lips. The young Nazi watched in horror as the mouth opened wide and began to plunge itself into his shoulder, biting and tearing at his flesh. He was horrified at the look of disease pouring into the fresh wound. The Nazi couldn't lash out and pry away the biting ghoul. He would lose his grip on the raft and be pulled to the bottom. He tried to use his other arm to curl around and pull the ghoul off by its hair, but he could get no grip on the slimy follicles. Blood poured down his arm as the teeth sunk deeper.

Then he felt the hands grab at his legs from under the water. Another ghoul was pulling itself up his body. He kicked at the thing, but it continued to climb. He felt the hands grasping at him, higher and higher, uncaring where they touched him, as long as they got higher.

This ghoul finally broke the surface, his face cleaner, less damaged. The clean cut look of a young gentleman defied the viciousness of the thing that it really was. It came up through the water like a shark. The Nazi sailor's wound already oozed blood into the water. Now this one came up and began tearing its teeth into his armpit.

The pain was immense, as the sailor felt his eyes roll up in blind terror. He tried to raise his arm, but they clung to it, tearing at the flesh, deeper and deeper. The Nazi slipped, almost releasing his grip on the remains of the raft. Bullets tore around him, but the ghouls didn't care. He felt the last of his muscles give way, and his arm rose at an unnatural angle until it started to snap and crack. The two ghouls twisted at it like a piece of chicken. He couldn't stand the pain, but his brain wouldn't let him pass out. Finally, with a sickening final crack, the arm came off and the two ghouls floated down and away with their prize.

Unbelieving, the Nazi struggled to pull himself out of the water and onto the flooded raft's floor. He flopped down. The bottom of the raft was folding and pooling with sea water, which quickly changed color to a sickening red as his blood swirled with the ocean. He tried to spread himself out, to help to float. He was almost completely out of the water.

That's when he felt the hands grab his dangling feet.

He screamed once more. The hands pulled at his body, slowly tugging him into the water. He tried to hold on with his one hand, but the raft was too slick. He reached out to hold with his other arm. His brain still felt it, he felt the arm reach out, to grab for a rope or rubber gunwale, but there was nothing there. His brain still thought the arm was attached, though it had floated away. His last scream came out from under the water with his last breath as the ocean turned black from his blood.

Krieg watched all this, having fired his magazine into the water and oncoming tide of the U*nmenchen*. The bullets only reached a few feet before losing any deadly effect, but he had seen several strike something under the water. Puffs of dark blood exploded in the low rolling waves that would later crash into the beach a few hundred feet away. In a moment of distilled discretion, Krieg noticed how the clouds of blood from the wounds stayed in the same place. The water under the waves remained relatively still while the waves on top rolled over until they broke in the shallows.

The boom of the flak gun getting back into action shook him from the dizzying revelry. Shells flew downrange into the shore, where hundreds of ghouls seemed to be standing. More waded in to the water, most from the north. The sea was turning black with bodies, all dead, but all still alive.

The flak gun wouldn't be able to decline far enough to fire into the water nearby, and Krieg didn't think it would do enough good. They had to be free of the shore.

As if in response to a demon's wish, the U-boat moved freely. They were in deeper water, and the boat began to power itself back. If he could get just a few more feet deeper, he would be able to steam freely to the south. Hopefully he would keep the tanker with him to fuel the U-boat as they traveled.

"*Schließen Sie die Luken. Nein, bleib an Deck.*" Krieg wanted as many armed men on deck as possible. He wasn't yet able to submerge. He still needed to finish fueling, but in deeper water. His sailors gathered around the hatches. The relative protection of the steel hull, sealed behind metal hatches, appealed to them after seeing their compatriots slaughtered and drowned by the zombies that could be under them already. The men jumped as the deck gun fired round after round, every two seconds pumping more explosive shells into the horde along the breakers. They were not used to being hunted. They weren't ready to fight for their lives, especially after being imprisoned in their boat for so long. One looked over his shoulder, jealously wishing to be on the mobile tanker still pulling away on the bow.

The sailors had to set their weapons down to secure the hatches. As one stood up from sealing the inner hatch, he saw a strange shape to the stern. A black blob was fighting to climb its way up the hull while being churned by the water that was stirred by the screws. The shape was so odd and out of touch with reality that it took him a moment to make out the thing's arm and head. It wasn't until it crawled and stood up on the deck that the sailor realized it was one of the zombies. They had made it to the boat.

The sailor tried to scream, waving and banging on the deck. He was unsure what to say. His voice was caught, not able to make a coherent sound. He finally pointed and the others looked. Sailors scrambled to their weapons. In a fit of terror, one sailor pulled the trigger on a reloaded MP-40 and poured the entire contents of his 32 round magazine in one squeeze of the trigger into the ghoul. The body splattered as it came apart on the deck.

Krieg screamed. "*Schießen Sie nicht auf das Deck! Wähle dein Ziel! Verschwenden Sie keine Munition!*" he worried about penetrating the deck and hull, as well as running out of bullets. There were so many of them.

And more were coming up.

Properly chastised, the armed sailors began a systematic cleanup of the U-boat. Targeting the slowly moving ghouls as they began to climb up the hull. Sailors pointed the weapons downward and discharged three round bursts into heads or the center of what mass they saw. In moments, the water around the U-boat ran pink with blood and flesh.

His boat had finally moved into deeper water, and Krieg felt that he had at least initially cleared the decks of the swarming *Unmenchen* long enough to continue refueling. He yelled at his remaining crew on the bunker tanker to hold position as the U-boat came alongside. The flak gun went silent as they ran out of targets on the beach. It was an ominous relative silence, with only the burble of diesel engines and the soft churn of the water. The bunker tanker sat only about thirty meters to port, past the roll of the forming breakers, in dark blue water, probably ten meters deep. Deep enough to steam away, Krieg hoped.

The tanker could maneuver more easily than the U-boat, so Krieg had them come alongside to begin the laborious process of pumping the marine fuel again. The deck was already soaked with diesel from when that American had detached the lines before. Sealing the hatches had only trapped the fumes in the hull. Krieg called the con to open hatches and turn on the fans to get the diesel vapor out of the interior.

The sailors on deck were still nervous. They had seen the ghouls crawl up over the hull to the deck. The Nazi crew paced the edge of the U-boat, with their weapons reloaded, primed, and fingers resting uneasily on the trigger guards.

"Die Fender absenken. Halten Sie die Rümpfe fest." Krieg ordered the two craft tight, so that none of the ghouls would crawl up between them. It was a dangerous position, but it offered less chance of those undead boarders coming up from the deep.

The crew restarted fueling apace. Most were now more than ready to get inside the U-boat and get under the water. A steel hull was their best protection from the zombie swarm that they no longer could see. With the attack from the ghouls, Krieg had no longer worried about being shot from the shore.

Krieg paced the deck. The fueling would only take a few more minutes. A low speed run under the water during the day, and passing the busy areas around Florida in the dark would allow them to pass undetected by anyone searching for them, if the Americans could even summon help. He would target to get to Montevideo, Argentina, which was allied with Germany. It would be a long slow run, but the fuel would probably last, if he could avoid heavy northward currents. Krieg had no idea whether the current political positions had changed as they had sat isolated in the U-boat, but it was his best bet. If he had to, he would run the U-boat up on another island in the Caribbean and simply change their clothes. Perhaps he could find an embassy, pose as current German sailors who were in a shipwreck. They would survive, which was his first goal.

If he had to, he would use his guns and torpedoes to attack a ship and gain their supplies and gear. Germany may have ended the war long ago, but he was still able to fight for the last remains of the Fatherland.

Krieg was plotting his return to the world, his long range plans of everything going right, while not being aware of what could still go wrong. He had to shake off his revelry when he noticed that the U-boat was blowing its ballast out. The sides of the boat began to froth with the bubbles popping from the tanks.

"*Räum die Decks! Wer hat die Ballasttanks geblasen?*" Krieg ordered his men off the deck, but then noticed the U-boat was not sinking.

"*Es sind nicht die Ballasttanks, Kapitän!*" one of the crew yelled, terrified as he looked back and forth between the captain and the waterline. Krieg wanted an explanation, but his question was cut short as the sailor began firing into the water. And then another, and another. Shouting came from the bow.

The water began to swarm with zombies. Arms reached up, hundreds of them, forming a thick ring around both crafts. Bodies, black, worn, waterlogged, climbed up long the hull of the U-boat. Krieg ran around the conning tower toward the bow, where already a dozen of the *Unmenchen* had crested the bow and were beginning to stand up. He saw them all, every eye a dark socket burning red with hate. Krieg unslung his weapon and raised it to shoulder height. He leaned into the rifle, firing in short bursts at each head. He rushed at first, firing three rounds at each approaching ghoul. He ignored the rosy splatter that came every time he hit his target. He just shifted from left to right, firing every half second. The first time he missed high, he stopped, took a step back, and calmed his now pounding heart. It was the first time he felt that in decades. The next seven ghouls went down in seven seconds as he blew their heads off. His MP-40 clicked on an empty magazine with only one ghoul still standing. More began to crawl up the bow to take the place of the fallen zombies. A shout from above at the conning tower warmed the captain.

"*Zurückgehen!*"

Whoever made the command didn't bother to wait for Krieg to move back. The high speed rattle of an MG-34 came from over his head. The deadly drumbeat poured bullets into the crowd of ghouls, knocking them back into the sea. The impacts tore some of the soft bodied ghouls apart, making the deck awash in spoiled guts and bones. The big machine gun ate at the zombies, tearing them to pieces. Krieg watched as the bullets went through the first wave, tearing an arm from one *Unmench* without slowing and impacting the one behind it in the eye. The head blew apart from the back.

Two sailors worked the unwieldy machine gun without a brace from the tower. It rattled on the metal gunwale, ringing the entire sub with an uncomfortable reverberation that the sailors felt from their feet to their teeth.

The stern began to tremble with more ghouls trying to climb up the sides. The sailors had attempted to concentrate on the aft with their hand held submachine guns. They fired bursts into the water which knocked the zombies back into the ocean. Their weapons were only made for short bursts, and they emptied the 32 rounds from the magazines quickly.

The flak gun team had seen the success of the two man crew and had picked up the other MG-36. They began to fire at the stern where another horde of zombies crowded up the deck. The machine gun was braced awkwardly along a rail. It rang with a metallic ping that sang a most inappropriate song as the bullets coursed through the bodies. It took only moments to turn most of the boat into an island surrounded by a sea of torn zombies, floating in a horrid gruel of body parts and blood.

Any wholesale death like that would break the back of an attack, Krieg thought. He discovered the *Unmenchen* had no fear of any death delivered to them. They had already faced it once. A whole new wave came pouring over the sides of the bunker tanker.

Krieg signaled for the men on the tanker to escape to the U-boat. He began to unhook the hoses, still pumping diesel, and ordered all lines cut.

Sailors started jumping across the deck to the U-boat. The decks were hot and slippery as they struggled to make it across. Some fell in the opening gap as the boats began to separate. Others were less lucky as the horde reached them on the ship. Each sailor still on the tanker went down to a gang of ghouls, all intent on getting a piece of flesh. They got all they wanted. One by one the screaming stopped as bloodied hands pulled the Nazis apart piece by piece.

"*Erschieß sie! Schieße in die Horde!*" Dead or alive, the remnants of his sailors would not survive much longer under the attack of the zombies. "*Innerhalb! Versiegeln und vorbereiten für das Tauchen!*" He was done. It was time to steam away and dive. Other problems would wait. Krieg would wash the decks of these carcasses and come up clean off the horizon somewhere.

The last of his men were trying to seal up the rear hatch, when the zombies made their way to them. Two of the Nazi sailors fought back, smashing at the ghouls' heads with the stocks of their machine guns. One just fell screaming; he was terrified beyond thought as the ghouls ripped him to shreds. When they stood back up, the ghouls were covered in gore, and the sailor was nothing more than a morass of bloody flesh and bone.

The other sailor bashed at the oncoming zombies, but he stood no chance against the overwhelming numbers. He had his weapon pulled from him as the ghouls began to pull at his arms. He felt the first one bite into his bicep, and then another at his shoulder. His clothes were being ripped now, and the teeth and hands were pulling at bare flesh. Trying to protect his body, his head ducked down until another ghoul dove its teeth into his skull. The teeth rattled onto his bone, unable to penetrate, but still scratching off his thick scalp. He knew he was done for. Crying in pain, he begged with his last words, "*Töte mich!*"

Krieg was left with only a sidearm, which he fired desperately at the sailor, until the young man went down in a bloody heap.

Krieg ran. He must get inside the U-boat. He may still stand a chance on the inside, if the ghouls could be kept out. He ran to the rungs of the conning tower, slipping on the deck as he struggled to get up and inside. Up three rungs, four, then pulling himself up toward the opening, and the relative protection. He screamed, just hoping that his crew inside would hear through the open hatch at the top of the tower down into the control room, "*Voraus! Vollgas voraus!*"

A hand reached for him. Krieg felt its grip on his leg. Looking down he was surprised by the vice he was in. The hand was small, with the bones and knuckles sticking out through stretched skin, which was pale white and phthisic, a skeleton hand covered in a filmy mucus. Yet it held firm. Another hand grabbed at him. Krieg looked up at the ghoul that held him. Stunningly, the man was in a suit, a torn and tainted white jacket. His hair was short, spiked from a second lifetime under the salt water. The man still looked like he was some rich clean cut traveler who had been caught up by mistake in a war that wasn't his. The only difference was that now his face burned with hate.

More hands pulled at him now, inexorably pulling away at his grip. Krieg fought to maintain a handhold. He was not going to let the *Unmenchen* win easily. He kicked out, striking a, woman?... Krieg was surprised at the shape of the ghoul, definitely a woman, in a frumpy brown dress, torn and sullied. She did not release her grip. His boot print was left on her soft face, a slimy flesh print across her cheek and nose.

The ghouls climbed up. They weren't striking at him like they did the others. He waited for the biting attack, the teeth, the tearing of flesh, but it never came. They just pulled at him. One began to pry at his hooked arm. It was bent against his will from around the rung. Krieg tumbled down onto the deck with his arms held tight. He could so nothing to lash out. Krieg waited for the end.

He was resigned not to show terror. He wasn't going to give in to their torment. Krieg was stunned when instead they lifted him and carried him, spread eagled, across to the stern deck, where they held him down. The deck was sticky and hot from the late morning sun and the diesel that still poured out into the water and over the wood planking. Krieg looked up at the ghouls that seemed to surround him now. The light of the day was almost blotted out by the bodies around him. His arms and legs, held down at his wrists, elbows, shoulders, ankles, knees, and thighs, had no motion in them. He was completely immobile.

The horde parted. Krieg was able to look up, at the far part of the stern, as one ghoul arose from the water. Dripping with both seawater and the bloody debris of the last battle Krieg would fight, he walked slowly, deliberately toward the pinned Nazi captain. Krieg saw in its hand was a small pistol.

It stood over Krieg, his voice trying to find itself after being full of seawater. The ghoul coughed and hacked, spitting a phlegmy vomit of seawater at Krieg's feet. It finally found its voice.

"I promised... I would send you... to Hell."

With a sure and confident hand, the ghoul raised Dan Howard's flare gun and softly popped off the bright red flare onto the deck between Krieg's legs.

The diesel fumes puffed to a flame as the bright red shell impacted just beneath Krieg's groin. The wooden deck, hot from the morning sun, had soaked in the fuel as it had spilled, and the vapors ignited immediately, rushing to any place that held fuel. Krieg felt his pants legs catch fire, and his ankles began to blister and burn. It took only moments for the flames to rise in a soft whoosh as the whole deck became awash in flame.

Krieg struggled under the grip of his captors, his former victims. He couldn't believe they would just stand and be burned. *"Was ist los mit dir Kreaturen?"* Krieg still refused to see them as people, just monsters.

The ghouls began to unlatch the remaining deck hatches. The fire began to spread. One simply unhooked the still pumping fuel lines and let it spill, a spray that vaporized and ignited, pouring a translucent flame into the hold. The fans that had tried to pump the vaporous fuel out only spread it farther. Krieg could feel sections of the inner hull thump as the air and the marine fuel mixed, burning out the oxygen. Gone were the German gutteral orders and hearty words. In place, through the crackling fire, Krieg heard the screams and cries as the last of his crew burned.

The fires took hold inside the boat now. They found purchase on anything flammable, clothing, oil, linen. The interior heated up as the oxygen got sucked away by the flames. Some of the sailors tried to escape through the open hatches. They were pulled up and into the deck flames by greedy hands in desperate desire to get at the Nazis. From his vantage point Krieg could see nothing over the burning flames around him except the stoic and ever forceful ghouls that held him even as they all burned. One sailor was passed from zombie to zombie, all throttling and shaking him like a dog with a torn rope. Krieg saw him out of the corner of his eye. The boy's body flew out of his vision. Krieg wasn't sure of what happened to him, but he heard the horrid thud of something thrown bodily into the conning tower.

Krieg felt himself burning now. More than just being burnt by flames, his body was starting to burn, to cook his flesh. The smell of burning wood moved to an aroma of charred deck and the putrid smell of his flesh cooking. Worse was the sight around him. The ghouls, the zombies, all around him, were becoming consumed. He felt the flesh cook and begin to fall from his ankles, yet the *Unmenchen* hands, themselves losing the rotted flesh to the fire, still held. A bony finger squeezed into his leg to hold back the involuntary spasms of his legs trying to get off the frying pan of a deck that his ship had become. Krieg threw back his head in anguish. His mouth filled with black soot, coating the roof of his mouth with a dry cake of ashed body parts. Eyes rolled back in his head, Krieg finally felt the pain that all those sailors, passengers, and crew felt with every torpedo blast, every time they hit the water. Only there was no icy release, nor savior of a life boat to come to him. It was just the agony of a death that would not come yet.

Faces stared at him, burning in the black oiled smoke. They all stared at him with ruby red burning eyes. Even though their mouths never moved, Krieg heard them. He finally heard them all. They screamed and cursed him, begged for help, or just cried as they died in fire or froze to death in the cold sea. The faces drew closer. The voices louder.

"Lass mich einfach sterben!"

A woman, burned almost beyond all recognition, climbed over him, face to charred face.

"You die when we say you die."

57

8:35 A.M.

OCRACOKE BEACH

Dan Howard had pulled a groaning Chief Jennifer Stone up to the top of a dune where the two had collapsed in fatigue and pain, unable to go even a few feet further. Dan had a vague idea of what might happen, but hadn't thought through much of the potential events. They had rolled down the back of the dunes to shelter from the attack on the wraiths. When the guns went silent, the two were able to crawl back up to the dune to discover the beach turned into a hellscape of pockmarked sand, where the shells had impacted the shoreline. Bodies of fallen merchantmen and other victims of the Nazi U-boat war covered the beach. There was a sickening smell of death in the air, stirred by the lingering dust of explosive shells. Salt air mixed with decaying flesh and a strange unfamiliar acid smell of the old Nazi explosives to make a sickening odor for Dan. Involuntarily, he took a deep exhausted breath of the air and retched. He had eaten nothing in over a day, and he only spit up a thin watery bile that left his mouth with a burning acid coating. He didn't even care, as the taste matched the pain the rest of his body had.

The two people were able to watch as the water turned black under the waves with a moving mass of the wraiths heading toward the submarine. They watched as the boats were able to pull off the sand bar and began to steam away toward deeper water. Stone thought that they would either escape or she would at least miss the final events in Captain Krieg's life. She was dismayed that she had no hand in the sinking of the U-boat. It was more fitting that the victims took the U-boat down, she understood, but there would have been something so satisfying in looking the Nazi in the eye before removing him from the earth, having left no loss of value for his exit.

When the smoke came, they knew the Nazis were finished. Smoke on a boat always meant the worst. The plumes of hot burning fuel went up into the blue sky, black and toxic like tires burning. Soon the water would fill with floating oil and the boats would bathe in the flames. Stone had seen it before. So had all the victims out there, she realized sadly.

Now the beach was empty of all the wraiths. They had all waded into the surf to meet Krieg and his goons. The artillery fire had drawn out some of the locals. Like times before, when the ships on the coast burned, they were drawn to the sounds and flame. The island was finally empty of the Nazi menace. They came to make sure the menace stayed off their shores for good this time.

Stone was cold despite the morning sun. An infection was setting in, and she felt the pasty feeling of fever sink into her body. She didn't ponder the minutiae of what was happening on board the U-boat as it burned. No one was escaping that inferno. She just wondered if the boat would stop and settle or if it would break apart from the heat. It was as if to her will that jets of flame spouted out the hatches, one after another, with a delayed crack and boom of explosions as something cooked off inside. The flames didn't dissipate. Things were burning off in the sub, Stone envisaged the conflagration going on inside the submarine. By now all of the crew inside would be long dead. Just what would be left…

The explosion hit Stone and Dan with a shockwave of impact, even at that far distance. One of the torpedoes had finally cooked off in the heat. The explosion came from the rear of the submarine, where the aft torpedo tube would have held its smaller arsenal. Water spurted hundreds of feet up, followed by an orange fireball. Within seconds two more explosions occurred on the bow. The submarine seesawed as it was lifted out of the water, broken in multiple places. Stone could see the tower fracture as it came apart from the center of the boat. The stern was a shredded mess as the main shafts split out like bones ripped from their metal flesh.

The bunker tanker fared no better, being split down the middle from the explosion. Its port half bobbed sideways as all the fuel was engulfed. It sank in a matter of moments.

The beach became a junkyard of scrap metal as the fiery mess rained down on the sand. Smaller pieces began to imbed themselves like shrapnel into the dune, while larger chunks flew up in a lazy arc, belying their mass, looking slovenly as they lazily tumbled through the sky. Dan looked at one particular wad of torn iron, stunned into motionlessness that the disjointed thing could even fly, let alone reach the shore. It crashed into the upper sand of the beach, kicking up the soft course white grains that normally made Ocracoke's beach so popular.

"C'mon, Chiefy, we gotta move," he said as he pulled the exhausted Coast Guardsman by her good arm.

58

9:00 A.M. TUESDAY, OCTOBER 1, 1985

OCRACOKE

Two days after the U-boat had exploded, after the Nazis had stormed off the island, and four days after the brush with Hurricane Gloria had brought all the hell to the island, power had finally been restored. Other restorations would take much longer.

The channel was declared clear so that ferry service could be resumed, but only for emergency service and residents. When the first relief workers got there, no one believed any of the story that the survivors told. There was no way 65 year old Nazis stormed the beaches of Ocracoke, only to be driven back by a horde of watery zombies. The story had simplified into that basic narrative by the locals who had to tell what happened from their own point of view, missing all the bits and pieces that painted a larger and much more horrific picture.

Chief Stone didn't even care. After the initial scoffing response, she didn't bother to explain her wound to her superiors. She simply said she was stabbed by "some guy" who was after her pistol, which was basically the truth, with a lot left out. Then she took another Tylenol 3. Tomorrow he would be able to go to Greenville to have surgery on her shoulder. Now she just didn't want to feel it. She wasn't much of a drinker, but a cold beer would be great today, if she hadn't needed the codeine to numb the pain in her shoulder.

This is the last one," she reminded herself as she swallowed the pill. She wasn't going to be able to sail with narcotics in her blood. It was well understood that some Coasties, as well as lots of other people who served on the sea, operated almost entirely on Tylenol and coffee, but narcotics were a black spot that if discovered would put a sailor on the hook, if not sent home in disgrace. Plus, she didn't like how it made her head spin.

She had gone out on a boat the day before. She had to see for herself. Dan Howard had taken her out personally, on his fishing boat. They had bobbed along the waves at low tide to look into the now calm blue water. Staring down in disbelief at what they found. Within the day, the entire U-boat had succumbed to the salt water, as if the over forty years of corrosion had happened in one night. A hollow dark bowl, a strange grainy stain under the ocean waves was all that was left.

Stone had forbidden the usual piracy of items found along the beach. No one was going to collect any of the tainted material left from the past few days. She even made it clear that no one was to go out over the sunken submarine, ostensibly out of fear of potential explosions, but in reality she just didn't want anyone to dive down and take anything. Not that anyone would put a toe in that water out of fear that a bony hand would reach out and snatch them to a watery grave.

Stone had little worry about that fear, though. The bodies of the wraiths were gone, too. A wealth of rank seaweed littered the beach. Kelp flies dined voraciously on the tangled wads. Stone wasn't sure where the bodies, or the animated wraiths had gone. Dan had pointed out that the seaweed lay on the beach like cooked sunbathers. He implied that the men and women had metamorphosed into the kelp weed piles. Stone scoffed at the idea. Though anything was possible, after what they went through.

The state police finally came in and investigated. They looked for the easiest answer, since the reality was so far fetched and unbelievable that there had to be something simpler. They simply blamed Eddie, since he was a good target. He had been arrested for looting the empty houses, and escaped, and he was now dead and gone. If he was violent enough to kill a sheriff's deputy, then he would have no problem stabbing a Coast Guardsman, too. He tried to escape on the one craft that could get him far, the fueled bunker tanker, and had blown himself up in the process.

Stone thought about how they were using Eddie as a scapegoat. Considering the choices Eddie made, he got what he deserved. Shot in the gut to die in a watery unmarked grave. She had no sympathy for the little toad. Stone had seen drug runners she respected more, and she loathed drug runners.

Everyone off the island simply decided Eddie tried to steal something on the beach from a washed up sailboat, or broke into the wrong fishing boat, got caught, escaped in the storm, and tried to flee on the bunker tanker after going on a murder spree. The story worked. It made sense to anyone who wasn't there, and since it made sense, the islanders let it be. Eddie's death put paid to a horrible time for them. It allowed them to at least stand a chance to move on, even if they couldn't put the events out of their collective memory.

The rest of Ocracoke went on. The islanders had long known how to tolerate loss, even when they couldn't stand the pain. Life went on, and people had to eat. It had always been that way. In the soft part of the days, they would cry, and at night they might huddle under the covers of a bed even when it was still warm out, with the windows closed and the doors locked.

Dan Howard went back to work, running the harbor, keeping the lines tight. He became more thoughtful about who came through the bay. Dan and Chief Stone had both suffered from the attack, but Dan's wounds were more psychological than physical. He had seen his family threatened firsthand. And he had done some very dirty work to right some wrongs that he only saw in his own head. Dan had felt better after a very long sleep and several meals, along with a quiet but heartfelt discussion with his family.

Chief Stone had been surprised to find Dan standing on the dunes the night before, staring into a late rising moon and twinkling stars out to the sea. Surprised at first, but then she thought, "That's right were I would be." They had waited against the tide, just to make sure. If anything ever came crawling back,

Stone knew she would be there, ready to beat it back into the ocean.

And let Hell take it from there.

EPILOGUE

5:56 P.M. MARCH 31, 1942

OFF THE CAPE HATTERAS COAST

The American steam tanker *Tulsa* cruised with worried merchant marine sailors above and below decks. The ship was returning from Venezuela, running low and heavy as it was full of crude oil. The off duty crew had just finished dinner.

Unbeknownst to the crew of the *Tulsa*, they had been spotted in the spring twilight by the Nazi U-boat U-857. *Kapitänleutnant* Reinhardt Krieg set a solution for his torpedo, aiming for the engine room and propulsion of the slow tanker. He watched as the weapon launched from his boat only to miss wide of the stern. Already he was plotting a more accurate solution, this time aiming amidships and using the lag time to catch the big tanker in the aft section of the hull.

The second torpedo ran true. It exploded in a horrendous crash, tearing through the engine room and flooding the entire aft section. In the radio room, Clifford Chesley tapped out the new SSSS call warning their ship was under attack. He radioed Norfolk to bring planes to find them, but he knew they would be too late. The boat was already lifting its bow upward. It would only take sixteen minutes for the *Tulsa* to go down in oil and flame. Captain Betts had given the Abandon Ship order, but it did little good. Of the 34 aboard, only seven would find their way to a raft on the icy March ocean.

Krieg waited until the ship had sunk to rise his U-boat. He steamed close to the raft and called out on his megaphone to the remaining crew, in lilted English, "What ship was this?"

A young man answered, Able Seaman Leroy Buzzell, though Krieg would not know the name nor care, answered back, in a strange Southern twang, "The *Tulza.*"

Krieg and the crew now late of the *Tulsa* watched each other in near silence as the sun sank on them. A member of Krieg's crew came up the tower and took a picture of the stricken men for a souvenir. One of the Americans turned his head, his hand up to avoid being photographed by the Nazis. Most of the others looked ashen and cold. They knew they would not be found out on the open sea. No ship would see them. None would stop for fear of being hit by the same U-boat. They were dead, all of them. It just hadn't happened yet.

"You can't just leave us here, " pleaded a young crewman. "You... you gotta give us some water, food, something. Take us to shore!" he begged.

Krieg didn't listen, or he merely didn't respond. If the men were fortunate, the current would pull them north toward the outstretched coast, and they may be spotted. Considering their current predicament, Krieg mused, these men would not be fortunate.

Krieg needed to submerge. The likelihood of an attack by plane was remote, but he would get underway soon. The setting sun would hide him soon enough. He began to retreat to the interior of the tower, as one of the men on the raft bellowed at him.

"You Nazi sonofabitches! You're leavin' us out here to die, you bastards!"

Krieg looked over his shoulder at the man yelling, red faced, fist clenched and shaking.

"I swear to God I will find you! There's nowhere on land or sea you can hide! As God as my witness, I'll find you bastards!

"And I swear to the Devil himself, I'll deliver you straight into Hell!"

ABOUT THE AUTHOR

John Martell has spent his life living on and exploring the sea. Growing up on the coast of the Carolinas, he swam and dove on the many wrecks off the shore of the Atlantic coast. A longtime explorer, he has traveled both the Atlantic and Pacific coasts, from the Mid-Atlantic to Florida, and from Mexico to Canada, in search of the last vestiges of history, from pirate treasure to long thought lost military events. Martell has been a swimmer, a diver, sailor, as well as an educator for children, youth, and adults, in an effort to help preserve and increase knowledge of history. He currently spends most of his time traveling with his wife and family.

John Martell has collected all of his gathered explorations in written form. This is the first book with his name on it written based on his experiences.

A NOTE ON THE EVENTS

On March 29, 1942, the *City of New York*, a passenger cargo ship carrying metal ore, wood, and forty-one passengers, was torpedoed by the *U-160*, captained by 26 year old Georg Lassen. As the surviving crew and passengers tried to escape the burning ship, Lassen fired a second torpedo into the *New York* as a coup de grâce. The crew of the Navy Armed Guard continued to fire at the U-boat as the ship sank. Their names were never recorded.

On March 22, 1942, the *U-123*, commanded by Reinhard Hardegan, targeted the *SS Muskogee*, an oil tanker, which Hardegan referred to as his "Sunday Roast." The ship was sunk about one thousand miles from the coast in deep water. Ten survivors boarded a raft and were photographed by the propaganda officer. They were offered no help and left to die. There were no survivors from the *Muskogee*.

The *U-857* was reported missing on or after April 30, 1945, off the North Carolina coast. It was possibly sunk by US warships or a torpedo attack by a blimp.

At 1:30 a.m. on September 27, 1985, Hurricane Gloria made her first landfall on the southern part of Hatteras Island, with her southern winds striking Ocracoke overnight. Gloria had formed off the coast of North Africa and became a tropical depression near Cape Verde on September 16. At her most powerful, Gloria had peak winds of 155 mph, making her a very powerful and dangerous hurricane, with little in the way of predictability except that she would strike the east coast. Evacuations ultimately were ordered from the Carolinas all the way to Maine.

When the hurricane hit the North Carolina coast, the winds had lessened, but the storm still caused massive damage to shores and houses, including new inlets cut into the islands.

Hurricane Henri formed in the Gulf of Mexico, but never made landfall, though its remnants did track through Florida and up the coast soon after Gloria. The addition of the full moon over the days and nights these events occurred helped increase the tidal surges, though by historical standards, residents of the Outer Banks at the time would say that these were somewhat typical, if not minor, events in comparison to other hurricanes.

These preceding events depicted in this book are historically fairly accurate, as are the basic locations of the roads and buildings at the time, though some author's license has been taken to make the book more readable and less convoluted.

The other events depicted cannot be verified, and if asked, Ocracoke locals of the time will deny that any of this actually happened.

Made in the USA
Monee, IL
14 December 2024

73741841R00184